SO-BFI-868

A VISIONARY NOVEL OF PLANETARY TRANSFORMATION

STEVEN M. ROSEN

STILLPOINT PUBLISHING
WALPOLE, NEW HAMPSHIRE 1985

FIRST PRINTING

Copyright © 1984 by Steven M. Rosen
All rights reserved. No part of this book
may be reproduced without written
permission from the publisher, except
by a reviewer who may quote brief
passages or reproduce illustrations in a
review; nor may any part of this book
be reproduced, stored in a retrieval
system, or transmitted in any form or by
any means electronic, mechanical,
photocopying, recording, or other,
without written permission
from the publisher.

This book is manufactured
in the United States of America.
It is designed by James F. Brisson,
cover art by William Giese
and published by Stillpoint Publishing,
Box 640, Meetinghouse
Road, Walpole, NH 03608.
Published simultaneously in Canada by
Fitzhenry & Whiteside Limited, Toronto.

Reproduction rights for **Print Gallery**
arranged courtesy of the Vorpal Galleries:
New York City, San Francisco, Palo
Alto, Laguna Beach, CA.

Library of Congress Card
Catalog Number:**84-71034**
Steven M. Rosen
The Moebius Seed
ISBN0-913299-04-9

For Andrea, David and Lesley

 # Contents

Acknowledgments

FOR THE ASSISTANCE THEY FREELY GAVE, THE inspiration they provided, or both, I would like to thank the following individuals:

Alan Azzara, David Bohm, Nick Capozzi, Leslie Carman, Arthur C. Clarke, Michael Cocks, Hugh Corbett, Paul Covington, Harriet Edwards, Ira Einhorn, M. C. Escher, Aristede Esser, Denise Falatico, Marilyn Ferguson, Joel Funk, Robert Gibbons, Alice Gooskos, Toby Greenzang, David Haight, Ruth Heber, Ken Keyes, Lawrence LeShan, Nicole Lieberman, Gary Mann, Magoroh Maruyama, Lynn Mason, Charles Muses, Marguerite Musso, Marian Nester, Karlis Osis, Johann Quanier, Oliver Reiser, Paul Ryan, Rupert Sheldrake, Michelle Sherry, Raymond Van Over, Francisco Varela, Alan Vaughan, and Miss Rhea A. White.

I give special thanks to Jim and Meredith Young for believing the project was feasible and lending it their generous support, to Myra Iris Schwartz for many hours of fruitful and heartening discussion, and to Kenneth Ring for the imagery his important work on near-death and out-of-the-body experiences helped evoke. It was Ken who introduced me to Caroline Myss, my brilliant and dedicated editor. The creative leadership she provided was indispensable in making *The Moebius Seed* more coherent and whole.

My deepest appreciation goes to Andrea Dichelle Rosen for all the time, talent and editorial acumen she has contributed to this project and for years spent patiently indulging my inward excursions.

This expression of gratitude would not be complete without acknowledging my first source of inspiration, Mr. and Mrs. Leon B. Rosen, my parents.

PART I

FIGUREground

© 1984 BEELDRECHT, Amsterdam/V.A.G.A., New York, 1984. Collection Haags Gemeentemuseum — The Hague.

. . . The community of self-seeing, all seeing selves does not yet see All, has not yet touched Self. A boundary still stands, a membrane unpassed . . . But they are approaching, coming close now to Self-impregnation . . .

They move through a tunnel. Darkness gives way to light . . . They move toward the open, to an Outside beyond inside and out. But the Planetary Egg is not yet fertile, the Moebius seed not yet conceived . . .

—Excerpts from the incomplete novel of Noel Innerman

 **1**

Flights and Deceptions

THE SENSATION WOULD BEGIN NOT LONG after she entered the twilight state of mind. Her toes were usually the first to feel the "pins and needles." Quickly and in no particular order, other regions of her body would pick up the pulse. The separate centers of vibration then would merge to set the whole of her atingle.

Normally, it was pleasant to surrender herself to this strange sensation — her own marvelous "shower massage" working from within. And the incredible experience that sometimes followed! But now she was not in the privacy of her bed.

Sandra Peterson was sitting in a crowded subway car on her way to the graduate center. Cradled in her lap was *The Principles of Physiological Psychology*. Within the hour, she would be taking the mid-term exams but was ill-prepared. The old pattern was reasserting itself.

The night before, she had opened the imposing textbook for the first time. A monumental effort was in order. But she could not

keep herself on track. Like a drunken driver apprehended and put
to the test, she valiantly tried to hold the thin line of concentration.
It was all to no avail. She could not stop drifting away. Disem-
bodied faces of friends, half-remembered dreams, fragments of
assorted conversations, or just formless reverie, all conspired to
destroy her focus on the details of neurophysiology. It seemed she
simply could not manage the mental discipline required of a
graduate student. Twice before, Sandy had begun study for the
master's degree in psychology; twice she had withdrawn. Now
she was in the process of playing out the third act of the drearily
repetitive script.

She should have quit last night, given in to the inevitable at a
reasonable hour. At least her embarrassing lack of preparation
would not have been compounded by fatigue. Her exhaustion
was also contributing to the present predicament. The tingling had
begun right there in public, amidst the two hundred passengers
closely packed into the uptown Lexington. One moment she was
in her seat, leaning sleepily against a window of the rhythmically
swaying train, the next brought those inner vibrations, and now
she was up at the ceiling!

Sandy had had this bizarre experience of "flying" many times
before. The first one she could recall was triggered by a dream
—the kind that can scare a five-year-old child out of her wits. She
was playing alone in a clearing in the woods. Someone was
coming . . . her mother or father, she thought. The unseen presence drew closer and closer, forming itself into an enormous
shadow ominously cast through the leaves and branches of surrounding trees. When the leading edge of the shadow began
creeping over the clearing in her direction, the nightmare ended.
Spurred by a terrible sense of helpless immobility, she fought her
way out of the dream, appearing to return to the normal environment of her room. However, the feeling of paralysis had not been
entirely dispelled and there was a curious tingling sensation
(which she later described as her "itchy body" to an incredulous
mother).

The next thing she knew, she was looking at everything from a funny angle. Why did her night table seem to be way down below her? How could she be seeing her toy chest and doll house as if riding above in an airplane? And she had never seen the *top* of that high red cabinet before. Then, looking directly beneath, Sandy was startled to discover a little girl curled up under her bedcovers. It was *herself*. There were two of Sandy, one "asleep" in bed, the other floating so closely to the ceiling that she could touch the overhead fixture with no trouble whatever. Using the globular light casing to push off, she propelled herself across the room toward the uppermost panes of the window. The wonderful feeling of exhilaration that this produced lasted until she made contact with metal. Palms thrust out, she had intended to stop herself against the iron window frame, but it would not contain her. After encountering momentary resistance — a sort of "rough air turbulence" — she went right through without breaking the glass. At that instant the little girl had found herself back in her body and was opening her eyes.

There was nothing exhilarating about Sandy Peterson's current condition. On the contrary, she was suffering from a peculiar type of claustrophobia. Close above her was the roof of the subway car — she had no desire to pass through that surface into the pitch-black tunnel. Equally unappealing was the prospect of being submerged in the sea of bobbing heads that lay below. So Sandy was more or less confined to the narrow channel in the ceiling that ran the length of the car. She hovered there uncomfortably, flanked by double banks of fluorescent lights and Madison Avenue platitudes. She was barely able to divert the "eyes" of her "second body" from the details of Kent's "micronite filter" or the "Sunbird's Whisperjet to Miami." And the whirring of the ventilating fans roared in her floating body's "ears."

Could she not re-enter the sallow, dark-haired form slumped in the seat by the window? Ordinarily, there was no difficulty; it required but an act of will. Yet the present venture out-of-body was far from ordinary. Again and again she urged herself, *Go back, Sandy, go back!* and every effort made in that direction met with frustration. Something was blocking her, a force was literally holding her back. She had the distinct impression of hands on her shoulders, though when she turned to look, there was nothing.

"Canal Street," called the mechanical voice from a remote location.

The sense of confinement was becoming unbearable.

"Eighth."

Only three more stops. Would she miss the exam?

"Fourteenth Street."

It occurred to Sandy that she might never return to her body. This fear had been in the background on each and every one of those fantastic journeys. Occasionally she had thought, *this is what it must be like to die.* Now the fear was taking control. She imagined herself swimming underneath a sheet of ice. She could scarcely breathe and time was running out. Overhead was an opening through which to rise and fill her bursting lungs. She strained frantically toward the circle of life, but the pressure at her shoulders weighed her down.

"Thirty-fourth Street."

One more stop. The train clattered tentatively away from the platform, then accelerated into the tunnel. Sandra knew she would have to repossess herself by the time she reached her destination or it would be too late. But no progress was being made. Alternately, she pleaded with her invisible captor and lashed out at it with dwindling mental reserves. It was hopeless. The Lexington Avenue express slowed down. The lights of the Forty-second Street station came into view. As the train screeched to a halt, Sandy remained in her state of suspended separation. . .

To the man who had been sitting opposite her, Sandy appeared to be sleeping. *Nothing special,* he had thought when the girl in the ankle-length dress and pea jacket had first stepped on. *She's too skinny.* Then he had looked again and seen her eyes: large, darkly lashed, and lightly glazed with a far-away sadness.

Soon the eyes had closed. After dozing quietly for a while, the young lady had begun to stir. The jaws remained slack, but the brow had become furrowed and she had started to squirm. Over the past few minutes, the restlessness had increased, prompting several sidelong glances from the pursed-lipped matron who shared the seat.

"Forty-second Street. Change for the shuttle to Grand Central Station."

Sandy's admirer was startled to see those mysterious eyes open so abruptly. The girl sat back awkwardly and stared into space for a moment. Then, gathering up the books at her feet, she lurched forward, straightened, and hurried past the irritated old woman. Slipping through the doors just as they were closing, she was gone.

Phil Myerson sat on the edge of his desk facing the class. He re-lit his pipe. Appearing relaxed, even detached, to his students, he waited for his last words to be fully absorbed by every member of the group. With the match held steadily to the bowl of the pipe, he sucked the flame into the tobacco. His attention was focused on his pipe so that no one in the class noticed the quick movement of his eyes. In a single darting glance, Phil gauged their reactions. A visual sampling of facial expressions, postural attitudes and levels of attention was instantly processed.

Satisfied with the effect he had created, Phil stood up and began a leisurely pace toward the large second-floor windows overlooking the campus. As he walked, he held his hands loosely clasped behind his back; his head was bowed in contemplation. When the next maneuver was calculated, he turned and spoke again.

"Who is to blame? Who is responsible for this sorry state of affairs?" Phil used the expected silence for dramatic effect. Waiting several more seconds, he rephrased the question.

"Do you mean it's just happening? Kids, adults, like vegetables, sitting hour after hour, day after day? *Seven hours a day*—the average American spends seven hours a day in front of the television tube. Do you know what that does to the brain? Small wonder that when they do manage to tear themselves away and converse with each other, all that comes out is 'Yaba-daba-do', 'dyn-o-mite!' and 'Where's-the-beef?' But it's easier than English, right?

"Next it's out to the movies and all you hear about for weeks or maybe months is 'the force'—'may the force be with you.' Can anyone tell me what the so-called *Star Wars* 'force' is supposed to be . . .? I didn't think so. But that's just it. Today it seems that nonsense is much preferred over sense, over rationality, and I want to know why. I'd like to know who the culprit is."

Again there was absolute quiet. The students were beginning to feel uneasy. Sensing with relish the building pressure for them to respond, the professor continued: "Actually, there is much more to it than what I've mentioned so far. Our language is dying and with it goes our capacity to reason intelligently and independently. But this death by trivialization is not only found in what comes through the air waves or out of Hollywood. You can see it plainly in the hundreds of trendy, pseudo-psychotherapy groups and crackpot religious cults that are cropping up. Do you want to 'open up your inner spaces', 'liberate your *kundalini*,' or just 'get into your head'? You can do it all at EST or Esalen, with TM, Zen, or the Hare Krishna—to name but a few.

"The point is that 'spaces', 'vibrations', 'energies', 'forces' and so on, are terms without referents—at least the way they are currently being used. In other words, they're pure crap—they don't *mean* anything. This garbage may not originate in the mass media, but the media is quick to latch on, to publicize, amplify, blow it all out of proportion. So you have your 'Age of Aquarius.'

"But we still have to get to the bottom of this. Where is it *really* coming from? Can anyone give me a clue?"

Finally a hand went up in the back of the room and was acknowledged.

"I think people are unhappy, dissatisfied with the 'rat race.' They're looking for something more out of life."

"That sounds very nice," Phil replied, "but why do they keep getting *less*? Could it be that they're looking in the wrong place?"

"Maybe," said the soft-spoken art major. "I don't know. There's a book I read on holistic health. It said that you should get into contact with yourself if you want to be healthy and that it's something spiritual, something you can experience but not talk about."

Phil smiled tolerantly and walked in front of his desk, positioning himself eye to eye with the student in the second row. The group shifted its focus in anticipation. An echo came, voiced in muted irony. " 'Something you can experience but not talk about.' What does that mean, Larry? Is it an experience that's very difficult to express?"

The student hesitated, averting his eyes. "I don't think so. It said that you *couldn't* express it."

"Then what *can* you do with it?"

"Well, uh . . . just *experience* it," Larry laughed nervously.

"See how it's got you going in a circle? You can't define it, communicate it, share it with me. You're stuck with it, whatever 'it' is. Some dead-end street you're on."

Larry shook his head in embarrassment and shrugged his shoulders as if to say, "*I'm* not on a dead-end street, I was just telling what it said in the book." He was relieved when the professor began speaking impersonally, to the class as a whole.

"Larry is right about one thing. America *is* in trouble. Something malignant is eating at us. But we will not solve our problem by sitting and contemplating our navels. Far from being a cure, this act of colossal self-indulgence is a symptom of the disease. Everybody's doing it—housewives, businessmen, professional athletes—giving in to nonsense, sloppily letting it all hang out. It's an epidemic. And it seems that every day another guru pops out of the woodwork to cash in."

When Phil paused, two more hands were raised.

"Maybe the laws could be stricter," suggested a coed. "Couldn't the government regulate that kind of thing?"

"That's censorship," another young woman admonished.

"Yes, but it might not be so bad. Maybe they could put a warning on books and TV programs, like on cigarette packs. 'The Surgeon General has determined that. . .' "

A fellow two rows back completed the slogan with exaggerated resonance:

". . . that watching *Star Trek* may be hazardous to your mental health."

The professor allowed the class its moment of hilarity, then interjected: "You're really missing the point." He pulled the chair out from under his desk and sat in it. Lifting his pipe from the tin ashtray, he began to work his hands in a fluid, rhythmic motion. The ritual had a hypnotic effect that changed the mood in the room. Phil did not speak again until he had cleaned his pipe thoroughly and was tamping in fresh tobacco.

"I think we'd better review our work on the Renaissance. You know it meant more than inventing the telescope or exploring the New World. What was happening in Western Europe around 600 years ago?"

"Humanism. A spirit of Humanism started developing." Freddy Wilson could always be relied on for a straight, factual response. Phil pursued the matter with his star pupil.

"Can you tell us something about Humanism?"

"Well, it brought people away from magic and the supernatural and worries about what would become of them after they died. It put the emphasis on what a human being can achieve in *this* life. The important thing is a person's power to reason on his own, without using religion or God as a crutch."

"Yes. Very good. Fred is reminding us that the Renaissance represented a profound liberation of human potential. It truly *was* a re-birth. For centuries before, man's senses had been dulled, his ability to reason tied up in knots by the doctrinal tyranny of the

Church. The dogma of Rome was like a powerful drug. It kept the mind in an otherworldly haze, preventing it from focusing on the real, the natural world. Then, in the Fourteenth Century, the Change began.

"I won't go back over all the reasons for the transformation. I simply want you to remember that the fog did lift, the air at last was cleared for independent thinking. And what was the result? Years, centuries of incredible progress. We've come up from the worst misery, ignorance, degradation. Because we've begun to really understand nature, we're finally at the point where we can stop being the patsy and start asserting ourselves. Today there's even the possibility of directing our own evolution.

"That's why the crap that's clogging the air waves and filling the bookstores is so frustrating. If it gets out of hand—and it seems to be doing just that—it could destroy everything that has been achieved—no exaggeration."

Phil let the solemnity of the moment register before proceeding.

"I'm honestly frightened by what's happening. A real danger exists. That makes it terribly important to recognize where it's really coming from. And you can't *see* it. . .?

"Well it is *we*. *We* are to blame. There's no point pinning it on the media or the Maharishi. In fact, that's the *worst* thing we can do. If you deny responsibility, if '*they* are doing it to me' is all you can say, there will be no hope whatever. We have got to get it into our thick skulls that we're doing it to ourselves."

Phil rose from the chair and moved around the desk to confront the class. His voice grew deeper, more sonorous. "It's been a bootstrap operation from the beginning. Six hundred years ago we managed to pull ourselves out of the mire. That was a hard thing to do and there's always been the danger of slipping back in. You have to work continuously at being an individual, at keeping your head clear and free despite the siren call of the primitive. It's so tempting to give in to that easy inertia. But your integrity is gone, your intellectual independence. . . you lose your 'soul' in the only meaningful way possible for a human being."

The professor looked up at the clock. "Well, I think we can end the discussion on an optimistic note. Someone *is* doing something. A new committee is being formed by concerned citizens —scientists, educators, individuals who can see the handwriting on the wall but believe there still may be time." Phil went to the blackboard and printed in large capital letters:

THE COMMITTEE FOR SENSE AND SANITY

"The name gives a general idea of the function. I won't say any more on that now. These people have their work cut out for them, but some of the best minds are involved so there is a fighting chance of success."

The bell rang, signaling the end of the period. "You will hear more about The Committee, and next time we'll get into Marx and the problem of alienation."

Phil arrived home that night in high spirits. For him it was unusual. But it had been such a satisfying day. He had made clear headway on the textbook he was writing. His classes had gone well. It was one of those rare occasions when he would allow himself the luxury of not working at sociology.

Even before removing his coat, he went into the kitchen of his two-room flat, sat the grocery bags on the table, and reached for the telephone. Lifting the receiver from the cradle, he dialed his own number and waited for the busy signal. When confirmation came that the professor would be inaccessible to any callers, he put down the phone and proceeded to the wardrobe to undress.

Clad in his comfortable terry cloth robe, Phil perused the shelf of audio tapes above his books for quite a time. Finally, he decided on Handel. After snapping his selection into place, he returned to the kitchen to fix dinner.

The meal was prepared with more ceremony than usual.

Every phase of the operation—cutting, trimming, slicing, season-
ing—was carried out within the stately context of the symphony.
The atmosphere of ordered harmony had its influence when the
food was eaten, giving a measure of deliberation and dignity to the
normally hurried process.

With supper finished, Phil went to the humidor on his large
oak desk, filled his pipe, and lowered himself into the leather
recliner. He shifted his weight to send the chair back to its most
horizontal position. The music became more subdued as full
orchestra gave way to an interplay of principal instruments. He
lifted the lighter languidly and struck the flint. The intricate pattern of tonal counterpoint appeared to lend meaning to the random
dance of the flame. He watched. He did not fire the tobacco. He
watched and lost all sense of time and space. . .

It seemed Phil was back in the classroom, speaking to his
students in his customary manner. Semi-rhetorical questions,
impeccably posed, were built into answers that exploded with
authority and finality. Although his lectures normally required
careful construction and measured delivery, words flowed out of
him now without much effort. He was not even conscious of the
specific ideas he was presenting, only of their seductive impact on
the class and the intense pleasure he derived from a strong sense of
potency.

Then a change took place. An edge of doubt entered Phil's
mind, a sense of being off key.

"All right, kiddies, what about alienation? How does it fit into
our little picture? Our *big* picture? By the way, do any of you
remember 'The Big Picture'? It was an old T.V. documentary
about the U.S. Army."

My God, what the hell am I saying, Phil thought. *I'm making a
fool of myself!* He struggled for control.

"Who can tell me about *aliation*—I mean *alation*."

The class began to stir. Muffled comments were exchanged
and a giggle escaped from the back of the room.

Phil knew what they were thinking. *What's wrong with Myerson?* He could feel the weight of their contempt bearing down on him. *He's really sick. Must be having a nervous breakdown. Maybe he can't take the pressure of teaching. Maybe he's just scared.*

They had exposed him. He was sure that they knew everything. He wanted to rush from the room, but his legs were no more obedient than his tongue.

"Please listen to me," Phil begged, abandoning his dignity. His eyes were wet, his voice pathetically thin. "Please, we're talking about . . . about *ali—aliation.*" He was thinking the right word yet just could not seem to say it correctly.

The class began to laugh at him openly.

Phil looked at the clock. He could not believe what he saw. Three minutes past five? Impossible! He had been in that room for at least an hour but the clock told him that only three minutes had elapsed.

He shut his eyes tightly. *This has got to be a bad dream. Please let me wake up. I've got to get out of this.*

When he opened his eyes, the dream had become a nightmare. All the angles in his visual field had become contorted, acute, curving in upon each other, converging severely to one central point. The room seemed to be contracting. Chairs, desks, windows, walls, and the faces of his students merged into a menacing collage.

"Aliation, what is aliation?" he pleaded with the blur of superimposed lines and planes. Icy sweat started down his brow as he heard a mocking chorus shrilly echo his words: "What is aliation? What is aliation, kiddies?"

Now the room was shaping itself into a funnel. The floor sank in the middle, all sides sloping steeply downward. Phil was being drawn into the chasm. He could not resist. A relentless force was tugging at his ankles and calves, dragging him down. And from the abyss, a demonic cacophony of screaming and cursing hysterical laughter could be heard, while above the din, he heard a rhythmic chant:

"Aliation, aliation, aliation. . ."

As Phil slid past the desk, he flailed his arms, frantically clawing the air, grasping for any solid object that would break his fall.

I'm not dreaming, he thought. *The bastards have drugged me. Someone has slipped me a wicked dose of acid.*

Soon though, he realized the futility of his efforts and did something uncharacteristic: he surrendered. With his body tumbling limply toward chaos, there was a strange sense of relief.

Let it happen, thought Phil. *At least I don't have to fight it any more.* But nothing happened. The room simply dissolved and he found himself standing on a deserted boardwalk. He looked up at a deep blue sky sparsely streaked with wispy cirrus clouds, then over at the ocean and a horizon brilliantly gilded by the ascending sun.

An offshore breeze sprayed him with a fine mist of sea air. He tasted the salt faintly and began to relive childhood summers spent at Rockaway Beach . . . hours of carefree play in the surf, barefooted walks back to the bungalow, the smell of wet grass in the back yard as soapy water drained off wooden slats and trickled under the stall of the outdoor shower. He could feel the crispness of fresh clothes against his newly-dried skin, sense his eager appetite leaping ahead to hot buttered rolls and the hearty meal that would follow when the family sat down to dinner on their screened-in porch. So guileless, so open, here he was alive. . .

Phil turned from the ocean breeze. Several familiar faces were approaching. He should have been surprised to find his students in that remote setting, but he was not. Their presence seemed perfectly natural.

Phil smiled easily and they returned his greeting. He began a leisurely stroll along the boards flanked by the members of his class. They spoke earnestly, seeking his views on contemporary

social problems and abstract questions of theory. Answers were
fluently given, but at the same time he tried to convey the broader
sense in which the answers did not matter. A deepening feeling of
serenity settled over the strollers.

As the process continued, it dawned on Phil that verbal
communication had ceased. It had become unnecessary. They
had begun to exchange ideas directly, their minds blending into a
collective awareness. They were drifting in unison through a
quasi-conceptual space. The boardwalk was gone. The beach and
ocean had evaporated. All that remained was a sea of free-floating
faces—the teacher's and those of his students. No distinct boundaries were maintained between units. One moment the faces
were detached from each other, the next they were fused into an
organic totality. And the movement of faces was fluid. Rhythmically, they dilated into oneness, then contracted into isolated
segments. With each union, the expression of unearthly contemplation appearing upon individual faces became magnified infinitely in a holy communion of wisdom.

But just as the mood was reaching a tantalizing peak of
intensity, a climax of revelation, Phil awoke.

The sense of cosmic unity rapidly decayed. A moment after
regaining consciousness, it was a faraway echo from inner space.
Then there was nothing.

But consciousness was not *fully* restored. Phil hauled himself
up and moved through his chores in a daze. He emptied his pipe
perfunctorily and crossed the room. With the stereo switched off
and cassette returned to its niche, he shuffled into the kitchen,
staying only long enough to run some water over food-caked
dishes. Unsteadily, Phil circled back to his point of origin, extin-
guishing the lights as he went. At last, bed! He pulled off his robe
and fell in.

The descent to oblivion began immediately. It hardly was
impeded by the fleeting glimmer of transcendent Oneness. Brush-
ing this aside, he sank into a dreamless sleep.

There she was again, his "Woman in White." Today she was all in flowing black. Chiffon blouse, ankle-length skirt, sandals, the perfect Gothic contrast of ebony on chalk. Her skin was so pale.

This apparition had been haunting him for months, it seemed. A dozen times she had appeared to him on campus: in the library, cafeteria, bookstore, in the corridors as he went from class to class. He had seen her on the crosstown bus, the subway, at the local cinema and once dragging an overstuffed bag of wash from the laundromat. At times he felt her eyes upon him, felt them penetrate, and he could swear she had been following him.

Now he was in the supermarket. Phil was on line waiting for the checker. The girl had come up behind him, her slender arms laden with more than they could manage. He was looking straight ahead, trying to avoid her, but could not help noticing a container of milk slipping from her grasp. In a reflex movement, he whirled and reached out with two hands, trapping the container against her abdomen before it could tumble away. They both laughed. Both were embarrassed.

"It looks like we're going to be here awhile. You don't have to spend the whole time juggling. Put your things in my basket."

She smiled reluctantly until an apple came loose and started creeping out over her elbow. "Thanks. Maybe I'd better. I wound up with more than I had planned."

Phil could have let it go at that, but his curiosity won out. "What are you studying at Franklin?"

"How did you know I was studying at Franklin?"

Oh, come on! She's playing dumb, thought Phil. "You mean you've never seen me before?"

"What?" She sounded genuinely surprised.

"Never mind," Phil said. He secretly applauded her performance.

"Psychology." Her one-word declaration broke the silence. "Undergraduate?"

"Graduate. I've started the master's program. . ."

"Good."

". . .for the *third* time."

"Oh. Well, that's all right. You want to be sure before you get too deeply involved."

She changed the subject. "Are you a teacher or something?"

"It shows, doesn't it? Too bad. I was hoping you wouldn't notice."

"But it's not your age. You could be a graduate student. It's just. . ."

"Just my style."

"That's right. I mean, it's nice. You seem very self assured."

Phil started to answer, wanted to keep the dialogue going, but in straining for a clever or witty reply, he came up blank. Small talk was so painful for him.

The line moved slowly. When they finally reached the checkout counter, Phil stepped aside to let her through. "You first," he said, with a gallant flourish. Thanking him, she slipped into the narrow aisle and began to sort her items from his cart.

"What do you teach?"

"Sociology." Each time she leaned into his basket, she brushed him with her skirt.

"Soc was my minor. It's pretty close to psychology, wouldn't you say?"

"People make too much of that. Each discipline has its own method and approach."

Outside, it was heating up. The sun had broken through the clouds, but the humidity gave no hint of compromise, at least as far as she could tell. It would be the kind of day where you could *smell* the heat, and she wanted no part of it. Her plan of action: a long, cold bath, then maybe a few hours in the recesses of the college library stacks.

As she started down the block, she heard his voice again.

"You didn't tell me your name."

"You didn't ask me. It's Sandra Peterson."

"I'm Phil Myerson."

"Doctor? Professor?. . ."

"Both. But I'll settle happily for Phil."

On the way home, Sandra puzzled over the strong emotions she was feeling. What was it about this man that she found so attractive? Certainly not his academic status. That kind of thing didn't impress her. Besides, he had seemed pretty pompous on that score—"each discipline has its own method and approach," she could hear the professor saying.

There *was* a hint of charm in the fellow, the promise of a real sense of humor that could be brought out, nurtured. She thought if she could get him to loosen up a little, Phil Myerson might turn out to be a delightful companion. But that still did not explain what she was *feeling*.

Could it have been a simple sexual attraction? Sandy wondered. Maybe that was it, she decided, something sexual—but if so, it was far from simple. Phil was not a bad looking guy -tall and slim, broad shoulders, dark curly hair with a dimpled, crooked smile—yet not nearly striking enough to account for her present emotions. *Then what do I mean by "sexual"?* she asked herself. *I mean something more than just physical, something deeper, an intensity, a yearning. Yes, there's a yearning in the man, as if he wants something badly without even being aware of it. Or maybe it's what he wants to become?*

Is it what I want too? mused Sandy. The spark of intuition was doused in the icy water of her tub.

The temperature rose to 105° F., unusual for the fifth of May. Speculation had it that this meteorological anomaly in some way was responsible for the phenomenon reported at Ocean's Edge Light, but Colonel Alan Hagger of the Central Intelligence Agency was convinced he knew better. Canceling a dinner engagement, he sat in his Washington office reviewing the disquieting facts that had been brought to his attention.

When the small Rhode Island community awoke that morning, no atmospheric disturbance was indicated. By noon, the sky had cleared completely and the chance of precipitation seemed remote. Yet before the hour of one, with still not a cloud to be seen, there was a distant rumbling of thunder. Events developed rapidly from there. A loud humming sound, which amplified in short order to unnerving intensities, was heard. A wholesale loss of electrical power then was experienced on the peninsula, accompanied by three earth-shaking explosions in quick succession, blasts that led residents to believe that a plane had crashed or a bomb had fallen.

This was followed by a visual extravaganza that triggered images of biblical apocalypse in some. Incandescent flashes transformed the familiar ambience, setting the air aglow with a silvery luminance tinged blue and red, and through this pervasive aura, three large balls of fire were seen sloping down from the heavens.

The electrical damage far exceeded the structural. Power lines were destroyed, voltage regulators fused, and all fuses linked to the transformer at the local power station were melted. Only in the immediate area of the lighthouse, the fireballs' area of impact, were *non*-electrical effects significantly manifested. In the old boardwalk that sank into the sand near the base of the tower, three round holes had been burned, forming an almost perfect equilateral triangle. Still more bizarre was the condition in which the lighthouse itself had been left. The upper portion of its convex dome had been severely stressed. Yet, instead of simply breaking apart, the dome had been partially *peeled back*, inexplicably made *concave*, so that its inner ceiling now lay open to the sky.

"Damn thing is turned *inside out*," Colonel Hagger muttered to himself, thumbing through the series of photographs that depicted the dome from various angles.

Yet despite its genuinely perplexing aspects, the Colonel did not feel entirely in the dark on the incident at Ocean's Edge. Of course, the sonic-boom interpretation had to be dismissed immediately, nor did the meteor shower hypothesis hold up much better, given the circumstances. But certain colleagues of the Colonel, operating under the sponsorship of his government agency, believed they understood the nature and source of the queer phenomenon. An "EYES ONLY" memorandum delivered to Hagger by special courier that afternoon had spoken of an exotic form of low-frequency radiation suspected of being transmitted from one or more secret installations in Eastern Europe.

It's a dangerous game, thought Colonel Hagger. *It seems the enemy is playing with fire.* Closing his folder on Ocean's Edge Light, Hagger vowed that the enemy would be burned.

A continent away, Supervisor Vladimir Malek of the KGB was conducting an investigation of his own. Unbeknownst to the Colonel, the Ocean's Edge episode had had a mirror counterpart. The same effects observed on the Rhode Island peninsula had been experienced simultaneously at a fishing base in the south Baltic Sea inside the Soviet Union.

It appears our adversary is courting disaster, thought Supervisor Malek. *If acts of sabotage are being perpetrated against the Motherland, they will not go unanswered.*

 **2**

Awkward Maneuvers

IN THE LAST WEEK OF MAY, THE UNDERGRADU-
ate cafeteria at Franklin College was closed for renovations,
and the professors were obliged to share their own culinary
environment with their students. Scanning the crowded
faculty dining room, Phil found only one vacant space at the
end of the table occupied by the psychologists. He nodded to a
few familiar faces, then settled down and started on the contents of his tray. But he was not uninterested in their topic of
conversation.

A full-time, tenure-bearing position was available to the
Department of Psychology, the first in several years. However,
the administration stipulated that the opportunity would have
to be seized by July first or be lost for the forseeable future, if
not forever. It was now the middle of June. Dozens of appli-
cants had been interviewed. The finalists had been re-
interviewed and observed at specially convened colloquia.
Hours were spent in deliberation, but the Personnel Commit-

tee was hopelessly deadlocked. Two votes had been cast for one candidate and two for the other, with the chairperson of that Committee steadfastly refusing to break the tie, "as a matter of principle," though the grounds for his repeated abstention remained obscure.

"It's not a question of politics," said the single Committee member present at the impromptu lunch table inquest.

"Then what is it? Your decision is going to have an impact on us. We have the right to know." The young clinical psychologist was indignant.

"Come on, Steve, you know how we have to operate. With two weeks to go, all we need are more problems. I violate the Committee's confidence, word gets out, and the line will *really* fly through the window."

Something he noticed from the corner of his eye gave Phil the distinct impression that the Committeeman had tacitly identified *him* in speaking of "word getting out."

The behaviorist presently entered the discussion. "If it's not politics, then it has to be the specialization. I've talked this over with Helmut and Paul. Clearly the Department needs another good Skinnerian. There'll be no grant money without a staff to carry out the research."

To the Committeeman, the sales pitch came as a welcome relief. Let the others speculate all they wished. He would sip his tea.

"Lester, I know this might break your heart," the clinician said, "but I don't think either of our two finalists is a Skinnerian."

Phil glanced across the table for Lester Pullman's reaction but was drawn instead to a swirl of gingham threading through the crowd. Once more, it was she. The same flowing, ankle-length cotton skirt, though now faded pink on white. The same thick, straight raven hair and open sandals. She was easy to track as she wound past clusters of fellow students, for most of them were of darker complexion, many with tans. Sandra Peterson's bare arms and willowy neck were as pale as ever.

". . . I think one has a strong background in social. Anyway, it would make sense. We haven't had a social psychologist since Margie Cannon retired. The course has to be taught. . ."

Her sinuous movement had a spellbinding effect on Phil. It unfolded as a visual drama fraught with surprise. Where would the next curve arise from what seemed to be straightness? At a calf? A hip or buttock? At the breasts? He had seen her many times before. Why had he never noticed her non-Euclidean aspects?

". . . They've got some kind of experimentalist in there. You can bet on it. And my sources tell me he's involved with biofeedback or some such thing. . ."

Enough. Phil had heard enough. He was badly in need of more coffee. He got up somewhat abruptly and started for the food line. Without being too rude or conspicuous, Phil used a shoulder here to wedge a path, an elbow there to pry an opening. Maneuvering in this "broken field" fashion, he pressed toward his objective. The last few steps demanded special agility since two strapping varsity jocks were approaching the end of the line from the other direction, taking enormous steps. But Phil turned the trick somehow, pretty much keeping his cool in the bargain. With that last bit of "razzle-dazzle," he slipped in behind the slender coed.

"It seems we're destined to always meet this way."

Startled, Sandy turned. "Oh, hello!. . .That's right, we're doing it again, aren't we?"

"Maybe we should try to break the pattern, arrange to bump into each other someplace else—*any* place but on a checkout line."

She smiled without answering.

"No planned encounter to foil the fates? Okay, what about a little coffee here and now? Or, if you're having lunch, you can use my tray. It'll be like old times."

Laughing appreciatively, she assented.

The search for eating space carried them to the far corners
of the faculty cafeteria. They circumnavigated the congested
room several times, steering a precarious course with cups and
silverware clattering. It was to no avail.

At last a single opening materialized and Phil rushed over
to stake his claim.

"Sit here," he commanded.

"What about you?"

"I've got to get back to the office anyway. I'm expecting
students."

"But I thought. . ."

"Yeah, well I only could have stayed a few minutes even if
there were room for me."

She cast a final glance around the packed dining area, then
wistfully tilted her head. "I guess it's hopeless."

"Looks that way," said Phil, "but I wasn't kidding before.
We really *should* meet, but not on any damned checkout line.
Then the fates will know who the masters are!"

"Right. Yes. I agree."

"Can you make it this Friday?" asked Phil.

The time and place were established. He would pick her
up at her apartment at seven-thirty and they would proceed to
Jagger's Restaurant. No definite plans were made for after
dinner. They would improvise.

As it happened, the schedule had to be slightly revised. In
the middle of the week, Phil learned of a reception for selected
faculty members to be held in the home of the college president. This invitation he could scarcely decline, and the event
was slated for the cocktail hour on Friday evening. He called
Sandy on Thursday night, asked her to meet him outside the
restaurant at eight, and told her he would refuse all offerings of
food at the president's party. The magnitude of the sacrifice
was impressed upon her—the president's reputation for
extravagant fare was widely known.

No promise had been made to abstain from drink. Phil arrived at *Jagger's* feeling uncomfortably warm and a trifle high. But he was well in control. His "Woman in White" was entirely so clad, except for a black and gold pendant that dangled far below the V-necked opening of her blouse.

"Ten after eight. Am I in trouble?"

She shook her head to the contrary.

"You're a very understanding person. Shall we go in?"

Taking her arm, he ushered her to the threshold. The riddle of her mischievous grin was solved the moment he opened the restaurant's door. Extending into the vestibule was a long line of patrons waiting to be seated.

"No! Another food line! I can't believe it! I won't accept it!"

Phil's caricature of stunned mortification was a comedic masterpiece that shattered Sandy's composure. She burst into hysterical laughter and Phil joined in, causing heads to turn. They backed out of *Jagger's* onto the street.

"Enough. Enough," said Phil. Both were breathless.

"We've got to remake our plans. The fates are more powerful than I calculated."

Putting his arm around her, he turned them in a southerly direction and they began to walk. They were heading downtown toward the parking garage that housed his car.

"Are you as warm as I am?" asked Phil.

"I'm suffocating."

"Good—I mean, yes. Me too. Why don't we leave the city. We can drive out to the beach where the air might at least be stirring a little."

"Sounds delightful to me," she replied, "but aren't you hungry? How much longer can a full-grown man hold out?"

"Honey, if I passed up the president's *hors d'oeuvres*, I can forego anything—that is, for a little while longer. We can stop for something on the way."

They were going to Rockaway, a ten-mile strip of sand, boardwalk and bungalows that had long been a warm weather sanctuary for New Yorkers who could not afford better or more exotic. In Phil's formative years, it had been the summer retreat for the Myerson family.

They took the Queensboro Bridge, stopped at a *McDonald's*, then continued south on Woodhaven Boulevard. Not a word was exchanged until the Crossbay Bridge. Words were a complication for Sandy. They did not seem to matter when she was feeling as she did, so content, so perfectly at ease. Inclined toward Phil in a semi-fetal position, her left arm was draped over the seat back, her cheek resting lightly on her arm. Eyes softly focused on the flickering night lights beyond the driver's window, she was rocked into a prolonged reverie by the periodic slowing down, the speeding up, the rhythmic motion of the car.

For his part, Phil was trying to reconstruct the texture of his youthful summers in Rockaway. He wondered how closely the Rockaway of the present would match the one he had built from memory, for he had not been there in twenty years. Lately though, he had begun to think a lot about those days, even dream about them. Now he was going back . . . on an impulse, he told himself at first. But conscious of the willowy figure beside him, he thought again. *Was* it only an impulse? Then why had he never had it when alone or with some other companion? Twenty years and never such an impulse. Was there something about this companion that made him want to share his private world, make it public for her? If so, he could not bring himself to tell her, to share it in words. She would have to see it for herself, and she would see Phil.

Squirming under his seat belt, he fished a quarter from his pocket and tossed it into the toll machine. They crossed the bridge, turned left, and proceeded along Beach Channel Drive.

This was a route he knew well, having covered it countless times in the family's rusty old Chrysler. The streets were numbered. Coming off the Crossbay, the numbers started in the nineties and went down. The Myerson bungalow was on Beach 38th Street, but "his sector" of Rockaway began on 45th. *His sector of Rockaway.* Phil remembered how the concept had evolved from mental games he would invent to lessen his misery on those steaming excursions. Once past *The Beach Shop*, the sprawling variety store on the corner of 45th Street, he fancied himself on home ground (though in actual practice, the farthest western outpost of his domain was Billy Elkind's house on 43rd Street).

In the early years on Rockaway, the heartland of his turf was in the upper 30's, the Myerson bungalow being its natural center. But when he entered adolescence, the center shifted three blocks eastward. The beach on 35th Street was where the "action" was, the gravitational hub of all post-pubescent longings and aspirations. Twenty-ninth Street was the eastern boundary. That was where the shopping district ended—how he had hated being dragged there by his mother to "put clothes on his back," or worse, to "help with the bags" on a sunny day.

Everything was normal above 70th Street. But descending through the 60's, Phil and Sandy began to notice a disappearance of life. Fewer and fewer people could be seen on the streets, abandoned buildings were turning up in growing numbers, and beyond the broken windows and crumbling storefronts, the bungalows were lightless.

Despite this prelude, Phil was unprepared for what he next encountered. Past Beach 55th Street, they went by a sign which made some terse and official statement about urban renewal. Then there was nothing. *Literally* nothing. It would have been sad, Phil brooded, if *all* the buildings now were boarded up and decaying, sadder if they had all been demolished and lay in rubble. But it was worse than that. There simply *were* no buildings . . . nor any sidewalks, trees, or boardwalk. The landscape had lost an entire dimension; it had been utterly leveled, save for the barest skeletal traces—the numbered lampposts on every corner, a few isolated telephone poles scattered haphazardly. Beyond that was only the naked sand, the pounding surf.

What a curious feeling, this loss of continuity. A chunk of his past had been cut away and in more than a manner of speaking, it seemed. Phil slowed the car to a crawl, at every block expecting that *his* Rockaway would appear on the horizon, that *something* would be left. But it was Hiroshima all the way. If he could never tread those paths again, never go back into that peculiar network of closed and open spaces where the poignant atmosphere of his youth had hovered, if the physical structures embodying his summer world had disappeared, who was to say for sure that it had ever really existed?

"God, this is spooky." Sandy shivered visibly. "Where have you taken me, you cad?"

"We just passed my bungalow. It's over there in the middle of that block." Phil was pointing back to empty space.

"You don't mean to say you lived here once? It's hard to believe. When did they start tearing it down?"

"I have no idea."

"You didn't know?" Hearing no response, she persisted. "Phil, you didn't even *know*?"

"How could I have known if I haven't been back?" He seemed to be getting irritated.

"But tonight you came back, with me."

Phil dipped his head matter-of-factly and opened the palm of his free hand to her and to their surroundings. She was stating the obvious.

"How long did you live here? How long *ago*?"

"The first sixteen summers of my life."

"Then you have to feel pretty—"

"I don't feel. I mean, what is there to feel?" His eyes were fixed on the road.

"Anyway," said Sandy, touching his sleeve with her fingertips, "I'm *glad* you brought me back here because I can see it, Phil. I can sense that it's all still here."

With that, he pulled the car over and cut the ignition. "Then you must be hallucinating," he said. Forcefully, he took her in his arms and they embraced.

Phil drove to 35th Street, made a right turn, and cruised until asphalt stopped and sand began.

"Bow your head; you're on hallowed ground," Phil intoned. "Imagine yourself sitting in front of a ramp leading up to a boardwalk. Those boards, the ones before your eyes, were a Mecca for everyone under 20 and over 12."

Sandy inquired if they could "go up," and obligingly, the driver got out and came around to hold the door. Before leaving the car, she took off her sandals. Phil followed her example with shoes and socks but warned her in his no-nonsense voice to be wary of splinters.

As they approached the edge of the asphalt, Phil slipped an arm around her. She would need help on that first treacherous step. Continuing in pantomime, he raised his leg with the exaggerated motion of a drum major and unexpectedly advanced.

It should have been rehearsed, for Sandy instinctively resisted the sudden pull at her waist. This caused Phil to break stride. He stumbled forward, dragging her down with him, and they landed in a heap.

For the second time that night, Sandy and Phil were in stitches. And—sprawled out in the sand, their bodies joyously entangled—they made it last. When they finally disengaged, it was at Phil's initiative. She had actually begun to take liberties with him—*she* with *him!* He straightened nonchalantly, brushed away some sand and began to roll up the cuffs of his trousers.

"I'll probably never get another chance to wet my toes in that ocean. Want to come?"

It was a cynical ploy. The moment they reached the surf, he moved like lightning. Sweeping her off her feet, he bore her into the shallow tide.

"I should have told you," said Phil, noisily huffing and puffing, "I'm a frustrated thespian . . . tonight it's 'From Here to Eternity.'"

The fierce battle she put up only encouraged him to go further. But soon he tired, and when the turbulent foam began to lap above his knees, Phil came to a halt. At the same time, Sandy fell silent. Coiled like a spring, she waited for her opportunity to strike back. Phil peered into her defiant face with wide-eyed innocence. "You do want to be my leading lady, don't you?"

She answered by unleashing a surprise volley of flailing arms and legs that sent them splashing to the ocean floor.

Supporting each other, they waded back to dry ground and collapsed in exaltation, barely able to breathe and soaked to the skin. Upon regaining her wind, Sandy arose and reached for the dripping hem that was plastered to her ankles. It was the natural thing to do, and she did it with the artless grace of a country child bending to pick a daisy. In a single fluid motion, the dress was off and being spread upon the sand.

"It shouldn't take too long to dry," said Sandy. The pendant that hung from her neck twisted and swung as she crouched above her work. It had an oriental look, he noticed.

"Would you mind doing some extra laundry?"

"Just a second." She was almost finished with her own. Sitting back on her heels, Sandy found the professor struggling with his waterlogged pants.

"I think it would be easier if you got up." He took her advice, secretly chiding himself for the awkward display. *I should at least have started at the top*, he thought fretfully.

Forcing himself to be more deliberate, he unbuttoned his shirt. Next, with one hand, he completed the job on his pants, holding the shirt casually in front of him as if it were anything but a screen.

Sandy received his wet clothes and turned to stretch them beside her dress. The moment the laundry was done, he was at her side offering assistance. As he helped her get up, he allowed an arm to slide across her back to her shoulder. Then, all at once, Phil was the master. She was being enfolded, gathered into a closing circle she could scarcely evade if she wanted to. Slowly, gently, he kissed her forehead, her eyes, her mouth. Using his tongue, he traced a winding path across her cheek and whispered in her ear, "I love you, Sandy."

In response, she became one with him. They dropped to the sand, never breaking their embrace and, for a short while, the tempo of ecstasy built within itself.

Then Phil started thinking. She was on top and that would not do. How could he get them inverted? Perhaps by raising his leg and elbow a bit, he could maneuver them into the appropriate position. *No. It's not working. I'm being too delicate. I must be more decisive. I can make it seem like it's part of the moment's passion*, he contrived.

Sandy was startled from her rapture by a jerk and a bump. He had reared up and flipped her onto her back.

"Sorry, honey. Guess I got carried away."

Now that things were set right, he would pick up where he left off. Mounted atop his woman, he began to caress her again, his hands, lips and tongue moving as before. But it wasn't like before. The more assertive he became—and he knew that this should be turning her on—the more she was deadened. Long and heroic efforts on his part bore no fruit. She remained impassive.

He finally stood up in a sweat. "What's the matter with you?"

"Probably fatigue—too much studying. Don't worry

about it." She sighed briefly and rolled on her side.

"I don't understand you," he said to her back. "One minute you're ready to go, the next you're dropping out on me. Did I do something? How about giving me an explanation?"

Getting none, Phil walked around to confront her face to face. Sandy was *fast asleep.* Shaking his head, he fell to his knees. *This is absurd!* Yet, what could he expect under *these* circumstances?

He looked at his watch. It was nearly midnight. Here he was, sitting beside a naked woman on a desert within the desert of his youth, and she was sound asleep. But he could not bring himself to laugh.

". . . a what?!"

"A parapsychologist," said Martin Curtis.

Phil rose from his desk. "They must be totally crazy. The heat must have cooked their brains. I thought they were considering an experimentalist?"

"He is. Or, more correctly, *was.* He was formally trained in that. Then he began flirting with the notion of mind control through biofeedback."

"Which means attaching electrodes to you so you can see a record of your brain waves, heart rate, and the like. Am I right?"

"Quite," confirmed Curtis. "And presumably, you learn to regulate your vital rhythms by simply viewing them on a monitor as they run off."

"Well, that doesn't sound so terrible," Phil said.

"No. It would not be if that's where it ended. But it seems the fellow has tried to tie it in with developing 'our latent psychic powers.' God only knows how."

"Ugh!"

"Wait, Phil, wait. It gets worse. Lately he's even dropped the *guise* of being scientific. Noel Innerman has apparently 'risen above' the need to do experimental research. You won't find him soiling himself in the laboratory."

"What *does* he do?"

"He philosophizes. He's concocted some sort of 'model' for THE INTEGRATION OF SCIENCE AND PARA-SCIENCE. A lot of pretentious crap that no one understands."

"I'll bet not even him," Phil added.

"Right, but here's the *coup de grâce*: to dramatize this business it seems the man has undertaken a *novel*."

Phil shook his head in disbelief. "What Chutzpah!"

"Huh?"

"Gall," explained Phil, "unmitigated gall. Tell me, where did Dr. Innerman earn his degree?"

"Can't you guess?"

"The University of California at somewhere."

"Yes, yes. . .," Curtis prompted.

". . .at Santa Barbara."

"Try again."

"Davis?"

"Bravo! The gentleman gets a cigar."

"But Martin, what really puzzles me is you. How on earth did you get so much information on the inner workings of the Psychology Department?"

"Thankfully, the psychologists weren't of one mind on the choice. I'm sure you know that. In fact, some of them feel rather strongly about the way things turned out. They don't want to see their Department destroyed. They argue convincingly that the credibility of the entire college is at stake."

"They spoke to you?" Phil inquired.

"I was approached and they asked me to contact you."

"You mean you didn't come to my office just to be sociable?"

"I was hoping you'd have some free time," said Curtis. "They're meeting in Pullman's laboratory and we're invited to join them."

"Now?"

"Yes."

"They want The Committee For Sense and Sanity involved?"

"Let's just go over there, Phil, and hear them out."

Three sweating men sat atop stools, the sleeves of their lab coats rolled above their elbows. They were fanning themselves. All around them were the regalia of modern research technology. Panel after panel of switches, dials, meters and small red lights covered two entire walls. Many of the shiny gray sections were interconnected by a multicolored network of crisscrossing wires. And in places where panels had been removed from the frame, an impressive maze of support circuits was exposed. On another wall were shelves of books neatly aligned from floor to ceiling and issues of professional journals arranged by month and year. There were tables loaded high with mesh-enclosed cages, elaborately equipped and occupied by creatures who could be heard scratching and scurrying about. And a special table was reserved for surgery, judging from the precision instruments that adorned it, the row of vials carefully laid out, and from the metallic insets apparently designed for the purpose of restricting movement.

Squatting in a corner of the room was an overstuffed wastebasket. A tremendous tangle of discarded read-out tapes spilled onto the floor and crept out in every direction. But this was no sign of disorder. On the contrary, it was an indication that much work had been done, that progress had been made here.

The only note of discord was struck by the drone of the ancient electric fan. It stood on the windowsill, swiveled through its arc at regular intervals, but did little to fill the function of the air conditioner that had broken down days before.

Phil was re-introduced to the long-suffering triumverate sweating in their technological wonderland.

"You know Lester Pullman, Barry Driver, Solomon Harrington," said Curtis.

Phil extended his hand to each. Driver was the first to speak.

"I want to make something clear. This sort of thing is a first for me and I don't like doing it. But Phil, I think you'll see there's no alternative. We are reaching a point of desperation."

"Barry's being a trifle melodramatic. Too worried about those grant dollars. If you fellas can manage a helping hand, *we'll* get it straightened out." The optimist was Solomon Harrington, an obese practitioner of behavior modification who spoke so slowly he was sometimes mistaken for a Southerner.

"What would you like us to do?" asked Phil.

"Barry is being *realistic*," Lester interjected excitedly. "I am on the verge of closing this laboratory. I will resign before I'll allow my name to be associated with pseudo-science."

Driver urged his colleague to calm down, then addressed himself to the guests.

"Grant money is at stake. I can hardly deny that. But there's much more to it. As it stands now, we're rated among the top twenty psychology programs in the country—"

"It won't be for long—"

"Lester, would you mind?" Driver composed himself and went on. "Over the years, we've earned respect by maintaining the highest standards. We get some of the finest students and can get them *placed*, which is saying a lot nowadays. Our faculty's research is published in the best journals. In short, we're a solid force and we want to stay that way. But it'll never happen unless extraordinary measures are taken because the damned vote is in."

"Outside intervention. That is the only viable solution," added Pullman. "Our esteemed president will never act on his own. He'll rubber stamp the Department's decision as he always has. But with some urging from the community, perhaps his paralysis can be cured."

"Phil guessed that you've asked for The Committee," Curtis explained.

"That's right, Phil." The behavioral engineer tilted his massive frame forward and opened his hands. "Let's let the community see that we've made a mistake and, with a little input from them, we're ready to own up and correct our error promptly before it can do any damage."

"And The Committee would bring it to the public," said Phil.

"Faster and better than any of us could." Harrington was now almost animated. "I'll bet your Stanford astronomer — what's his name?"

"Forrest Reynolds."

"I'll bet Reynolds can move mountains with the local press."

"Slow down a second. If he's available, Forrest could help. But we shouldn't be overestimated."

"Also," said Driver, "the politics of the matter are kind of delicate. Obviously."

"*Obviously.*" Harrington chuckled as he echoed the gratuitous remark. Driver continued. "We have got to protect ourselves at all costs. It can't get out that *we* summoned The Committee. That would be the worst thing that could happen — even worse than letting in that oily Svengali."

"But Barry, how will Martin and I stay out of it? People know we're connected with The Committee. Won't they draw the natural inference?"

"I guess we can't stop them from speculating. But who could be sure?" said Driver.

Harrington interceded. "Look, my friends. I've seen your Committee in action—truly a wonder to behold. Nothing gets through those far-flung nets of yours. I don't have to tell *you* that your Committee has investigated several faculty appointments in this area alone and on campuses where nary a Committee member could be found. I don't see why this couldn't seem like just another item on The Committee's busy agenda."

"Solomon, please don't use the word 'appointment.' It is still in the hands of the president," Pullman observed. "There has been no official appointment yet—thank God!"

"Which is our problem," Driver asserted. "How could The Committee investigate a decision that hasn't been made public without a *private* information source? It could look quite bad."

"But it doesn't have to if we do it up right," protested Harrington. "Naturally, The Committee won't talk 'appointment.' It hasn't happened and won't, if we're sensible. And it can't talk 'vote' since it has no inkling of that, does it? But what's to prevent The Committee from merely commenting, in its own inimitable style, that a fellow with rather dubious credentials has been interviewed and is being considered at Franklin College? No one would expect that to remain a secret for very long. After all, this Innerman character is pretty well known in some circles. The Committee could have been tipped off by any one of a number of folks who know what he's up to, people *outside* the college."

"I see where there'd still be a doubt," said Curtis, and Driver noted darkly, "That would be enough. Small doubts often lead to big trouble."

"Is that Confucius?" asked Harrington.

After several moments of silence, he rose from his stool with surprising alacrity.

"Gentlemen, eureka! There's no need to print a single word about Franklin College. These hallowed halls can be left entirely out of the picture. All we require from The Committee is a feature article on Noel Innerman, or at least one that mentions him prominently. If the piece is given the proper slant and circulates widely enough—"

"—into the president's office—" Pullman inserted.

"—Yes, if it does that, I think we can rest easy."

Driver was smiling broadly for the first time. "I like it. What I mean is, I think it will work. That on top of the split vote should turn the trick."

"Of course, you would need the right kind of man in the president's chair," said Curtis. "A bit spineless, highly susceptible to the changing winds of public opinion, phobic about controversy. Do we have that kind of man up there?" Curtis answered his own question. "I believe we have."

Only one conspirator stood mute. Interpreting, Curtis said, "Believe me, Phil, none of us is happy about this. But what options do we have? I don't have to tell you that if Innerman finagles his way in, the psychologists won't be the only ones to suffer."

"I'll call Reynolds tomorrow," said Phil.

"Bravo!" Harrington led the cheers, then suggested, "Why not try him tonight? I don't want to push this thing too hard, but we may not make it as it is. The decision from the 'Oval Office' could come down before the week is out."

The process went like clockwork. The call was placed, the article was written, tailored to perfection, and three mornings after the conclave in Pullman's sweltering laboratory, it made *The New York Times* and the president's desk—a shining example of efficient informational flow and big name media clout, in Harrington's estimation.

They had been right about the president as well. With Reynolds' smooth dismissal of Innerman's career, sanctified by *The Times* and inscribed for all the world to see, Anderson could not bring himself to sanction the Department's decision. The full-time, tenure-bearing line was awarded to the social psychologist who had been runner-up. Confident that the Department and College had been saved, the conspirators rejoiced.

Just one miscalculation marred the triumph. Apparently,

The Times article had not discredited Innerman thoroughly enough to prevent the president from seeking a compromise. A bone was thrown to the disaffected Department majority. They were informed that Innerman might have the president's support if an adjunct position were sought for him at some future time.

 **3**

The Omega Expedition

LATE IN THE SUMMER, *THE OMEGA EXPEDITION* had its gala premiere. It opened simultaneously in California and New York and was billed as the definitive step beyond *Close Encounters of the Third Kind* and *2001: A Space Odyssey*. The science fiction spectacle had been seven years in the making. Its director, Merlin Mises, had discontinued his patented line of "psychological shockers" and their sequels to gamble on an entirely novel approach.

The Omega Expedition went into eclipse at its Los Angeles opening. With klieg lights sweeping the night skies and limousines pouring forth high-fashioned luminaries moment by moment, the film itself became something of an afterthought. Much later, when cinematic images finally found their way onto the screen, they could barely compete with those seated about the theater.

The pageantry attending the New York premiere was not quite so distracting. Promply at 9 p.m., the curtain rose to an audience that included a scattering of celebrities and critics, a larger contingent of avid science fiction buffs, and the reliable breed that will never miss a first performance. The showing also attracted a fair number of serious cultists and students of the avant-garde for, in addition to the massive commercial promotion of the film, it was being touted in more exclusive circles as an unusual prospect, one that might break new ground.

The audience got down to business before the credits began rolling, even before the lights were dimmed. No preliminary chatter could be heard that night. The house was primed to a state of high expectation, ready for a total experience. They could not know how total it would *be*.

The theater was thrown into blackness and the title of the movie came into view. At the same instant, an amplified thumping commenced along with the cadence of deep, protracted inhalation, exhalation. There was nothing more for quite a while except the players' names, lettered conservatively and shown at long intervals. Then fuzzy flecks of yellow began materializing. As they grew in number, the staccato rhythms of life receded into the background.

Softly, "a star exploded" in the galaxy of inner experience being portrayed. Muted streaks of yellow, blue and white splashed across the screen. A moment later, darkness again predominated, only to be followed by another liquid flare-up. These ethereal pyrotechnics continued until the last credit faded out.

A panel opened, a square of intense white light was exposed. Next, the sound of water sloshing, a silhouette bobbing up against the luminous frame, climbing out of the enclosure into a laboratory.

The "psychenaut" was handed a towel. Unsteadily, he moved to a chair and the dialogue began.

A most peculiar research venture was under way. *Project Lazarus* was an experimental rescue mission aimed at "retrieving" a government scientist who had been lost before he could complete his pioneering work in the area of laser technology. The scientist had died. But that was not necessarily an insurmountable obstacle from what the government had learned in its top secret inquiry into the relations among matter, energy and consciousness. They had actually discovered the hidden source of ordinary waking reality: a paraphysical reservoir of unfocused energy occupying a higher dimension of space and shared collectively by every member of the human family. The Project Director explained that when the brain is at rest, the person goes down into this well. Return to the sharply-focused, familiar level of consciousness occurs when the brain is reactivated. Of course, if it ceases to operate, if the brain cannot be reactivated, there can be no return. This is called "death." The living possess the capacity to refocus energy, the dead possess it no longer. That is the only difference. As one of the psychenauts put it, death is just consciousness irreversibly thrown out of focus, a sleep beyond sleep.

Now there were methods for reaching that state of cosmic awareness *deliberately*, and that meant maintaining an element of control. The psychenauts had come to understand that this had been the true purpose of all esoteric practices—Yoga, Zen, Christian and Jewish mysticism, Sufism and all the rest. The critical task was to empty the mind, to liberate it from the dominion of the senses: "Outward hearing should not penetrate further than the ear . . . thus the soul can become empty and absorb the whole world . . . use your inner eye and inner ear to pierce the heart of things." So spoke Chuang Tsu, a Chinese sage of old, and it was the credo of the mission.

Project Lazarus thus was founded on an extraordinary combination of frontier science and occult wisdom. The psychenauts comprised an elite corps of theoretical physicists who had been training intensively in the art of meditation. The vessel for plumbing the depths of inner space was the sensory deprivation tank. Suspended for hours on end in their lightless, soundproofed environment, these psychic submariners were learning to systematically shut down their physical, sense-receptive machinery while staying mentally alert. In this way, they hoped to make contact with the field of collective energy, then use their own brains to "tune in" their particular target.

A voluntarily induced sort of "spirit possession" was called for, one requiring the acumen to discern the contour of a given personality, entangled as it was in the subtle cosmic blend of all personalities, and the transcendental balance of a Wallenda. Could a droplet of water long retain its separate identity when cast into an ocean? That would be the challenge the psychenauts would face upon entering the ocean of consciousness.

Merlin Mises had met his own challenge. From the opening sequence, the audience was under his spell. The magic only grew more potent as the plot progressed. Then they were taken back into the tank for the *coup de theatre*.

Again there were the pyrotechnics, the liquid light show of the mind. Darkening by degrees now, these rainbow eruptions through gauze were becoming enshadowed, the somber psychedelics slowly contracting to a point. Next came blackness, enduring and pervasive.

The viewers now were ready for a singular moment in cinematic history. The unremitting darkness transformed the theater into a large-scale approximation of the psychenauts' tank. Without visual cues, the patrons were thrown back to their own subjective resources. When enough time was allowed for the locus of reality so to shift, images were projected again, pulses of cool luminosity oozed and flowed, but not upon the screen. Somehow they materialized in the very midst of the audience and not as thin, flat, pasteboard pictures. They were full-blown, three-dimensional forms obeying the principle of parallax by which they changed their appearance in relation to the position from which they were seen.

For a while, these ameboid apparitions continued in sinuous flux, assuming no greater definition. A kind of differentiation then followed, one seemingly achieved by means of light alone. At first there was simply an increase in contrast. Certain portions of the shapes shimmered more brightly than others. But in the ensuing process of luminous molding, the silvery outlines of humanoid figures could gradually be discerned.

Integration came next. The beings of light that hovered above the gaping spectators rapidly reproduced until all the spaces between them were filled; and still their number increased. Growing to impossible densities, the crowd of phantoms melded. What a jarring incongruity to see form pass through form with no regard for boundaries or the notion of private identity.

As the merger neared completion, a scream was heard. It was not on the sound track. A woman stood up, pushed her way to the aisle and ran from the theater. Others followed suit, though not all at once. The sporadic exodus had a peculiar aspect. Straggling to the door, the patrons seemed disoriented. They left the building like a dispersing band of somnambulists—glazed eyes, blank expressions, some even muttering queerly to themselves.

In the orchestra section, a violent quarrel broke out. A woman was shrieking at her male companion. Slapping and rebuking him, she called him "daddy," though he was clearly her contemporary. Elsewhere in the house, someone started sobbing mournfully and, in yet another section, a man reached for the dazzling overhead projection, then collapsed to the floor.

The New York premiere of *The Omega Expedition* was aborted at that point. Who could deny that the first dramatic application of cinematic holography had been effective? After dozens of interviews with those who had been in attendance, an incredible story emerged. The witnesses contended that they had not been merely decomposed by the unexpected use of a powerful new technique. They insisted that they had *seen themselves* in those undulating forms. Their thoughts, hidden feelings and fears, subjective impressions, had been *objectified*, put on public display! None of the participants found the experience easy to explain. More than one said a sense of being *turned inside out* was the closest they could come to describing what had happened.

In the ranks of the Committee for Sense and Sanity, there was little surprise. What could you expect from the motley crew of sci fi nuts and self-obsessed occultists who showed up for that opening? Of course, they were not all on "Angel Dust" or LSD, and probably not more than a few were genuinely psychotic. Simply ultra-impressionable, the Committee reasoned. It was clearly a case of mass hysteria among individuals so perfectly ripe for that sort of thing that they might have been picked by hand.

The Committee was not entirely displeased by the affair. It had confirmed the members' judgment on irrationality, on the potential of the New Nonsense to create havoc. Accounts of so-called "synchronous phenomena" were seen only to strengthen their position. In the days following the *Omega* episode, stories of similar aberrations were rampant. Claims of "seeing my feelings on the screen," of being "turned inside out," were made by theatergoers from Montreal to Manilla. In none of these cases had the hologram technique been used. Indeed, the same effect had allegedly been produced on hundreds of television screens. One woman was even convinced she had seen her "life" on her lampshade, and a child who had been taking a bath said he "saw all about himself" when he looked in the water.

It could not have been a hoax. Too many people were involved on too broad a scale to doubt that the reports contained a kernel of sincerity. While it was gratifying to have its prognosis supported, the Committee had not anticipated such *massive* support. A full-blown epidemic had been precipitated, a collective psychosis of immense proportions. And, apparently, otherwise reliable channels of communication also had been seriously infected, for sources were advancing a preposterous notion. They were suggesting that the hallucinations all had been experienced simultaneously! Why didn't the media people carefully check out their facts (as the Committee planned to do, though it knew already what it would find) before conveying the impression of some kind of a *participation mystique* at work? Why did they choose a time like this to be so naive about the way information spreads in our modern world?

In another quarter, a very different interpretation of the Omega affair was being entertained. Colonel Alan Hagger did not share the Committee's confidence that the incident was simply the outcome of weak-mindedness, social pathology, fallout from the New Nonsense. It was more than a widespread delusion, he suspected. The forces at play were decidedly real and bent on wreaking havoc in the camp of their opponent.

The results of the Colonel's frequency analysis glowed on the monitor of his computer, key phrases identified from the dozens of response protocols that had been collected:

. . .SEE MYSELF, SEE MY FEELINGS, MY WHOLE LIFE FLASHING ON THE SCREEN, FELT LIKE BEING TURNED INSIDE OUT—

"Turned inside out," he whispered, his eyes stopping on these three words. Colonel Hagger gave his computer a new command and an unfamiliar term appeared.

CIRCUMVERSION. DEFINITION: TO TURN INSIDE OUT.

He puzzled over this for a moment or two. "What in hell does it mean?" the Colonel muttered, thinking of the lighthouse at Ocean's Edge.

Next, for the third time in as many minutes, the computer was asked to display the map density chart showing the geographical correspondence of Omega-related incidents to low-frequency waves detected in the atmosphere. The correlation was disappointingly low, inconclusive. Colonel Hagger shook his head in frustration. The whole truth was eluding him, but it did not necessarily mean he was on the wrong track. Information was still coming in, any and every account conceivably related to Omega was being funneled to the Agency's data base for storage and analysis. While the process continued, no conclusions could be drawn. Naturally, he would keep an open mind. . .

One piece of data never was made public, never brought to the attention of the Colonel or the Committee. On the night the "disease" first erupted, a symptom had appeared in an unlikely place. A sociology professor and member of the Committee was home alone, listening to Beethoven, when his mind had begun playing tricks.

The initial hypothesis was that something was wrong with the tape. Perhaps he had put on the *Moonlight Sonata* one time too many, for a warp had seemingly developed. Subtle but unmistakable, the foreign element persisted with every replaying of the piece. What disturbed him was that it was not a mere random distortion. A *melody* was rising up from the background, a tantalizingly familiar theme. Though he could not quite make it out, he knew it was not from the pen of Beethoven.

For over an hour he strained his ears, racked his brain. Then he gave up. The professor went out for a walk. Strolling to the corner of his block, he looked up at the night sky.

"And we're lost out here in the stars. . ."

The song from his childhood! The tune that had run through his mind for months after his mother, as a special treat, had taken him to see a local revival of an old Broadway musical. What was it doing mixed in with Beethoven? How had it gotten from the inner recesses of long-buried boyhood abstractions onto the ferrous oxide track of his audio tape? Back in Phil's apartment, the tape was rewound a final time, and the *Moonlight Sonata* unfolded with flawless fidelity to the master who composed it.

Sandy Peterson was excited. She hadn't felt this way since entering freshman psychology, where new horizons were to open for her. What she had actually found was a myopic "behavioral scientist" reading in a monotone about aversive conditioning and the gradient of reinforcement, his thick-lensed glasses never more than inches from the page. All her life, she had been trying to discover who she was. How unoriginal. Wasn't *every* member of her alienated generation purportedly looking for the same? Yes, but for her, the problem was tangible and immediate. Those unrelenting bouts with "separation" *literally* left her identity "up in the air."

Therefore, in her erratic, half-hearted fashion, she had continued with psychology. What other subject was there for what she wanted? Additional courses had been taken, a B.A. finally earned, followed by still further work toward the Master's—but never any true enthusiasm. There was only inertia, perpetuated by feeble rationalizations about what the *next* course might bring, or possibly the next.

Couldn't it be different now? Sandy thought. In the spring, the psychology department was to offer a course in *parapsychology*. She was certainly no expert on the subject, but not long before, on a night she had planned to devote to an upcoming exam, she had gone through a fascinating book instead. It could have been written about *her* for it was called *Journeys Out of the Body*, and the introductory section had been written by a *parapsychologist*. Then was there a field of psychology that dealt with her special concern after all? In a matter of days, she had devoured every parapsychology book the college library possessed, with no loss of interest. Her appetite had merely been whetted. She had begun to understand that there was much more to the riddle of identity than even her own queer experiences suggested.

And now the psychology people had announced they were giving an entire course on the topic! She'd be there at registration for the opening bell—at the head of the line, if she could manage it. But this promising turn of events called for *more*. It was Sandy's time to act aggressively, however unnatural it was for her.

She had an inspiration. After a month of procrastinating, her stop in the office was made. Sandy learned that the instructor hired for the course was not scheduled to be on campus until the spring semester. However, he was in town and, when the secretary called him, he readily agreed to meet with a prospective student.

Noel Innerman handed the menu back to the waiter and turned to his dark-haired companion. "This is some treat for me. I never expected to get such an early taste of student concern."

"Well, I'm fascinated by the subject. Nothing will stop me from taking your course. But to be honest, there's also a personal side."

"Do you feel you have a special talent?" asked Innerman.

"I don't know if that's the word for it. Talent is something you can control."

"Out-of-the-body experiences?"

There was a long pause. "I'm very impressed," said Sandy, blushing deeply.

"Don't be too impressed. They're actually quite common and most of the people who have them can't control them. I made a good guess."

She remained impressed nevertheless.

"I'd be happy to listen," said Innerman, "if you want to talk about your experiences."

"Yes, but not just talk. I thought I might do a *study* of OBE's, if you'd be willing to sponsor it and give me supervision."

"Is there a way to get academic credit?"

"*I'd* get credit—it would come under Independent Research. But I'm afraid there'd be no return for you . . . I know it's a lot to ask . . ."

"You're wrong. There *would* be something in it for me. I would be getting my feet wet at this college. I'd like to give it a try."

"Outrageous!" Sandy exclaimed, smiling joyfully. "You are a very nice man."

"And you're a delightful young woman. But let me try to pin you down. Have you had any specific ideas yet about the project?"

"Nothing really specific. Not yet. I wanted to speak to you first."

"And now that that's done," said Innerman, "I know you'll agree that it has got to be *your* project. Sandy, you can do a lot with it, both academically and personally. There's no need to separate the two areas of development. You can get them working together for you in tuneful harmony. But before anything constructive can happen, there's a critical preliminary."

"You don't have to tell me. I know what I have to do — something I've never been able to do. Get control."

"My turn to be impressed," said Innerman.

"But how do I do it?"

"You start by asking yourself if you really want to *have* out-of-the-body experiences. You don't have to. You can control them in a *negative* way, learn simply to switch them off."

"That wouldn't leave us with much of a project," Sandy commented.

"Right. And you wouldn't feel quite so vulnerable any more."

"I can't close myself off to something that's there. It would be like making myself less than I am."

Sandy lowered her eyes to her coffee. Absently, she began to twist a strand of hair around her finger.

"You're not sure," Innerman gently observed.

She was slow to respond. "Yes, you're right, Dr. Innerman. Perceptive as usual. I'm really not sure I can handle it. I could panic at any time and run away. But I'm sure I want to *try*."

How could the relationship continue after the fiasco on the beach? From a strictly sexual standpoint, of course, it could not have gotten any worse. Some slight progress had, in fact, been made, with Phil as the chief beneficiary. Otherwise, the entanglement had become an utter disaster now that first-date amenities had been dropped.

Sandy and Phil were, nevertheless, all but inseparable, and no one who knew them could understand the phenomenon, least of all Sandy and Phil.

The Halloween party was typical. It should have been an evening of lighthearted pleasure. Students and faculty had come together to let down their hair following a week of mid-term exams. The mood was hardly serious, not even *before* the smoke began to billow and the wine to flow. But one student had brought along her Tarot cards to celebrate the occasion, and Phil could not let that go. When she began her reading, half-stoned as she was, he felt it his duty to educate her and all present on the evils of irrationalism; in truth he was a trifle intoxicated himself. This student happened to be Sandy's friend. Phil did not take kindly to the defense Sandy mounted, modest as it was. Directed at her, his sarcasm became loudly abusive. In response, she walked out, leaving him in a circle of gaping spectators.

Another time, Phil was slated to speak before the New York Academy of Sciences—a major address, an important milestone in his career. As the day of the momentous event drew near, his relations with Sandy improved dramatically. The speech was *the* topic of conversation. And the rapport that developed between them as they anticipated it together made for an almost healthy liason. She encouraged him warmly, glowed with optimisim on the impact the presentation would have, declared she couldn't wait to occupy the front row seat he had reserved for her. Then Sandy overslept and never showed up. She had forgotten to set her alarm, was her feeble explanation. She didn't expect him to accept it, and he didn't.

And there was the visit to the psychiatric center. A graduate student known to both of them had failed to come out of a hashish-induced depression and had committed himself. In mild weather, patients and their guests were permitted to stroll the grassy hospital grounds. Flanked by the illustrious professor and his winsome coed, their arms supportively hooked under his, Harry Seligman was just beginning to feel the benefits of their solicitous concern when the whole picture changed. Before Harry realized what was happening, Sandy and Phil had withdrawn their attention from him and were at each other's throats. Afterwards, neither could recall what had set it off, but it turned out to be quite a bout. God only knew where Phil's judgment had flown, for he ended by making such a clamorous display of his emotions that a nurse appeared and told him to go to "his room."

Their relationship went on that way until the Christmas recess, when a climax was reached. They were to take a couple of days in the mountains, a time to breathe before facing the last grueling week of the semester. Yet Phil was unbearable from the start. There was no special reason; he didn't need one. The usual accumulation of minor headaches and obligations was enough to get him going. With a blemish left in his latest manuscript, a disgruntled student petitioning for a higher grade, or too many uncorrected term papers waiting on his desk, living with Phil could be hell.

He began warming up on the thruway to Vermont, with rancorous grumbling about the "comatose condition of Sunday drivers." The topic of billboards was next on the program. Obscene commercialism! There was just no escaping it, not even on the open highway, driving out to "God's country." When they passed a bigger-than-life advertisement for a book called *Psychic Mysteries of the Bermuda Triangle*, he almost went off the road.

The onslaught continued relentlessly up to Mount Hope ("the middle of nowhere"), into Mercer Township ("a depressingly quaint little hick town"), to their "terminally dilapidated" hotel. Phil had the room changed twice, stiffed the bellboy for "indifference" and said, "Never again!"

And all the time his agitation had been escalating, Sandy was playing the game she knew best, *detachment*, but she had added a dangerously provocative variation. Without responding to him directly, a counterpoint had been established. Opposing his caustic irony and gloomy disdain was the bright enthusiasm of the consummate tourist enchanted with everything she saw: the pine trees lushly clustered on the lower mountain slopes, those adorable village shops she would *have* to visit before they left, the charming rustic decor of Sky View Lodge, and so forth.

Miraculously, there was no major upheaval. The soliloquy in parallel simply ran its course. Once they were settled in their room with the door shut, no more of it was heard. Sandy began unpacking and Phil headed for the shower.

As the water streamed over him, his passions subsided, or rather, they were *transformed*. Suddenly, he was feeling very sensual. He *wanted it*. The new setting, the strange room, made it exciting. He was going to get it. *But think. Don't get carried away*, Phil instructed himself. A scenario was composed, down to the last detail of what he would say and do.

Ready for action, he opened the bathroom door only to find her on the floor, her eyes closed, her body twisted into a highly improbable position. It was that blasted Yoga routine she had picked up from her new mentor, the parapsychologist. Phil crossed the carpet clad in a towel and seated himself at the picture window, his back to the irritating contortion.

He still was not impressed with the mountain panorama of icy blue over green. It did not rob him of a single breath. He shut one eye, and the sweep of verdant woods and towering peaks became flat.

Smiling thinly, he was remembering an old "Amos 'n Andy" episode. For a mere "bag o' shells," d'Kingfish had sold Andy a palatial estate. Unfortunately for Andy, the "mansion" was nothing more than a two-dimensional billboard on an abandoned lot—like the billboards that polluted the thruway all the way up to Vermont.

Someone was tapping his shoulder. "Can you tear yourself

away from the scenery long enough to lend me your body?" She stood with her hands on her hips, wearing only a bra, her standard Yoga "costume." "I know it's a tough decision, but please hurry, Phil, I'm *freezing*. What will it be, the lady or the landscape?"

"The lady," said Phil. He left the towel behind when he rose to enfold her.

But in bed, nothing worked. Sandy's effort was monumental. She fondled, stroked, massaged, squeezed tenderly, slapped stingingly. It all came to naught. Even the snake-like workings of her tongue could not sustain him. And he fared no better in his attempts to rouse himself. Ordinarily, a few minutes spent at the right places—breasts, saucy buttocks, the firm, smooth flesh of her inner thighs—were a guarantee. Ordinarily, but not now. The struggle was over when he tried to pump himself up with hastily-woven mental erotica. These forced images flickered hollowly and died, and he with them. At present there was *no* hint of life, not even the pathetic stirrings that had been managed hitherto.

Sandy disengaged herself and slipped under the sheet.

Staring up at the ceiling, Phil said, "What do you really get out of those exercises?

"Sandy?"

No response.

"Do you have to be so boringly predictable?" said Phil. "Change your act, God damn it, or I'll explode."

Sandy finally broke her silence. "Yoga is something you should try, my dear. It might keep you on a longer fuse."

"Well, you can be my guru, guide me on the 'Path to Enlightenment.' "

In a show of supplication, he stretched his arms above his head with open palms: "Oh master, raise me up from ignorance!"

"If that could only be."

"Okay," said Phil. "You insist on taking it seriously, so tell me what it's all about."

"Everything. Everything is, or can be, Yoga. The exercises are just a beginning. They help to turn things around."

Again there was silence.

"*That's* the explanation?"

"It isn't so easy to explain."

"Don't let it trouble you, honey. Even the great Innerman probably can't explain it."

"It's that we're forever reacting, Phil. We're at the mercy of every stray thought or outside stimulus that happens our way. But it's important to be able to *act*. That's what Yoga does. It helps you develop your potential to *act*."

Phil climbed out of bed and crossed the room.

"There," he said triumphantly. "I was feeling cold. I got up, went to the window and shut it. *I acted*. Yoga?"

"No. Phil, honey, when you take directions from your body, because it's cold, or hungry, or tired, that's *re*-acting."

"Now I'm lost. You're telling me that cold and hunger are *ex*ternal stimuli? Then what would an *in*ternal stimulus be?"

"Something called *will*."

"Uh oh, you're going metaphysical on me. I'd better try something else." He dropped to his knees, began flapping his arms like a bird, then pumping more vigorously, he leaped into the air.

"Not hunger, not fatigue—just sheer insanity. Am I getting any closer?"

"A little bit, in fact."

"Then Yoga is sheer insanity," he concluded.

"Oh come on, Phil. Your performance was far from insane. You were improvising."

"All right. Yoga is improvisation. Is that the whole deal?"

"There's more."

"What? What's the 'more'?"

"I don't know if I can put this the right way."

"*Try*," Phil urged impatiently.

"Okay. You chose the bird routine from your repertoire. But once the choice was made, did you *think* about what you were doing with your body?"

"No. Was I supposed to? Didn't I give a convincing

performance?"

"You were acting out of habit, Phil, like putting on a pre-recorded tape. It was the standard bit we all learned as kids and that's what I mean by '*re*-acting.' "

"Then for God's sake, tell me what 'acting' is."

"Did you ever see Marcel Marceau?" asked Sandy.

"Pantomime isn't my bag. Of course I've *seen* it."

"Well, that's Yoga! The power of active imagination. It goes into every muscle moved by a mime. If he wants you to think he's flying, and he's good at it, he can bring you pretty close to real belief."

Sandy handed him a stapled booklet from her night table. On the cover page was printed:

YOGA AND THE IMAGINATION
by Noel Innerman

"That really says it, Phil. Try the passages I underlined on page three, just for an introduction."

Phil fought back his resentment and grudgingly began to read.

A habit is a handy thing to have at your disposal. If it fits the situation—and it very often does, more or less—you just plug it in and play the sequence out. No fuss, no bother; it works automatically. So we spend most of our lives running on automatic pilot. To the extent that the human being is a biosensory machine, you can't knock it; it's necessary.

But don't expect too much from habits by way of richness of expression or qualitative depth. The job may get done, but in terms of the lowest common denominator. And there is always the danger of forming the "habit" habit.

Squirming, fidgeting, not being able to concentrate or even sleep because you cannot stop distracting yourself with a thousand trivialities or because you can't resist the temptation to scratch or pull at some part of your anatomy one more time—that's the least of it. There is overeating, oversmoking, overdrinking or drugging

— over-reacting, *in general. It all comes from too much blind habit, from not being able to truly, humanly, open your inner eyes and* act. . .

Phil looked up and met her expectant gaze. "So Yoga cures it all," he said sardonically.

"It helps you to break the '*habit* habit.' You're able to live more deliberately because your *mind* is controlling your *body* for a change."

"That '*habit* habit' thing is very catchy. What else did you commit to memory here?"

"Phil, I sincerely believe it's an answer. Try it yourself. Just *try* it, and I bet we'd do much better than we did before."

"Uh huh," he said, flipping through the pages of Innerman's offprint. He had been leaning against the bureau on the wall opposite the bed. Now Phil straightened and affected a shudder.

"You know it really *is* cold in here. My hands are freezing." If he hadn't been holding the booklet, he simply would have been rubbing his palms together. As it happened, *Yoga and the Imagination* was being methodically crumpled into a ball.

Now he dropped it casually into the ashtray on the dresser and reached for his lighter. "I hope you don't mind. I have to have *something* to warm up these hands."

Calmly, but without a word, Sandy got out of bed. She packed her bag, put on her clothes, and was on the way to the train station long before the fire went out. There had been only one attempt to communicate, an obscene gesture made with her middle finger prior to shutting the door to their room. But it had gone unnoticed. The professor's eyes were fixed on the hypnotic dance of the flame.

 **4**

On the Subject of Love

I<small>N A BACK BOOTH OF THE</small> *CIRCUS PUB* <small>SAT A</small> group of Franklin College students with a member of the faculty. The candle-lit alcove was brightened by the picture, a pastel portrait of a gayly grinning clown. Yet the merriment spread across the comical face was not reflected in all who were present. The glum countenance of Arthur Rosenberg stood in stark contrast. Somberly, he was running his finger around the foamy rim of his half-empty beer stein. As the barmaid passed, he quickly drained his mug and deposited it on her tray, pleading, "Lower that racket would you, or change the music; it's giving me brain damage."

"This is really a personal thing with you," Mindy Harris commented sympathetically.

"It's a personal thing with *you*. Don't you see that? It'll affect every one of us personally."

"But can any of us do anything about it?" remarked Sandra Peterson.

"That's just it, that's why it irks me—because I can't do a damned thing about it."

"But it's not true, Arthur—you're doing plenty," Mindy encouraged, "more than any human being I know."

"Right," he replied ironically, "Students for Peace, Common Cause, Citizens for Survival, and the list goes on. But what does it amount to? It isn't making a dent, not even a chip. The process seems to have a life and logic of its own . . . just no stopping it. One shoe drops, then the next, and the next . . . and nothing said or done seems to matter."

Sandy noticed a familiar head bobbing toward them through the crowd in the front of the pub. It was Paul Flax. The lanky biology major hooked his goose-down vest on a peg of the coat post behind their booth, then laid a copy of *The New York Times* on the table. Squeezing into the seat beside Arthur, Paul arrived at the correct diagnosis with a single glance at his comrade.

"Premier Provokin?" he asked.

A rueful nod was Arthur's confirmation, and as he gave it, he rolled *The Times* into a tube and shoved it under the arm of its deliverer. "I don't have to see that headline again."

Paul removed the newspaper and put his hand on Arthur's shoulder. "My friend here worries about the big problems like the Soviets pulling out of the nuclear arms talks, and I struggle with the smaller ones—like where my next joint will come from. Actually, Arthur, tormenting you was not my main reason for bringing the news. I wanted Professor Innerman's reaction to another item." Handing the paper across the table, Paul pointed down the third column toward the bottom of the page. "PENTAGON PROBES APPLICATIONS OF ESP," the headline announced.

"So it's made the front page of *The Times*," said Noel Innerman, after reading the three short paragraphs.

"What has?" asked Mindy Harris.

Innerman passed her the *Times* piece and she read the title for everyone to hear.

"If you want *my* reaction," Arthur volunteered, "I think it's all part of the same insanity."

"That might very well be true," said Noel, "and not just as a generality."

Sandy requested an explanation.

"What he means," interjected Paul, "is that Provokin's decision could be tied to our government's psychotronic research."

"Psycho. . .?"

"—tronic. The technology of mind control. ESP, psychokinesis, the engineering of exotic radio waves, that sort of thing."

"You're kidding." Mindy was incredulous.

"They're not laughing about it in the Pentagon," said Paul.

"Then Premier Provokin's pullout is the Soviet's way of protesting."

Affirming Sandy's interpretation, Paul added, "Seems they're as deadly serious as we."

"And probably as paranoid," smiled Innerman.

"Yes, but you don't think it's *just* paranoia?"

"Sandy, I'm not sure. My guess is that a lot of dangerous deception is involved."

"But couldn't there be something to it?" Sandy wondered. "Couldn't *something* be happening?"

"Something might be happening," Noel said quietly. "I believe something is. And it could be a fairly momentous development at that. But I don't believe it's what they think. And I'm afraid they may be holding it up, obstructing the process."

"What process?" Arthur craned his neck toward Innerman, straining to comprehend.

"Did you know I was writing a novel?" Noel asked his companions. "What a challenge that is, because you really can't *write* a novel; you have to let it write itself. I mean, you can't engineer it, you've got to collaborate with it. Try wrestling it down, controlling it, and the spontaneity will vanish before your eyes. If anything happens at all, what you'll get will be contrived, tinny, nothing authentic. You need to give yourself over to the process to get any genuine results."

"What does that have to do with ESP?" Arthur pursued.

"I'm describing the creative process. It can happen for an individual or a group. Who knows, maybe even an entire species can creatively transform, as a kind of metamorphosis. That sort of change would be nothing if not spontaneous, a merging that —once the ground was paved—would be consummated in a flash, the way the inspiration for a novel or a work of art comes together, the way any great idea is born. When parts come together like that—all at once, in an organic rush—what you have is more than a mixture. The parts interpenetrate, fuse to form a brand new compound. And yet. . ."

"And yet. . .?" a befuddled Arthur echoed.

"I was thinking that the 'parts' of such a process actually would need to be full *participants*. They'd be creating *themselves* in conscious collaboration with each other and with the process itself. They'd be helping to write the 'novel' in which they themselves were the characters. What open souls they'd have to be—is it *possible* to be as open as that, surrendering your old self so fully, giving it over so freely . . .?"

"Well, that's very nice poetry," said Arthur, clearing his throat in discomfort, "but I still don't see the connection with ESP."

"What if ESP doesn't work like transmitting a wave, sending a message from one separate mind to another? What if it works like creativity? Parts leap *together* when an idea is born in the mind of a master. But in the case of ESP, a greater genius would be at work, since the parts or participants freely rushing to organic unity would be minds themselves. Sheer fantasy, or is it what reports of psi phenomena are really about . . . hints of an 'embryo' being formed, a creative birth, maybe the birth of a species? Could this be the 'something' that Sandy senses happening? If it's true, the engineering approach should hinder more than help, since it's designed for the status quo, to serve the *old* self, which is the very self you'd have to let go of."

Paul was shaking his head. "Now I have to admit I'm lost."

"Please say a little more," Mindy asked Noel, "because I kind of understand, I mean, intuitively, but I'd like to get it clearer."

Arthur wanted Innerman to be more specific about the "creative coming together." "Would it have any definite pattern or structure? What would it be like?"

"Rather like that," said Noel, pointing to the remaining pretzel in the basket before them.

When the group reacted with frustration, Innerman reminded them that it was time for class.

Professor Barry Driver slipped into the classroom a few minutes after the period had begun and seated himself in the back. He tried to be inconspicuous as he removed the evaluation form from his attache case. It was faculty examination week. Once each semester, all non-tenured members of the Department were observed by their tenured peers. Driver had accepted his assignment with strongly mixed emotions. He had drawn Noel Innerman.

Gathering his wits for the task at hand, Driver shaped his first impressions: *What in the world are they doing? Is this parapsychology or arts and crafts?*

Innerman was sitting in front of his class, close to the first row of students. On the plastic surface hinged to the arm of his desk chair were several sheets of blank white paper and a roll of cellophane tape. He was working with a pair of scissors. Every student was similarly equipped and engaged in the identical activity. Students and teacher were cutting out ribbons of paper.

When each participant had snipped off two long, narrow sections, Innerman instructed them. "We'll start by making an ordinary ring." He lifted one of his strips, brought the ends together, and fastened them. Again he waited. After every student had formed the paper ring, Innerman demonstrated the construction of what he called a *Moebius band*.

"Bring the ends of the strip together, just as in making the ring. But before taping them, give one of the ends a half twist; turn it through an angle of 180 degrees."

The instructor stood up and repeated the exercise for everyone to see. Now all but two members of the class had successfully fashioned a Moebius strip. Innerman went to the aid of the stragglers, then returned to his place and held up both finished products.

"A cylindrical ring and a *Moebius band*.

"You still have some paper left that's intact. Take an uncut sheet and notice that it has width and length, but of course, not much thickness. We'll disregard the thickness entirely, assume it's negligible. Then the paper surface gives a simple model of a two-dimensional space."

Innerman put down the ring and its twisted counterpart and raised the paper leaf to the class.

"Naturally, our space isn't like this one, ours is three-dimensional. Which only means that in *our* world, you can find three directions to measure in. Measuring is observing, observing is experiencing—it's nothing more."

Becoming quite animated now, Noel moved laterally across the front of the room. He was displaying his model with deliberation but also a springy spontaneity that brought the group's attention fully into focus upon it.

"Can you imagine your experiences confined to a *two*-directional space? Suppose you're a 'Flatlander.' You live in an infinitely thin universe. You're stuck in this surface, so you can move your ruler back and forth or measure up and down, but . . .?"

"But no more," said a fellow in the second row. "The third direction couldn't be conceived."

"Like *we* can't imagine the fourth," added Mindy Harris who was sitting in front.

"Hey, wait!" Innerman cried comically, feigning chagrin. "You stole my fourth dimension! That was my dramatic climax. Forget what Mindy said, class. We have to get back to Flatland."

He continued over the subsiding laughter. "Actually, the situation isn't what you might expect, not if you go by the model of Flatland we've started with. There *are* Flatlanders who seem to lead a purely two-dimensional existence. But others are talking about the *higher* dimension."

"How do you know that?" a student asked.

"Come on, Pat, Flatland is us." The comment came from the biology major who sat in the rear. "It's just an analogy," said Paul Flax.

"Yeah," Innerman agreed, addressing himself supportively to Pat Loring. "And you know what Mindy said. Give her credit, even though she upstaged me."

"Because she mentioned the fourth dimension?" asked Pat.

"Exactly. I don't have a fourth direction to lay my ruler in, but Mindy *spoke* about it, if only to say that it couldn't be imagined. If her experiences were *strictly* three-dimensional, could she even begin to *talk about* the fourth?"

Innerman said no more. He hoped the students would draw the next conclusion on their own. But their responses were not forthcoming.

Gripping the paper at both ends, he pulled it taut to accentuate its level two-dimensionality. "Can this be the final word on what a Flatlander might experience?"

A moment later, a new voice was heard. A freshman haltingly suggested that the Flatland model must be wrong. His thought was completed by the aspiring biologist. "If Flatlanders can talk about the third dimension, Flatland can't really be entirely flat!"

Observer Barry Driver had not the faintest idea of where Innerman was going with all this Flatland business. On the scratch pad clipped to his evaluation form, he had recorded a question mark next to his notation of the "Moebius band." Now he wrote, "relation to ESP," and after it, another question mark. In fairness though, there was no denying that the instructor was getting his students involved.

When Driver looked up, Innerman was at the window. Staring out, he appeared to be distracted by what he saw on the street below.

"Would you please come over here," said Noel to the class. Not a person in the room made a move.

"Everyone come on over," Noel waved insistently, "I want you to see this before they go away." Paul finally broke the ice, and the rest of the group reluctantly trailed along, Barry Driver bringing up the rear.

Arms encircling waists, two lovers were strolling down the block. The coed's lissome neck was curved to the shoulder of her escort on a long, delicate line. The forms yielded so gracefully to one another, they appeared to be a single form.

"You think that can happen in Flatland?" Innerman remarked. He went back to his chair, the students following suit. Noel sat down with a blank piece of paper and started to draw. "I want to get personal about this. Say I'm a lover . . . Hot blooded . . . Very passionate. Look what happens to me in Flatland." The simple cartoon profiles Innerman displayed were frowning in frustration. Sketched in close proximity, full-length male and female figures strained toward each other with arms outstretched, drops of perspiration forming on their bodies, oversized tears falling from their eyes. A hidden barrier seemed to be keeping them from contact.

"Is this love?" Noel asked, raising his voice above the mirth. "Suppose we have a drawing contest. Free lunch for the best pair of lovers. But if you decide to enter, please go easy on the anatomy. No hard-core porno because I get embarrassed and besides, I like my job here."

Innerman distributed paper to the gleeful group. "You'll have about five minutes . . . It's a game. Be playful, but serious too, all right? We could make a nice point."

The class went along with him, despite some restiveness and snickering. When the last request for extra time had been honored, he collected the work and examined each submission. It was not before a second perusal of the entire lot that he lifted his selection into view. Growing from a common torso like petals from the stem of a flower that had not fully opened, a woman and man were shown twining and merging in a liquid caress.

"What is it?" someone sardonically commented.

"Everything *my* masterpiece is *not*," replied Noel.

Mindy now observed, "They're not in love with each other, they look like they *are* each other," and Innerman delightedly applauded her remark.

"But," he added, "that can't happen in Flatland."

"Because there it would make no sense. I can't be you if I'm me." Arthur Rosenberg's pronouncement led them quickly to the first law of Flatland:

$$A = A; \; A \neq \text{not-}A$$

A thing is equal to itself, it cannot be other than what it is. In terms of space, it cannot be other than *where* it is. No person or object can occupy more than a single location at a given time, and matter cannot pass through matter—"not without making a bloody mess," Noel declared.

"That's what *my* picture showed," the instructor continued, "matter trying to pass through matter and being frustrated in the attempt. *This* picture shows something else." He held it before them again, then turned it around for his own reappraisal. "But how can it happen in Flatland? Authentic love is not possible in Flatland. Can we occupy each other's space, share identity, interpenetrate?"

"We can't but we *do*. Thank God we do," said Paul. "I'd go out of my gourd if my love life always resembled the *professor's* picture."

"It doesn't have to make logical sense," Mindy interjected. "Maybe you can't explain it. But if it *happens* to you, you don't have to."

"Tell us about it, Mindy."

"It's over your head," she told the heckler who sat behind her.

The next person to reflect on the winning entry was older than the others. She spoke in a tremulous half-whisper, noting that this kind of "love" was not limited to sexual relations. She and her husband had been married for twenty-five years, and a mental bond had developed between them. Each frequently knew beforehand what the other was going to say or do. They shared each other's thoughts, even shared dreams. What evidence did she have? The evidence of her lived experience. She didn't expect anyone who had not lived it to accept or believe it.

"Which is just the trouble," retorted Arthur, playing the devil's advocate. "I *haven't* lived it, though I'm taking this course. So what should *I* believe? To me, it could be a string of coincidences or a lot of distortion and wishful thinking. When people live together, they learn a lot about each other. They can read the smallest signs and not even know they're doing it. Can't *that* be love?"

"Mm, but Greta's kind of love is found somewhere else," Noel said. "In the last place you'd expect it, as a matter of fact—in the physicist's laboratory!"

Noel went to the blackboard.

"They call it 'non-local behavior.' It never seemed to happen a hundred years ago, when scientists could only study the more or less large-scale world."

"Didn't they have microscopes then?" a student asked rhetorically.

"Right. But the cells and crystals that were examined microscopically are unimaginably immense compared to what modern physicists now have under scrutiny. They're taking apart the stuff the world is made of. Atoms, subatomic particles . . . and this is where things begin getting bizarre."

Chalk dots were put on the board, one at each end.

"Two well-separated subatomic particles; electrons, let's say.

Must they be two? Is there any way they could be the *same* particle?"

"They could be the same one at two different times," Pat suggested.

"Okay, but we'll assume that we're seeing an instantaneous picture."

"Then how could it be?"

"By 'non-local behavior.'

"Flatland physicists are tearing out their hair! It seems absurd, but there's no escaping it. Decades of hard thinking and experimenting tell them that before a particle is observed, it must exist in a peculiar state, in effect, be in more than one place at a given time." Innerman pointed from one dot of chalk to the other. "Conventional wisdom says these have to be different entities. Yet the finest minds of the century insist that, under certain circumstances, they're also one and the same."

"Now you really lost me," said a student near the window, and another closed his notebook and left the room. Mindy Harris appealed to her classmates. "It's like the lovers. You and your lover go into a special space. In that moment, you're sharing identities."

Responding to Mindy, Innerman drew a circle around each point of chalk. Next, he projected an arrow from one and dropped a cross from the other, endowing the subatomic particles with gender.

"'Special space' is right, is very accurate," Noel said. "Particles cannot be intimate in Flatspace."

"Because A would have to equal not-A," said Paul, "which is against the logic of Flatland."

There were those in the group who wondered how the new physics could be valid if it were not logical. Paul answered that all logic was not Flatland logic, and the freshman first to question the Flatland model now spoke more boldly of the need for a *new* logic. There was no going back, they agreed.

"Not after seventy-five years of Einstein, Planck, Heisenberg and the rest," affirmed Innerman.

"Then why is this class the first we hear of it?" The doubt raised from a member of the skeptical faction drew a scornful reply from Paul.

"Because there's an Establishment, dummy. The vested interests depend on your ignorance."

"That's paranoid crap," said the skeptic.

"—It's a great time for a *break*," Noel interceded. "We'll pick up the thread in fifteen minutes."

During the brief recess, Noel returned to his office and the students dispersed. Arthur and Mindy went out together for coffee, while Paul rushed off to the library to pay for an overdue book. Only Barry Driver remained in the room. He had added nothing to the notations he had made early in the session. The page of his pad was blank but for the two phrases, "Moebius band?" and "relation to ESP?" Driver now retraced the first question mark, accenting it. In spite of his puzzlement, his misgivings, he had to admit he was fascinated, and more importantly, so seemed most of the students. In fact, fascination was too weak a word for what some appeared to be experiencing.

As the class was reassembling, Innerman came back into the room carrying a plainly bound academic volume. Settling into his chair, he deposited the text on the floor beside him and immediately set to work with paper and pencil. He was transposing the illustration that had been left on the blackboard. With the facsimile completed, he rose to present it to the group.

"I bet you spent the whole recess racking your brains over Mindy's special space, the problem of how to get there," said Noel. "So what about these Flatland particles? Can you see how to put the male and the female on intimate terms?" When no one responded, he proceeded to demonstrate the union of sexual opposites. He folded Flatland over on itself and the particles coalesced.

"A similar example was given by a Princeton physicist," said Noel, pointing to the book at the foot of his chair. "John Wheeler showed how 'wickedly intimate' things can get in the microcosm, where space can curve back on itself. Notice that the moment I start bending the flat surface, I'm using the dimension *perpendicular* to it—the added third dimension of space."

Laying his latest specimen aside, Innerman searched through the pile of papers on the desk and retrieved his first illustration on the subject of love, the cartoon profiles straining to make contact. "This is as intimate as lovers can be in a flat world."

The remedy was now obvious to everyone. Folding one upon the other, Innerman put the suffering twosome out of their misery.

With unexpected forcefulness, he spoke again. "There's a point to all this paper folding that I'd underline in red. It has to do with separation and true union. Suppose a rendezvous is planned. The would-be lovers live in distant cities. One must take a plane, the other a train and a bus. As the meeting time draws near, the distance between them is closed, and in the final scene, they leap across a sunlit field of flowers into each other's arms. *Nevertheless*, if the space they occupy remains flat, they cannot be truly united, they won't come to share identity in a fundamental way—they should have saved themselves the fare because, in the important sense, they'll be as far apart as they were before they left.

"There's only one way for meaningful intercourse to occur: by a folding of flat-space through an *added dimension* of space. The real separation, the real obstacle to communion is not a given distance in flat-space but the inaccessibility of the higher space. And when movement in this fresh direction becomes possible, there can be core-to-core communication—love."

Moments of silence followed the completion of Innerman's thought. The vacuum was filled at last by a student wanting clarification on the folding of space. "How does it really happen?"

Noel sighed. "Not quite like my paper folding, huh? Yes, I

agree. A giant from another world does not come along and fold our space the way I folded Flatland. It's not that simple. Or maybe, in a way, it's actually simpler, because the 'giant' isn't needed."

Innerman was busy again with paper, pencil and scissors. He sketched another pair of cartoon profiles, this time drawing only the heads. Cutting them out, he taped them nose to nose on an uncut sheet. "Behold my final rendition of frustrated lovers in Flatland," said Noel, exhibiting his work to the class.

"*What* is it that's keeping them apart. . .? Not the distance between them in the two-dimensional surface, is it?"

"It's the *higher* dimension," a student asserted.

"Right. And if the third dimension is truly the barrier, there's a better way to show it." Noel untaped the masculine cutout and refastened it to the other side of the paper. Holding the sheet above him, he turned it to and fro to expose the lovelorn figures alternately.

"They're on opposite sides of Flatland now. The only way for them to commune is by moving in the added direction from one side of space to the other . . . which they cannot do."

Innerman noticed Pat shaking her head in the negative and invited her to comment. "I don't understand why they can't just come around to each other," she said.

"You mean leave their surfaces?"

"I guess they would have to."

"They *could* . . ." Noel peeled the tape from the male profile and lifted it. ". . .But it wouldn't be natural. Do you see why?"

Getting no reply, he retaped the figure and hoisted the paper aloft once more. "What is this thing? . . . Isn't it Flatland?"

"Yes."

"And what does Flatland represent?"

Pat responded tentatively. "Nature?"

"*Yes.* For the moment, it's our model of nature. And if you stick with it, if you believe the model, you can't believe in love."

Greta Jurgens raised her hand. "Why must I worry about believing and models and nature when love is something I *experience?*"

"A hard question. Experiencing does beat modeling, if you're not kidding yourself about your experience. Greta, I don't think you are."

Noel stood beside his desk chair, gazing at the tangle of drawings, constructions and paper cuttings, some of which had fallen onto the seat. His face softened in a wistful smile. Now he took the refuse pail and brought it beneath the edge of the desk surface, cocking his open hand as if about to sweep the surface clean. There the action froze. "You know why I won't do it? Because I buy the sappy old song about the world needing love sweet love, needing it now, and for everyone, not just for some.

"But Greta, a model will operate. There'll always be a set of assumptions, hidden perhaps, yet working all the time. Our Flatland model does affect our experiences. For the vast majority of people, the range of experiencing is drastically cut down. The others are pariahs as soon as they become too open, too honest about themselves."

"I thought we switched to a *different* model," a student said, "weird acting particles and the like." In the exchange that followed, students came to see that the process had only just begun but that there was a real potential for new vistas of experience to open.

"After all," Noel remarked, "modeling *is* experiencing, though of a limited kind. So for many individuals, the first step toward experiencing love might be a symbolic one. It was for me. You find the right model, the right blend of poetry and logic, and it can help set the whole thing in motion.

"At the moment, of course, the logic of love is not that widely understood. Love is 'supernatural' then. And if you don't reject it, you'll have to imagine mysterious forces operating outside of nature, like a super-dimensional giant folding your world, or imagine you can somehow detach yourself from your space and leap out into the void.

"It gets much simpler when the logic is seen, when the model of nature is extended. Actions in or from the 'void' become unnecessary for transforming the space of your experience. The simplified model of space is one in which space can fold or transform *itself*." The paper with the taped-on profiles was again displayed. "But this thing isn't going to fold itself. And if lovers find themselves on opposite sides of it, there'll be no natural way for them to merge their identities, because nature is *two-sided* in this Flatland model."

Innerman rummaged through his paper jungle and came up with the very first construction they had done, the ordinary ring formed by joining the ends of a narrow strip.

"Here's another two-sided surface," said Noel.

The students were asked to make a pair of lovers for their own ring models and stand them on opposite sides. "You put the girl on one side, the boy on the other, and have them travel around in their circular paths. Would they ever come together? Not in a million years. They might like to fly to each other, to leave the surface of the ring and link up through the added dimension. But in this illustration, the surface of the ring is their reality, total and exclusive. And it's a *two-sided* reality; the sides are mathematically segregated from each other. So round and round they go on their lonely ways. Any thought they might have of leaving their side and traveling to the other could only be a flight of fancy."

Grinning, Noel put down the ring and squatted beside his desk chair. He began tidying up. Stray scraps of paper from the seat and the floor were gathered and dropped in the wastebasket. He sorted through the unruly accumulation of drawings next, separating his own work from the contest submissions, arranging the latter in a neat pile with the winning entry on top. When Innerman finally rose to face the class, he was holding the twisted counterpart of the ordinary ring.

"The peculiar looking Moebius band you made before happens to be a *one-sided* surface. Mathematicians call it that and that's why it looks so peculiar—opposite sides of the Moebius strip do not conform to normal expectations. Instead of remaining distinct as they do in the ordinary ring, they twist into each other to become one."

"Sounds like good news for the lovers," commented Paul.

"You're so right. But try the experiment yourselves."

They played with the Moebius model for several minutes and were amused and befuddled. Manipulating little paper profiles on that eccentrically shaped surface was an awkward operation. A few students laughingly resigned; others continued the struggle with no definite results. In the end, Arthur was the one to make the point with greatest clarity. "If you send the figures out in opposite directions, they come around to meet each other."

"Wonderful!" cried Noel. "Opposites *do* attract. The right-facing male and left-facing female get superimposed. They embrace each other, come to share each other's identity. And no supernatural force is needed to fold them together because they interact in a space that, in effect, *folds itself.* Sublimely romantic, but also realistic. To love, you don't have to leave the Moebius world; you simply follow its natural contour into the added dimension."

Still, one fellow could not comprehend what all this had to do with parapsychology, the course for which he had registered. "It has to do with *love,*" explained Mindy, "and a psychical experience is a kind of love."

"Yes, *genuine* love," said Innerman, "not mechanical pretenses. A perfect example is Greta Jurgen's bond with her husband, their intimate marriage of minds."

The class was quiet for a time. Then Arthur offered his reaction. "Very clever. I mean it's nice. I'm enjoying myself."

"But no telepathic flashes," said Noel, and Arthur nodded wryly. "Because we have only been modeling, working with what's easy for us, with what we can see with our eyes—the second and third dimensions of space, instead of the fourth."

Innerman was sensing a certain amount of resistance in the group. "I know. It's hard to take in all at once. But please listen. The 'fourth dimension' is just the part of your experiencing that isn't seeing. All seeing is experiencing, but not all experiencing is seeing—nor hearing, tasting or touching, for that matter."

"Or smelling," said Mindy.

"Or smelling," Noel said, returning her smile warmly.

Now he hooked his Moebius specimen onto the end of a pencil and extended it for the class to inspect. "Here. You're *seeing* the natural way to enter another dimension—by a Moebius-type twist. You can see it because the transition it shows is only from the second dimension to the third, and human seeing is *already* three-dimensional."

"But if I were a Flatlander . . .," Pat began.

"If you were a Flatlander, you'd only see in *two* dimensions," said Paul.

"You would never be able to see a Moebius twist," Arthur chimed in.

"Yet," said Mindy, "you should be able to *experience* it. I mean, if your space isn't really flat, if it does have the Moebius curve."

A nursing student entered the discussion for the first time. "Wait, though. That kind of experience is rare. Wouldn't it be a rare exception?"

Mindy replied that she did not think it was so rare.

"Rare enough," said Paul. "If space has a twist, it's usually lost on us."

Arthur made the next contribution. "You wouldn't notice the curve if it was very *gradual*. I'm thinking about traveling in a plane, say from New York to Tokyo. It might seem that you're traveling in level flight the entire time, but actually you're going around the world."

"You're not aware of the curve," observed Paul, "because your awareness covers just a small section of the globe."

"Yes," Arthur said, "only one section at a time. Covering a short distance on a large sphere gives the same impression as covering *any* distance on a flat surface. To notice the curving of space, you'd have to expand your horizon."

Innerman was beaming. "For a change, I'm speechless . . . well, *almost.*" With his free hand, he pointed to the fingers of the hand that held the Moebius. "You see my thumb and forefinger? They're on opposite sides of the strip. They cover just a small portion of the total length of the surface. At that or any local cross section, the Moebius strip is no different from the two-sided ring or flat sheet of paper. Limit the Flatlander's experiencing in that way and the Moebius nature of his world will be hidden from him. But if his horizon is expanded, his awareness stretched along the length of the surface, he will experience opposite sides becoming one side — the twist in the new direction."

"The 'creative coming together'?" asked Arthur, thinking back to the discussion in the *Circus Pub.*

Noel acknowledged this inside remark with a smile and continued addressing the class. "If I—three-dimensional Noel Innerman—wanted to sample the fourth dimension beyond my seeing, that's the way I'd have to stretch my awareness. I'd enter an altered state of consciousness, and it would be equivalent to extending myself along *our* Moebius twist. There has to be a twist at our level. If love is real, if it's natural and genuine, there has to be a twist."

Barry Driver leaned out of his chair, poised as if ready to exit. Noticing his observer's behavior, Innerman looked at his watch and was startled. The period had come to an end. "We'd better clean up this mess," he said, and when someone waiting in the hallway for the next scheduled class began rattling the doorknob impatiently, Noel dashed from desk to desk, shoveling paper cuttings into the refuse pail. Not until the room was more or less in order and students were heading for the door, did he remember the contest.

"Stop. I owe someone lunch. Whoever you are, come claim your work."

Innerman left with the winning contestant. He gave her a choice of local restaurants, but she opted for the school cafeteria. However tempting his offer of an elaborate meal, she would stay with her itinerary: a light lunch, an hour or two of studying, a nap and some yoga. That evening, Sandra Peterson had an exam to take.

 **5**

Foiled, and Foiled Again

I'M NOT GOING TO BE A HATCHET MAN, BARRY
Driver resolved. Walking back to his office, he cursed the whole
complicated affair. Why did it have to get *more* complicated?

It was not that Innerman had been a paragon of scientific
clarity —far from it, with all that business about consciousness and
added dimensions. Science is not philosophy. But the presentation
had had a certain appeal. What was it? Maybe that it seemed so
logical in spite of itself.

And Driver could not ignore the fact that the instructor had
reached his students with those oddball drawings and constructions of his; he had gotten many of them to think and be involved.
Then how could the observer bring himself to write a completely
negative evaluation? Let the politics be damned.

Harrington and Pullman were disappointed. Soon the Personnel and Budget Committee would meet to consider reap-
pointments of faculty for the coming semester. Would they see the
obvious when they read the observation report, despite its positive

features? Would they see that Innerman was doing philosophy though he had been hired to teach psychology? Any reasonable panel of psychologists would see that. They would recognize that speculative fiction was no substitute for sound, scientific fact, however entertaining the former might be. They would remember the needs of the students seeking admission to graduate school. The department's primary mission would not elude them, and they would act accordingly on Innerman's reappointment. "But these were the same bloody fools who had appointed him in the first place," raged Lester Pullman.

It was going to be difficult now, but the Harrington group did not intend to shirk its responsibility. Too much was at stake. The problem of Innerman would have to be solved.

"They were not all mesmerized," said Pullman to Driver. "You mentioned that one of them actually walked out."

"Right."

"Well, who was he?"

"How the hell should I know?"

Solomon Harrington intervened. "He's got a good one up his sleeve, Barry. Lester wants to know the ones who weren't dazzled by the ol' black magic. Can you identify that fellow who walked?"

"I suppose I *could*, but. . ."

"A petition would be ideal," said Pullman. "We simply need to learn the boy's identity. If you could just point him out to one of our people from Student Government, the boy could be approached and reminded of his rights. He has got a legitimate grievance and should be encouraged to air it."

"He'd put it in writing," Harrington explained, "and get his buddies to sign."

Pullman earnestly felt that such a document could influence the Personnel and Budget Committee.

"Especially if this 'document' says at the bottom that a carbon copy is going to the president," added Harrington.

But Driver was as unwilling to be the finger man as the

hatchet man. They understood. Harrington suddenly remembered that his lab assistant had a friend in Innerman's class.

The assistant was prevailed upon, the friend contacted and carefully questioned. He would not commit himself. He claimed he had nothing to say, that nothing was terribly amiss in the parapsychology class. As for the fellow who had left in the middle of the lesson, he had only been to class that one time; never before, never after.

When Harrington and Pullman decided that a general "reconnaissance" was in order, the third member of the triumvirate made his own decision to withdraw from active participation. A long-neglected manuscript cried for Barry Driver's full attention, so he could not assist his colleagues in their attempt to get Innerman's class list from the Registrar. Steadfast in their determination, the remaining two would press forward. With names and addresses at their disposal, they could mail a simple but properly worded questionnaire. This should be an effective way to gain a foothold.

The request of the Registrar sounded plausible. A new and unconventional course was being offered. Naturally, the department was interested in its students' reactions. But the investigators found that it wasn't so easy to obtain another instructor's class list if they were not acting in the official capacity of the Personnel and Budget Committee. Two weeks after the request was made, Pullman received a sealed envelope from the Registrar. It was a politely written refusal. In the same delivery of departmental mail, Harrington discovered an unsealed envelope that contained a photocopy of the class list! The attached note did not elaborate. It said only, "With compliments," and was signed, "Noel Innerman."

"The fool thinks he's invulnerable," Harrington chuckled. "What would Bennett call it? . . . an 'Icarus Complex'?"

Pullman saw it from a simpler perspective. "It's his colossal ego, and it will be his undoing."

But would they have time to *use* the list so thoughtfully

provided by their colleague? The meeting of the Personnel and Budget Committee was now only eight days away. Once the reappointment was made, the movement of mountains could not get it reversed. It was clear that a mailed questionnaire was no longer practicable.

Glancing over the class list, Pullman did a double take. He nudged the stout Skinnerian with his elbow and pointed to the last column on the right.

"A sign from the Lord," said Harrington, reverently rolling his eyes toward the ceiling.

"I never noticed telephone numbers on these lists."

"That's just the point, my friend. They're a brand new feature, put there by Divine Providence to guide us and for our convenience—Innerman would understand this sort of thing."

They would conduct a telephone poll. In the spirit of the modern psychology laboratory, a standard introduction was composed, followed by a series of questions designed to procure the desired information. The stimulus material was recited verbatim by Harrington's trusted research assistant. All responses were recorded on tape.

The results: largely inconclusive.

It was sad, but a number of students *had* been caught in Innerman's web—sad, yet entirely expected. What they had not expected was the spinelessness, the wholesale apathy shown by the others.

"No, I can't say I'm ever completely confused," one student had replied. "It can seem vague at times. Other times I think I know what he's saying."

Or take the girl who'd whined, "Facts? He *does* give facts. He just spends more time on his concepts and models."

" 'Facts? He *does* give facts'," mocked Pullman, fuming over this gutless reaction. What were the kids afraid of? Why wouldn't they take a stand? Only one question brought a nearly unanimous response from the students who would be applying to graduate school. They agreed that the "parapsychology" entry would not exactly beautify their transcripts. To any responsible P and B Committee, this would mean a great deal . . . to any *responsible* committee, Pullman brooded.

But there was a student who had not been called in the initial poll. Apparently, he had dropped the course, for his name had been crossed off the list. Perhaps he had had a good reason.

When the fellow was contacted, he could barely contain himself. In his opinion, the course was a total waste of time. The subject matter? Really bad, of no practical value whatever, and abstract as hell. Worse yet was the instructor. "He never explains anything, just stands there, high and mighty, laying it on. Maybe he thinks we can read his mind. But a lot of us are just out of it. I'm thinking of making it official, of dropping the credits."

Thinking of dropping? Then he was still in the course! Innerman had Harrington's admiration. A sly dog, that Noel. He had somehow gotten wind of their investigation. There'd been a method to the madness of sending them a copy of his *own* class list. It was aimed at preempting their attempt to secure better information, information that had not been censored. Nice try, but Harrington could now smell the kill.

He would pay a personal call on their star respondent, a considerable sacrifice for the corpulent professor to make. He was not in the habit of traveling beyond a three-block radius of his apartment, which was only yards away from the college; in fact, he had not done so in over a year. But an heroic effort was indicated by the promising development.

So Harrington lumbered aboard the congested uptown bus, suffering stoically the assault upon his senses—the bumping, jostling press of alien human flesh, the noises, the odors, the continual swaying and jerking, starting and stopping. He endured the trek past crumbling tenements, withstood the loathsome mustiness of the dilapidated lobby and, worst of all, the two-flight climb to his respondent's loft. That, too, he survived.

Pausing at the top of the stairs opposite the student's flat, waiting for his breath to return, Harrington mused sourly over his ordeal. It was all so terribly distasteful or, perhaps, *unappetizing* — yes, that was the better word. But he composed his most paternally persuasive smile and knocked on the door.

The ordeal of Solomon Harrington was by no means over. With the patience of Job, he sat through nearly half an hour of insipid conversation and herbal tea, served to him with a bowl of Lorna Doones that he showed the poor judgment to sample. In the end, however, it was the turn of the dialogue that brought on his sudden, acute attack of indigestion.

". . . so I'll be getting out of Franklin in about a year, if I don't get messed up again, like what's happening in para."

"You won't," grinned Harrington, "because you've learned your lesson. Am I right?"

The student responded to Harrington's wink with a shrug of the shoulders. "I guess so."

"But how 'bout *other* people, Billy? Can't they get suckered the same way as you?"

"I guess, but what can I do?"

"Glad you asked. The answer is '*a lot.*' Ya know, Billy, it isn't that easy for me to get around town. I made the trip up here to offer my department's sincerest apologies for what you're experiencing in our course —which can't get you back a minute of the time you lost." Harrington smiled regretfully, staring at Billy with a penetrating frankness that finally drew a nod from the undergraduate. "But there's a more constructive side to my mission, as I think you'll agree. I'm going to show you what you can do to help your fellow students."

Harrington opened his attache case and withdrew a prepared sheet of paper. It was dated for two days hence and addressed to Professor Garrett Rush, Chairperson of the Personnel and Budget Committee. At the bottom, on the left, was the standard indication that carbon copies were being sent to the Dean of Faculty and

College President. Below "Sincerely" on the bottom right, space
was provided for multiple signatures. Only the text of the grievance remained to be inserted.

Harrington saw the boy's reluctance and was not surprised.
Hadn't his classmates declined to commit themselves, even on the
telephone? Nevertheless, there *were* others who felt the way Billy
did about the class—Billy had confirmed that. Perhaps the
professors had only themselves to blame for the failure of the poll.
They must have blundered the semantics, shaded their questions
too crudely—Pullman and his blustering ineptitude. The num-
skull should have been kept out of it.

Well, now he would be. The matter was in cooler, more
capable hands. A properly worded complaint would be drafted,
and if a mere half dozen names could be mustered up and affixed,
wonders might yet be worked with Personnel and Budget. At the
very least, the Committee could not simply ignore an effectively
packaged letter of protest from a seriously aggrieved student.

The mountainous behaviorist struggled from his chair and
went to the student's side. The instrument of impeachment was
laid before Billy.

"This is the way you can help," intoned Harrington, resting his
hand on Billy's shoulder. "It's your right, son—your *obligation.*"

"I don't know if I . . ."

"Are you the only one in the whole class who's having
trouble?"

"No, but . . ."

"All right then. You won't be in it alone. We'll write it up till it's
just the way you want it. I'll have it typed, and first thing in the
morning, you come by the office. There'll be a hot cup of tea
waiting for you . . . that's the least I can do to reciprocate. And
Billy, when you read the thing over, if you change your mind, I'll
understand. You can just get right up and walk out. Otherwise, it
gets signed and passed along to your classmates . . . believe me,
son, you'll be doing them a favor. They'll be grateful."

"I . . . I hope you're right."

"Billy, I'm dead certain. So let's get the show on the road, okay?"

Harrington handed him a pencil and a blank sheet of paper. Ignoring the boy's persisting uneasiness, he fixed his gaze on a cobweb in the corner of the ceiling. A small insect was trapped in the web and the professor thought, *such perfect symbolism.*

After a moment more of silent contemplation, the dictation began:

" 'We the undersigned, as students enrolled in Parapsychology, would like to express our. . .' "

"—*Site*—"

"What's that?" Harrington asked.

"Uh, para-*site*-ology."

"What are you talking about?"

"The biology course I'm taking, Dr. Harrington. It's 'Parasitology'."

His arches had begun to ache. After a time, the throbbing reached the threshold of recognition, and Phil Myerson was reminded of what he was doing to himself: waiting in front of her building for God knows how long, moving back and forth and in circles to keep warm in the biting pre-snow chill. He hadn't even had dinner yet.

Christ, it's nine p.m.! thought Phil. *What time did I get here? Eight-thirty? Eight? She's got to be back here soon, the bitch. She can't be out on a date on a weekday night. Unless the "guru's" got her. Very unlikely. Not that scoring with a student is beneath that hypocrite. But he knows where he stands with us; he'd never take the chance.*

Maybe she's up there. She doesn't answer her phone or the downstairs bell. The light is off in her room. But maybe she's there. She could be up there in the dark doing her nude yoga—standing on her head or twisting in the shadows, deep in a trance, oblivious.

Phil went back into the vestibule and jammed his thumb against the button beside her name, pulsing it frenetically as if to jar her from her stupor. The intercom remained maddeningly impassive. Three more times he called with long, plaintive bursts of the buzzer, then gave up.

The vestibule was warmer than the street, but there was little room to move about. Phil went out again.

Five more minutes and I've had it . . . What am I doing here to begin with? I don't need her. I'm not even sure I want her. 'The Woman of Mystery.' Bullshit! She's just a screwed up, gullible little brat—and how she tops it off with her arrogance!

Sandy had shut him out of her life. In the weeks that had passed since Sky View Lodge, there'd been just those few grudging moments on the telephone. Hindsight told him the call had been ill-advised, though he'd only intended to pacify her to patch up their relationship. Phil was even prepared to offer her an apology he didn't believe she deserved. But she'd hung up on him in a rage before he'd had the chance. And all he had done was ask a few questions about her parapsychology class, at Solomon Harrington's request.

Who the hell does she think she is? Phil shivered, eyes stung by a sudden blast of icy wind. The times he'd tried to reach her since that phone call came back to him. There'd been other calls, too many to count, but always with the same result. Nor was this his first stakeout. By trial and painful error, he was becoming a pro. It was amazing how much he'd never known about the rhythm of her life that he now was finding out.

Up shopping early in the morning, then riding the Lexington Avenue subway to the college. Going from class to class, to the School cafeteria and back to class. Going to Macy's "Curiosity Shop" on Wednesdays and weekends, for her part-time job selling toys and magic. These were the constants, the features of her routine he could more or less count on.

A greater challenge were the variables. On any given day, would she proceed to the library after her classes or go straight home? No regular pattern discernable here. Which were the evenings she tended to dine out? This was an easier question: never on weekends, probably to avoid the crowds. And what about those late night walks? *They* were a puzzle. She'd gone into the park one night and stretched her arms into the frigid sky. What for? Was it Innerman's dementing influence? Why had she smiled that way with parted lips at the indifferent stars?

Phil had resigned himself. Some things about her he'd never comprehend, though he was learning more all the time. But to what end? *There* was the question about *himself*.

Why this insanity? His car was demolished on the first day of surveillance. Then days spent on buses and subways, midnight vigils . . . For what? So many hours lost, so much work neglected, *important* work, and lately, not even any real contact, just watching from a distance, unobserved.

He had tried to make contact. In the college bookstore, once he'd tried at length to break through to her. But she made him feel invisible. He gave up only when he realized the Dean of Students had been viewing the entire spectacle.

Or the day on the bicycle path . . . another cold day. She was jogging. He'd come up alongside her in his sweatsuit, matching her stride for stride, hoping that she'd find some humor in the situation or appreciate his originality. She never turned, though, never cracked a smile or broke her gait, and before very long he was left behind, wheezing in a crouch.

With these humiliations, it should have stopped. There was nothing whatever to gain from becoming the world's foremost expert on the life and ways of Sandra Peterson. The stupidest pigeon in Harrington's laboratory would not lift a beak without *some* reinforcement. What had been his?

Well, he had had enough. That didn't mean he was accepting defeat, not at all. Phil reminded himself that tonight he was going back to the direct approach, and it would be different, of that he was sure. He had something to tell her he knew she could not resist.

I just want you to know, he heard himself say sincerely, *that I'm taking your advice. I'm signing up for yoga.*

In fact, he was also planning to try meditation but wouldn't need to mention that now. His inspiration was really quite brilliant. Two birds killed with one stone. He would reestablish himself with Sandy and launch his own sociological investigation into the New Nonsense. Maybe, in time, he'd even be able to show her how badly misled she had been.

But screw it, where is she? My toes are freezing. Five more minutes. I'll give her five minutes more and that's it. . .

A half hour later, Sandy showed up and he was encouraged. She paused for a moment in the vestibule to listen to his pitch. But then, without a word, she unlocked the door to the lobby and entered the building.

He plodded back to the bus stop against the glacial wind. It swirled about his cheeks, relentlessly filling his eyes with tears, blinding him to all but the look he had seen on her face as she'd vanished up the stairs.

When Solmon Harrington lost his composure—a rare event since his days as a student—the symptoms were invariably gastrointestinal and devastating. An entire week elapsed before he could venture from his apartment following the ill-fated uptown excursion. Yet, no one could say the man lacked resilience, that he did not persevere; he'd made it through graduate school on just these qualities. So Harrington returned to the college full of fresh ideas and a keen appetite for putting them into operation.

A program of adjunct involvement was instituted by the psychologists. It's purpose: to bring part-time members of the staff into the mainstream of departmental life. Too long had they come in just to meet their classes and collect their paychecks. This was debilitating to the department as a whole. It seriously weakened the "team spirit" necessary for peak effectiveness. Adjuncts would now be asked to attend all faculty meetings, serve as advisors, accept committee assignments; in short, make themselves more accessible to students and colleagues. Officially, it had been argued that the high ratio of adjuncts to full-time instructors created a special need for the policy. An added benefit, mentioned strictly off the record and with considerable relish, was that it might bring some "prima donnas" down to earth.

While the department had no legal authority to mandate participation, there was the clear implication that future personnel decisions would be affected by non-compliance with the request. That was enough to keep adjuncts on campus, though the vast majority were less than enthusiastic about it. Only two instructors actually seemed to welcome their new role: the psycholinguist, who began inviting groups of students to his home on a regular basis, and the parapsychology professor, who, among other things, proposed a departmental student/faculty research journal and a series of open seminars, volunteering himself as coordinator of both.

"He must be a pervert. Of course, who else teaches a perverted subject?"

"Don't believe that, Lester," Harrington smiled.

"Am I supposed to believe this Great Philosopher is seriously interested in a departmental research journal?"

"He's *toying* with us, man, having his little game. But relax and enjoy—it's our ball now. He wants seminars? All right, that's just what he'll get."

When the topic of open seminars was raised at the next department meeting, Harrington was the first to speak. Professor Innerman was warmly commended for his fine, constructive suggestion. The department was asked to endorse it unanimously and, further, to approve Innerman as coordinator of the series. And, waxing poetic, Harrington insisted that the architect should be given the honor of laying the "foundation stone," that the inaugural presentation should be his. Naturally, Innerman could not be expected to coordinate this initial seminar if he were to be its principal attraction. Someone else would be needed for advertising, scheduling and the like, and to serve as the moderator.

Dr. Pullman proposed that Harrington himself might assume these responsibilities and the big behaviorist graciously accepted.

The days of preparation that followed gave Harrington the opportunity to put his natural talents to use. Delegating all routine matters to his faithful assistant, he applied himself with gusto in the field he knew best: the engineering of behavior. The particular test of his prowess was to persuade certain independent-spirited members of the college faculty to be present on the day of the seminar, at the given place and time, to play a given role. It was no mean challenge. Yet through a series of clever gambits and political twists of the arm, he got just the people he wanted.

Only two weeks after the department's approval of the open seminar idea, students and faculty assembled for the premiere event, Professor Noel Innerman's colloquium on "The Geometry of Nonsense." Innerman stated his intention at the outset: "I'm going to speak today about 'nothing.' "

Following his introduction to Eastern philosophy, other "absurdities" were entertained: clairvoyance and precognition, mind over matter, synchronicity and seriality, "black holes" in space. They then were led from the ridiculous to the sublime, to higher dimensions, self-transforming consciousness and to his Moebius notion. The lecture ended with a quote from the *I Ching*: "The essence of mysticism is to *feel* . . .that $0 = \infty$ and $\infty = 0$."

Even before the speaker could be thanked for his "provocative presentation," hands were raised all around the hall. Harrington's invited guests from the Physics and Math Departments were first to be recognized. They fretted over the extravagant use of analogy, especially of the "fanciful" kind—that is, if Innerman were attempting a serious statement, which Innerman did not deny. Of course, analogy has a part to play in scientific progress but only in its earliest stages. Speculative propositions need to be formulated analytically and put to the test. Ultimately, experiments have to be devised which permit carefully controlled observations. The difficulty with "higher dimensions of space" and similar curiosities is that they are unobservable in principle and therefore inappropriate for serious scientific consideration. Higher dimensions may be great fun, but they are not science any more than philosophy or religion is science.

"I wonder whether *science* is science nowadays," Innerman replied.

He spoke of the zero-point energy field which Einstein had hinted at. He mentioned the ethereal microworld described by Erwin Schroedinger's wave equation and Werner Heisenberg's "state vector"—the very stuff of physical reality, according to contemporary physics, and all "unobservable in principle." *Mind Stuff* was the term one celebrated physicist had applied.

"Using denial won't help," said Innerman. "The problem of unobservability is real. It won't go away and can't be solved, at least not by conventional scientific methods. But suppose science itself were evolving. Couldn't this mean that 'unobservable' is a *relative* limitation? Wouldn't the restriction, 'unobservable in principle,' lose its force when principles change?

"You could say there's something primitive about frontier science," the speaker continued. "And this same undeveloped quality can be found in many of the notions I've presented today. They're primitive. But not by any standard of development that currently exists. On the contrary. Their whole significance is that they point to a *new* set of standards, a new methodology still on the horizon."

Sitting at the dais behind Innerman, the moderator smiled a moderator's smile at the sprinkling of applause. In fact, Harrington was in discomfort and had been for quite a time. Halfway through Innerman's lecture, he had surreptitiously begun popping antacid tablets and now was perspiring visibly. But some relief was on the way.

Innerman was asked for an indication of what the "new methodology" would involve. Grinning, he talked about doing research in altered states of consciousness, and this cost him dearly, as Harrington estimated. Whatever credibility he had earned among the mathematicians and physicists was certainly lost.

"After all, you can't study 'non-sense' with your senses," said Noel. "You need yoga. Scientists will have to become alchemists again."

The scientists in the audience looked at each other, and the moderator gazed at the ceiling.

Now we've got the ball rolling, thought Harrington. Hard questions started coming down the pike, questions to separate the men from the boys, and old Noel wasn't equal to the challenge. He could not write a single equation to back himself up or even suggest what a propositional calculus for "deeper consciousness" might entail. He felt it should relate to his Moebius notion. Beyond that, he flatly admitted he hadn't a clue. On renormalization procedures, energy density calculations and projection operators, a total blank was drawn, and the issue of measuring synaptic transmission frequencies was a mystery. They were speaking a language he didn't understand and he confessed it openly.

Too openly, Harrington suddenly thought. His gastrointestinal barometer took another violent dip when he realized what was happening. The twits were actually being disarmed by this "candid" display of ignorance! Innerman was creating a vacuum and they were filling it. They were taking up *his problem,* the problem of mathematically expressing the so-called "consciousness." In short order, he had them babbling about "radically non-linear cybernetic systems", "families of partial differentials", "phase spaces", and "non-distributive lattices." And when the speaker reasserted himself to propose that the question of infinity could not be ignored, they took to bickering among themselves. Was Innerman correct? *Would* the idea of infinity play a major role in a physics of consciousness? How? What sort of infinity . . . Newtonian, Cantorian or some other variety? What the devil *was* infinity, anyhow?

"Pure fiction," a professor of electrical engineering stridently declared. On these discordant notes, the allotted time expired.

Twenty minutes later, Harrington returned to his office from the men's room. He was refreshed now and ready to consider the colloquium in an objective light. He would call it a draw. True, the scoundrel wasn't hamstrung as he should have been . . . slippery bastard. But neither did his messianic image go untarnished.

Well, they'd have to play their ace. Harrington contemplated this prospect and quickly regained his appetite.

 **6**

Bert Biggs: Live!

HALF AN HOUR TO SHOW TIME, THE AUDIENCE for *Bert Biggs: Live* was led down a corridor to a door which read, "POSITIVELY NO ADMITTANCE. ON THE AIR."

Sandra Peterson was the last person to file past the as yet unilluminated sign.

Light glared brassily in the refrigerated room. *It's a little incongruous*, Sandy thought. *Shouldn't light go with warmth?* The enveloping columns of air chilled her to the marrow, for she had encountered a cloudburst on her way across town and her hair was still wet.

Sandy had failed her "screen test." While members of the audience who had been chosen to participate in the program were given seats in the first two rows of the small television studio, she was ushered to an aluminum chair in the back. Earlier, when the group was being held in a waiting room, the director had come in with her clipboard asking, "Who's got a psychic experience?" Those who had ever had one should make themselves known. This Sandy did, hoping that later it could be helpful to Noel

Innerman. But when the woman in the man-tailored suit impatiently asked, "What's yours?" Sandy found it impossible to put on the requisite Gothic performance. She could not manage the proper mood on such short notice. Maybe someday, when she had studied yoga long enough . . .

They were being warmed up, Sandy realized. The emcee had come out in his vested Pierre Cardin pinstripes to tell them it was "T.V. time."

"I *do* feel good today," Bert Biggs said, proceeding to make contact with his audience. Twisting his tie to an easy angle, he chatted with selected individuals.

"How are you feeling today? . . . Where are *you* from? . . . Do they believe in ghosts where you come from? . . . Perfect weather out there for the show, isn't it?"

With five minutes to air time, the group was asked to vocalize its sentiments on the topic of discussion.

"Wooooo!" came a chorus of compliant spirits.

"Not too bad, but try again. I need more feeling."

"Wooooooo!!"

"Yeah. That's good and weird. I want to hear that every time I say, 'Audience, what do you think of the show?' Okay? So, audience, w h a t   d o   y o u   t h i n k   o f   t h e   s h o w?"

"Wooooooo!!"

Seconds to go now and the countdown began. Emcee Biggs scampered onto the carpeted rostrum where five upholstered swivel chairs, each with its own microphone, were arranged in a semicircle. Taking the middle seat, Biggs composed himself as the numbers regressed on the studio monitors.

"Three," beep.

"Two," beep.

"One," beep.

"Ladies and gentlemen, welcome! Here's Bert Biggs, live!"

The familiar boyish image, casual yet sincere, appeared on the screen. He told his viewers that a treat was in store. They would be led on a "fascinating journey to the dark side of the mind."

"Is the ability to read the future locked inside all of us?" Biggs wondered aloud. "Do we possess the capacity to mold matter using only our minds? Or are new claims of paranormal powers simply part of a new wave of nonsense sweeping our country, taking a lot of us in because we want so much to believe?

"Some awfully intriguing questions. And today we'll be looking for answers with the help of our studio audience and invited guests.

"All right audience, w h a t d o y o u t h i n k o f t h e s h o w?"

"Wooooooo!!"

After a commercial, the guests were introduced, beginning with the most prominent. At once, Sandy saw a resemblance. Dr. Forrest Reynolds—Stanford Professor of Astronomy, author of the best-selling *Galaxies in Eclipse*, habitue[1] of numerous prime-time talk shows—reminded her of their host. Reynolds had the same kind of boyish good looks, the same air of confidence of the man who knows he has made it. Remarkably, his complexion and build even matched. The scientist wore no pinstripes, however, and his suit was a little less tailored.

Reynolds took his place to the right of Biggs and the next member of the panel made her entrance. She was Gwenevere Sturgess, the editor of *True Reality Magazine*. Mrs. Sturgess also styled herself a psychic investigator and spiritual consultant. As she glided to the chair on Bert Biggs' left, Sandy noticed that she was nearly a head taller than Biggs and Reynolds, yet slender to the point of vanishing within the folds of her floor-length black cloak. At her neck swayed gold earrings bearing the Maltese Cross, and her eyes spoke of other-world involvements.

Lord, what a sterotype, fretted Sandy. *This is starting to look like a cartoon.* All that remained was the introduction of the supporting characters. On the side of science was Dr. Paul Krantz,

Chairman of the Committee for Sense and Sanity, and assigned to the opposition was parapsychologist, Noel Innerman.

"We've got an action format we think you're going to like," Biggs enthused, speaking into the camera. "Besides our distinguished panel, I'm told there are some fascinating people out in the audience, with some fascinating stories to tell. We may even get a demonstration or two. The panelists have agreed to keep debate among themselves down to a minimum and take their cues from the folks in the gallery. One more word from our sponsor and we'll be ready to go. Tell me again, people: W h a t   d o   y o u   t h i n k   o f   t h e   s h o w ? "

"Wooooooo!!"

Sandy was becoming upset. It was going to be a real carnival. They simply had *lied* to Noel when they had asked him to be on the show. The situation here was utterly hopeless. There would be no way for him to make his point.

She felt like getting up and walking out and might have done that, had she not caught sight of two of her parapsychology classmates sitting on the other side of the studio. The glimpse of Mindy Harris and Arthur Rosenberg encouraged her to stay. They appeared to be as miserable as she.

Biggs talked to his viewers once more, then the house lights were raised. He went into the audience now, calling for their *experiences*, and the hands went up. Off camera, the director gestured emphatically to an alluring blonde in the second row. The emcee approached.

"Stand up, dear . . . Don't be nervous, stand up."

Clad in a décolleté blouse and tight black slacks, the doe-eyed beauty towered over her interviewer.

"Your name is . . .?"

"Carolyn Batkin." Carolyn spoke in a high-pitched tremulous voice.

"From?"

"New York City, I guess . . . actually, the Bronx."

"You mean a person can encounter the paranormal even in the Bronx?"

"I guess so," quavered Carolyn, "'cause I did." She shifted her weight to the other foot as the audience tittered.

"Then tell us about it!"

"Actually, I'm wearin' it." With this, the girl smiled gorgeously, glancing down to her bosom.

"Uh, is that what you mean by 'paranormal'?"

"*No*! It's the necklace. My gran'mother's necklace." When the laughter abated, Carolyn explained.

"I had it since I was nine. My gran'mother gave me it when she went to England, so I never take it off. So about a month ago I was sleepin' y'know, an' I guess I started chokin'. The thing was chokin' me! I started turnin' blue an' couldn't breathe an' everythin'. They were gonna call an ambulance but I snapped out of it. So next mornin' we get this call from England, y'know. They tell us my gran'mother died at eight o'clock that mornin', which was three o'clock in the mornin' our time. I mean, it was just the time her necklace was chokin' the life outa *me*!"

The audience buzzed and Biggs allowed their reaction to play itself out before turning to the platform, where an amused Forrest Reynolds patiently held up his finger.

"Just one question. Was this the only time she ever had this kind of problem with the necklace?"

"I would say yes, when it was really chokin' me. Sometimes it can get a little tangled up, when I'm sleepin', make me cough a little. That's all."

"Does anyone *die* when this happens?"

"No, but I don't choke or turn blue neither."

Mrs. Sturgess now intervened. Her words were measured, her delivery sibilantly theatrical.

"We have just been given a prime illustration of the extraordinary order of communication that is possible upon release of *soul-energy*. Such cases have been authenticated many, many times in the annals of psychospiritual research. Therefore, we would be ill-advised to regard them too lightly."

But Chairman Krantz of the Committee for Sense and Sanity did not seem impressed with the admonition. He wanted additional information about the girl.

"What other kinds of 'psychospiritual experiences' has she had? If there's more, let her tell us."

"Have any more, Carolyn?" The emcee tucked his arm around her waist to demonstrate his support.

"Uh, no, n-nothin'."

But it was clear to Biggs she had something. "You trust me, don't you?" he said.

"Yeah, but . . ."

"So are you gonna keep us in suspense forever?"

"It's just that it'll sound so stupid on T.V. in front o' my ol' man n'all."

"Then if it's that embarrassing, forget it. We'll understand."

"—No, I'll tell it. It's that I hear things sometimes."

"Things?"

"Voices."

"What kind of voices?"

"One voice, really. A woman's . . . boy, this is gonna sound dumb . . ."

"But the suspense is killing us. Carolyn, *whose* voice do you hear?"

"The Virgin Mary's."

Mrs. Sturgess appeared highly offended. Was it the girl's claim that was disturbing her or the audience's skeptical reaction to it? Host Biggs wanted to know. He invited her to express herself. But clasping her hands tightly in her lap, the spiritualist would say not a word. Noel Innerman, being the only panelist not yet heard from, was asked for his comment and gave it. "Carolyn looks pretty honest to me. I guess the Virgin Mary spoke to her."

"And you believe the experience was valid?" Dr. Reynolds asked ironically.

"Or do I believe it was a fantasy," said Noel. "Belief is such a vicarious thing compared with actual experience. Will you excuse me if I don't make a judgment?"

"'Judgment,' or do you mean *commitment*? This wouldn't be a cop-out, would it?" said Reynolds.

Noel smiled but did not reply.

The tone was set and the program unfolded accordingly. There was a couple from rural New England who stolidly insisted that they had been telepathically spirited into a flying saucer and whisked to another solar system by the citizens of the planet Astrogon. There was an octogenarian who contended that the pyramid worn on his head had been used to keep his razor blades sharp for over a year. An aura reader was followed by a tarotist, and a warlock from a coven in Hopatcong—without too much urging from Biggs —intoned the Litany of Lost Lemuria. If it happened that an audience participant did not thoroughly discredit himself, Reynolds and Krantz were there to oblige with the question or comment that would close the case.

Mrs. Sturgess, for her part, did not remain taciturn throughout. On occasion, she broke her stony silence, but her remarks were never too closely related to the issue at hand. Instead, she spoke of prophecies and perils, the advent of an anti-Christ and of the grave necessity of spiritually arming oneself for the cosmic confrontation that was certain to come.

During one of Mrs. Sturgess' sermons, an exasperated sigh had escaped from the rear of the studio and had drawn dagger-eyes from the producer. Among those glancing back toward the source of the distraction were Arthur and Mindy. When they saw who the culprit was, they understood at once and grinned to each other.

How Sandy Peterson was suffering. What a monumental effort it was for her to contain herself. *Sighing is better than screaming*, Sandy thought. That is what she *really* wanted to do, scream out loud. The freak show was driving her mad, and she was convinced she would have yielded to madness already were it

not for the twinkle she could discern in the parapsychologist's eye.
"Ladies and gentlemen, we've saved the best for last. I'm told
there's a Child of Geller among us."

At Biggs' prompting, a fellow in a wrinkled raincoat rose
unsteadily from his seat and stepped out into the aisle. Tony Sikes
looked as though he badly needed sleep. By way of introduction,
Biggs said, "Who isn't familiar with the Uri Geller sensation—the
uncanny power the Israeli is said to have of twisting forks into
pretzels, stopping watches and clocks, and the like. But here is a
man who can tell us about the *Children* of Geller."

"I guess I must." The gaunt young man smiled weakly. "I was
like everyone else until six months ago, Bert. I had a normal
interest in the paranormal. That was all. Then came the night at the
Coliseum. My girlfriend wanted to see Uri perform in person . . ."

"And he stopped your watch."

"Right, and messed up my life in the bargain. *I* can stop
watches now, bend keys and do other fun things. Except, is it fun
when you lose your job?"

"Explain that, Tony."

"It's simple. The car lift at the South Shore Service Station
doesn't work any more when Tony Sikes is around. Neither does
the transmission tester or the electric drill. *Nothing* works at South
Shore when Tony is around. So Tony isn't any more. They didn't
invite him back."

"Wow!" said Biggs, playing to the camera.

"Yeah, and there's plenty more. I'm ready to show it to the
world. I *tried* hiding it and it's just been dragging me down."

Biggs stared at Tony for a moment.

"You're not alone in your predicament, are you?"

"That's what I've heard."

"How many Children of Geller would you say there are? A
rough estimate."

"God only knows."

"Fair enough," said Biggs, turning to his viewers. "My friends,

stay right where you are. Mr. Tony Sikes is coming up on our stage
to exhibit his incredible powers—after these messages from our
sponsors."

They began with a demonstration of mental telepathy. Biggs
himself was the subject. He was asked to write a number from zero
to nine on a pad. Sikes covered his eyes and turned away. From
the angle of his head in relation to the pad, it seemed clearly
impossible for the Child of Geller to see the digit being imprinted.
Yet he correctly identified it and seven subsequent numbers, for a
total score of eight out of ten. The audience showed its
appreciation.

Sikes appeared in command now. He announced that the
telepathy demonstration had been a mere preliminary. He had
been warming up. But he was ready to begin in earnest, ready for
the watches and clocks.

Any timepiece would do, Sikes assured the audience. He was
not particular. He could start the ones that had stopped or vice
versa. He was happy to work with whatever they gave him. Of
course, it was not too likely that members of the audience carried
impaired watches around on their person or that they would be
willing to sacrifice ones that were operating. The home viewers
therefore were invited to participate. For the present, Sikes would
focus his energies only along constructive lines.

"I'm in enough trouble as it is," explained Tony to Biggs. "I
don't need your viewers to swamp me with watchmakers' bills."

While he was preparing himself, the people at home would
have the opportunity to bring out their broken timepieces.

The disciple of Geller required little—a comfortable chair,
which Krantz relinquished willingly, and a pitcher of water, since
Sikes claimed he became dehydrated by the use of psychic
energy, though he did not know why. Taking his seat, he squirmed
for a moment. Then his eyes fluttered shut and he slumped
forward, his chin dangling above his chest. Tony's breathing

audibly deepened as stagehands placed a table before the panel. The pitcher and a glass were set in front of Tony, while at Biggs' end of the table, a beeper phone was installed to allow viewers' calls to be put on the air.

Almost immediately, the switchboard at the station was ablaze. The calls that passed the producer's screening procedure included one from a woman who excitedly reported that ticking away on her wrist was a ten year old watch she had just fished out of a drawer where it had lain inoperative for the last two years. Another caller could not get over the fact that she had been planning to take her watch in for repairs just that afternoon. "No need to *now*," was the phrase she kept repeating until Biggs politely eased her off the air. Even an old Grandfather clock entombed in an attic corner had been set in motion, although its resurrection was short-lived. And the whole time these accounts were pouring in, Sikes, the professed power behind them, sat in his state of apparent oblivion.

After a dozen calls were permitted, the emcee got a signal from his producer. She had Nicky, the stagehand at her side, and holding him by the wrist, had his left arm raised aloft. The object in Nicky's hand was an ancient alarm clock discovered on a shelf in the maintenance room. He had tried winding it without success. Nicky was brought on camera to explain the circumstances, then the clock was put before Sikes.

The Child of Geller did not respond at once. He continued in his torpor for many seconds. But just as Biggs began to fret about the problem of "dead air," the mask of serene insensibility grew furrowed and tense, Sikes' mouth started twitching, the muscles of his arms and legs tightened noticeably, as if being fueled for a herculean effort.

In short order, a climax was reached. Sikes erupted from his stupor. Lunging forward, he slammed his palms on the table. Then, though his eyes still were closed, he took hold of the alarm clock. Turning it down on its face, he slid it toward him. A ritual was now performed. Slowly, with his left hand, he rotated the clock 180 degrees in a clockwise direction. Switching hands, he reversed the operation. Five times the ceremony was repeated, after which the timepiece was returned to its upright position. At last Sikes opened his eyes and, nodding once to Biggs, poured himself a glass of water.

"It's ticking!" the emcee exclaimed when he went to examine the clock. And as he extended his microphone for all to hear, the alarm went off.

By Biggs' yardstick, audience reaction measured ten on a ten-point scale. They were unnerved. A shock wave of over-wrought laughter, mixed with gasps of amazement, had been set off. In the flush of this magic moment of television programming, host Biggs stripped the watch from his own wrist, waved it with a flourish, and handed it to Reynolds.

"The scientist will verify that it's in perfect working order."

Reynolds so affirmed.

"It hasn't missed a beat in three years," added Biggs, now depositing it before Tony Sikes. "Do with it what you will."

". . .But I might not be able to start it up again once it stops."

"Don't worry. I accept the risk."

Sikes never actually touched the watch. After briefly re-entering trance as if to charge his psychic battery, he merely passed his right hand in the parallel plane above it. Right to left, left to right and halfway around, moved the palm. Then left to right, right to left and a half turn in the opposite direction. It was a variation on the alarm clock ritual with rotations reversed. And as the basic pattern was reiterated, the fingers grew taut and began trembling, as though a hidden source of energy were being tapped.

Sikes suddenly rose to his feet. Upon draining another glass of water, he addressed himself to the host. "It's done. I'm sorry, Mr. Biggs, but you asked me to."

The wristwatch was closely inspected. Biggs shook it vigorously, held it up to his ear, and shook it again.

"Five hundred dollars, guaranteed for life, and dead as a doornail!"

"Don't lose hope," smiled Sikes, in the wake of another ten-point audience reaction. "Later, I'll try to restore it. But can we do something else with it first?"

"In its present condition, what?"

"What time does it say?"

"The moment of expiration was 10:45."

"10:45," Sikes announced, seizing the timepiece from Biggs and holding it up. Then he laid it on the table and simply stepped back. "Bert, please look again."

"5:20! But what about doing the trance?"

"Once I'm warmed up, it's automatic. I'm in trance right now."

For Sikes' final demonstration, a tray of spoons and forks was brought in from the studio commissary. In the frenetic style of his master, the disciple of Geller scooped up a handful of utensils and scampered into the audience, passing them out to be scrutinized. It seemed that the testing of samples had barely begun when Tony was back on stage, spreading the remaining utensils across the table in haphazard array.

He guzzled still another glass of water and shouted for attention. "Please!"

When all activity ceased, Sikes extended his arms above the flatware. There they hung suspended until aquiver with indwelling tension. As the hands started their descent, the cameras dollied in on the table top.

At this point in the proceedings, Sandra Peterson was as engrossed as everyone else. The transformation of forks and spoons that ensued gave her the impression of a bizarre botanical garden. Everywhere on the surface the metallic "flora" were bending and contorting grotesquely in sudden spurts of "growth." The slightest finger-tip contact was enough to bring a dramatic change, and as Sikes' fingers continued to fly, a new stage was entered. The "plants" began to break, to snap at the stems. When his work was finally done, the Geller Child appeared exhausted. Before him on the table lay a heap of metal scraps.

Biggs took great pleasure in the ovation that followed. He hated to interrupt it and loved being in the position where he had to. But time was a real problem, he informed his audience. Regretfully, the panel's reactions would have to be condensed. Two speakers only could be given their say, one from each side.

The honor of first reply was extended to Professor Reynolds, who promptly passed it to the opposition. The spokesman for science wanted Mrs. Sturgess' opinion before giving his own, and she was more than willing to oblige. There was no question that the spiritual consultant would be chosen over Noel Innerman, though Noel had also shown an interest in commenting.

"We have had the privilege of witnessing an extraordinary occurrence," said Gwenevere Sturgess, "the pure energy of *soul*, working its influence upon matter. This is the energy form we alluded to earlier. Rarely do we see it manifested so boldly. Of course, the energy itself is not rare, and to the spiritually advanced, it is always discernable.

"Dare I say that I was not unprepared for what we observed? For me, 'observing' has come to mean more than mere looking with the eyes. There is an unmistakable aura surrounding Mr. Sikes, a vibrant field of energy. Intense white light. I noticed it the moment he stood up."

Thanking Mrs. Sturgess for her observations, Biggs turned back to Reynolds, and a close-up of the scientist came onto the studio monitor. The brief interlude before Reynolds began was time enough for Sandy to read the expression on his face.

"Oh no," she murmured, "don't let him do it." In alarming realization, her eyes flashed to her classmates on the far side of the room and she found them returning her stare. From her pained grimace, it was clear that Mindy also could sense what was coming, and the long-suffering Arthur simply shrugged his shoulders and helplessly opened his palms.

Reynolds directed a question to the spiritualist. "This *aura*, can you see it around him now?"

Mrs. Sturgess hesitated. Her suspicions were aroused. Sikes moved in front of the table and out to center stage, as if opening himself for easier inspection.

"Is it there? Do you see it?" persisted Reynolds.

"I have already explained. Those possessing the gift of inner vision will see what others cannot."

Reynolds nodded facetiously. "In a funny way, it makes a lot of sense. You see Mr. Sikes bathed in glowing light. Well, Anthony Sikes has been in the spotlight on many occasions, though normally, he uses his stage name, *The Astounding Antonio*."

Taking his cue, Sikes bowed deeply to a stupefied audience.

Mrs. Sturgess was also moved to action. "Satan!" she shrieked. "The treachery of Satan!" Bolting up, she wrapped her great black cloak around her and raged off the stage.

The host exuded more charm than ever in this hour of triumph for *Bert Biggs: Live*. The smile seen by thousands was both mischievous and apologetic, and, at the same time, comically perturbed. "All I can say is my mind is blown. We have only two minutes left, but if we can get some answers, we're not going off the air, not if it costs me my job! Dr. Reynolds, *talk to us*."

Reynolds was pleased to provide a thorough debriefing. The first demonstration, the impressive display of "number telepathy," had worked on the principle of *peeking*. When *The Astounding Antonio* had covered his eyes and turned away from Biggs, he had peeked through his fingers. True, Sikes had not been able to see the actual numbers Biggs was printing on the pad. But a trained mentalist can do quite well by observing the mere movement of an arm from the corner of his eye.

"A well-trained magician should also be equal to the repertoire of Uri Geller," remarked Reynolds, continuing his account. It was common knowledge among watchmakers that an impaired timepiece will often start again as a result of simply being handled, especially if handled in particular ways. That was why Sikes was able to start the alarm clock while the stagehand could not. As for stopping Biggs' watch, a magnet concealed in the "Geller Child's" palm had halted the movement of the balance. The production of the seven hour time lapse involved a bit of stage magic that was scarcely worth mentioning. A moment's contact with the watch was all Sikes had needed to pull out the stem and give it a twist.

"More preparation had been required for the climactic illusion. Professor Reynolds confessed that some of the utensils brought from the commissary had been given special treatment before the show. These forks and spoons had been forceably bent back and forth to fatigue the metal. Certainly, they were not the ones the audience was allowed to sample. Skill and showmanship were demanded here. In choosing the utensils that would be inspected, the magician could not betray the fact that he was discriminating, selecting only the items that had not been specifically marked.

The Astounding Antonio's mysterious "unquenchable thirst" had also played a useful role. Beside adding an interesting touch of eccentricity to the performance, it made the presence of a convenient prop seem necessary and perfectly natural. Taped inside the hollowed-out handle of the water pitcher had been a capsule of diluted nitrate of mercury. Upon raising the pitcher for the last pouring, Sikes had broken the capsule with his nails, permitting the substance to ooze out onto his fingers, which were coated with an invisible protective cream. This substance, lightly applied to the already weakened metal, had been the catalyst for Sikes' spectacular finale.

"My Lord, that is just amazing!" said the breathless emcee. "We've learned some lesson today—my hat is off to professional magic and to science!"

As Biggs extended his arms to the audience to solicit their applause, the theme song of *Bert Biggs: Live* rose in the background, cuing the wrap-up.

"Whew! It's been a fabulous show. Thanks to all my guests for making it possible and to *you* for just dropping by. Tomorrow there'll be *more. A bientot.*"

The host was out of his chair, shaking hands while the program credits quickly rolled on the monitors. In the closing message to the viewers at home, the studio scene faded to black, and three rows of white lettering appeared. It was the address to which interested viewers might write for further information, the address of The Committee for Sense and Sanity.

 **7**

Epilogue/Prologue

At 5:20 P.M., THE CITY STOPPED. THE POWER failure came while Sandy was in Bloomingdale's. She had been in the posh department store for several hours, had not bought a thing, had not even been seriously looking. It had been a convenient escape from the raging elements—the driving rain, the thunder and lightning—and from the after-images of *Bert Biggs: Live*.

But Sandy found herself out in the storm again in a matter of minutes, for the management of Bloomingdale's had decided that drastic action was necessary to safeguard its merchandise. To avoid the possibility of looting, a cordon of employees was deployed and the patrons forceably herded to the exits. So for the third time that day, she was getting a drenching.

Sandy had just begun her struggle across town, head lowered to the relentless walls of wind and rain, when a cab driver pulled alongside and waved her into his already crowded car. She accepted his kindness, struck by how a crisis can bring out the best, as well as the worst, in people.

Crossing town in the other direction, astronomer Reynolds sat alone in the back seat of his limousine. He was irritated by the unforeseen turn of events. A colossal traffic jam had quickly mushroomed in the wake of the blackout, throwing him far off his schedule. The situation at the airport would probably be worse, assuming he ever got there.

What annoyed Reynolds most was the effect the episode was likely to have on the next edition of *The New York Times*. If the paper went to press at all, it was doubtful there would be space for his story. Since he left the television studio, he had been contemplating some interesting possibilities for tagging his piece. T.V. EXPOSE[6] OF PARAPSYCHOLOGISTS was one viable alternative he had envisioned. Or maybe, PARAPSYCHS LEARN A PUBLIC LESSON. PARAPSYCHS PUBLICALLY DEBUNKED was the headline he had finally decided on, and it was just after this moment of gratifying closure that the city had gone black. Perhaps the article could be featured later in the week, but this prospect offended his sense of timing.

"Can't you find a faster way out of the city?"

"Impossible, professor. You got a rush hour here and no traffic lights. We're locked in solid."

Reynolds said no more to the chauffeur, though the fellow's attitude was definitely unacceptable to him, and he planned to report it. Despite the urgency of the situation, the cretin seemed perfectly content to inch along, listening to those idiotic "news bulletins" pour out of the radio. Multiple blackouts were supposedly occurring across America and in Western Europe. A major earthquake had rocked Iran, there was a typhoon in the Philippines, and numerous sightings had been made of "UFOs" at widely separated locations throughout the world.

Preposterous! thought Reynolds. *What a perfect example of yellow journalism—grossly distorted facts hysterically mixed with fancy. And dangerous. It's dangerous to do that when the city is in a state of emergency.*

The scientist pressed his head back into the plush upholstery of the limousine and tried to think of the triumph he had scored earlier in the day.

Expecting that power soon would be restored to his blacked-out laboratory, Lester Pullman waited in the semi-darkness, playing host to Solomon Harrington. They were discussing the satisfying outcome of the *Bert Biggs* media event. It was Reynolds who had orchestrated the highly effective sequence with *The Astounding Antonio*, but the program itself had been conceived by the two behaviorists and, with the influence of the Committee for Sense and Sanity behind them, they were able to bring it to fruition. All of their recommendations for panelists and format had been accepted and successfully implemented. Harrington and Pullman were proud of the valuable educational experience they had helped to promote in the public interest.

"Old buddy Noel barely opened his mouth the entire time," remarked Harrington.

"What could he say?" Pullman replied. "With the truth staring him in the face, was there anything to say? You know, I'm not happy about the way we, uh, set him up, but —"

"—We had a whole bunch of choices," Harrington sarcastically injected.

"We *had* no choice," agreed Pullman, "none whatsoever. The Department's survival depends on getting him out of Franklin College."

"And there's a damn good chance of it, now," said Harrington.

"Yes, happily, that's true. But the point I'm making here is that maybe Innerman *himself* gained something from the experience."

"Well, I bet you it's knocked him down a peg or two," Harrington grinned. "Got him off his high metaphysical horse and rubbing elbows with the likes of . . . what was that gypsy's name?"

"Gwendolyn or Gwenevere, something like that. But what I

mean is that, let's say the man really was on to something. Just for argument's sake, suppose he really did have something new to offer, some sort of seminal idea."

Harrington raised his eyebrows at his colleague.

"Solomon, this is hypothetical. I said *if* he had something to offer, then the experience on *Berts Biggs* could have brought him down to earth with it, taught him an important lesson: that he can't just thumb his nose at us—at *the scientific method*, that is—and expect to get away with it."

"Come on, Lester. You know he's doing more than thumbing his nose. It's a big religious thing with him. Don't you see that the man is a dangerous fanatic? Thinks he can walk on water or something."

"Do *you* think he can walk on water?" Harrington snidely inquired.

Phil Myerson sneezed again. He gingerly dabbed at his nostrils, then dropped the used tissue into the paper bag next to his bed. Two other bags sat on the floor in the kitchen, both stuffed to capacity.

Five days had passed and there was no relief in sight. Over this period, Phil had not written a word, had met none of his classes, had read not a single passage from the sociology journals piled on his night table. For the most part, his time was spent just lying in bed or reclining in his big leather chair, with Mozart, Beethoven and Shubert providing the therapy.

Only the therapy was not working. Inside he felt like the planet Venus—oppressively dense, watery and all clouded over. Never had he had it this bad, nor had it ever been this persistent. So dulled were his senses that Phil barely noticed the abrupt cessation of Shubert's quartet for strings. The piece ground to a screeching halt, but seconds went by before the event fully registered, minutes before he could mobilize himself to investigate.

The stereo had lost its power, as had every other electrical appliance in the flat. Outside, an angry trumpeting of auto horns told Phil the problem was not his alone.

He went to the window. At the corner of Mercer and Hudson, the traffic light was out, and it seemed to be every man for himself. *Paratroopers*, Phil blearily associated, *you wait your turn, then take the plunge.* The continuing downpour added a further obstacle to the course of earthbound maneuvers. When a driver saw his opening, he had to sprint across an intersection that was treacherously slick, then pull up short behind the next line of cars stacked up for a subsequent run. Much skidding and swerving, spinning of wheels and squealing of brakes accompanied the truculent jangle of horns.

After witnessing three near-accidents, Phil returned to bed. What else was there for him to do?

Twilight was becoming a somber charcoal in the darkening apartment. Through thickened, half-closed lids, Phil watched deep shadows deepen. *Lightless room, lightless city. Lightless. . .*

Yet there was *one* light. The luminous dial of the wristwatch lying on the night stand. He squinted but could not make out the position of the hands. Painfully, he squinted again. 5:20? Could it be that early? Phil wondered. Lifting the timepiece to his ear, he listened. Nothing. He shook it, tried winding it, still heard nothing. An odd coincidence. The electrical failure had been coupled with a mechanical one, and Phil's isolation was complete. His own separate space, his own separate time.

Effortfully, he sat up in bed. In the mirror on the opposite wall, Phil saw his reflection. He saw it so clearly: hair comically disarrayed, mournful graveyard pallor, eyes peering from their hollows, perplexed by the impossible glimpse of themselves they were getting. The hallucination soon passed and Phil dropped into a light sleep.

An *esprit de corps* had quickly formed among the westbound passengers and their driver. Packed into the slow-crawling cab, the group had abandoned itself jovially to an ongoing analysis of New York City blackouts, past, present and future. Sandy's participation was marginal. She nodded and smiled at the appropriate times but was thinking about her professor.

Hadn't Noel mentioned *The Astounding Antonio* to the class on a couple of occasions, something about meeting him at a symposium on magic and psi? Then he could have recognized Sikes from the beginning. He *must* have . . .

He'll quit the college now, thought Sandy. *Why should he stay on? Does he need to play these ridiculous games forever? . . . He'll go where I won't be. I want him with me. I want him.*

The answer is the special space. Can't it be? A mental bond develops and geography doesn't matter. But it's too bloodless, too pale, too much like air. I want to feel his presence, feel him inside me.

. . . S-o-o-o-o. Two. Three. Four. Five. Six.
H-a-a-a-m. Two. Three. Four. Five. Six.
S-o-o-o-o. Two. Three. Four. Five. Six.
H-a-a-a-m. Two. Three. Four. Five. Six.

Time and space were gone but there was rhythm.

. . . S-o-o-o-o. Two. Three. Four. Five. Six.
H-a-a-a-m. Two. Three. Four. Five. Six.

Where there might have been chaos, there was organization. A certain *volume* woven by mind was flickering within, expanding and contracting resonantly with Phil's breathing. He was doing yoga. He allowed himself to reflect briefly on the irony of it before re-entering the flow.

Later that night, the rain stopped, but the city was still in the grip of the power failure. Sandy was imagining smoke. She saw it around her bed, swirling mysteriously, black on black. She felt it envelop her. Then she went out of her body.

The projection was unlike any she had ever experienced. It must have been the blackness, Sandy guessed. In the absence of *physical* illumination, the familiar setting was sensed in a most peculiar way. Like viewing a blueprint in an early stage of drafting? Or a half-finished drawing done with chalk on ebony slate? A better analogy occurred to her, one of a photographic negative, indistinctly formed so that the lines of demarcation were fuzzy and riddled with gaps.

There was something else, something even odder about the experience. The room was not right. As far as she could tell from her vantage point near the ceiling, it *was* her room. As far as she could "see" through the eyes of her second body, the usual objects were in their usual places—armoire, bureau, table and chairs, bookcase, windows, bed. Yet the angles were wrong, as if . . . as if *what?*

The clock seemed correct, in any case. Power had been lost at 5:20, a fact to which the hands attested. But wait. Was she looking at the clock? A moment of utter confusion, then a realization. She had been looking in the *mirror*. Her gaze quickly shifted to the unreflected counterpart whose numbers she found to be reversed.

A chain of reflections was triggered. *Alice Through The Looking Glass*, thought Sandy . . . *Through A Glass Darkly* . . . Robert Monroe traveling astrally through his mirror world, *Locale III* . . .

The Flatland Lovers rose now to consciousness, left and right-facing profiles twisting together in hyperspace on Noel Innerman's band of Moebius. Sandy pictured *herself* as one of the profiles, as if she were one of Noel's creations, a character in the novel he was writing.

Was that his sleeping form in her bed? It was not her own. A male was curled up in the place where Sandy should be! *My God, it is* Phil. *Then where am I?*

Two miles away in his own blacked-out flat, Phil peered down at Sandy and asked the same disturbing question. But the feeling of distress passed quickly once each understood that at last it was possible to truly be one with the other.

PART II

GROUNDfigure

 **8**

Meltdown

THE INCIDENT AT AMALGAMATED EDISON'S
Hackensack facility began with lights blinking red on the master
board and a siren whooping its warning to the technicians in the
control room. At 2:17 a.m., the giant electrical turbine "tripped,"
shut itself down automatically. No one was alarmed, for it had
happened before—a normal aberration somewhere in the complex system. It would be found and easily corrected.

On the same night and for the first time, the plant's external
security system was operating by computer control. With the
services of the gate crew no longer required, the men had been
dismissed from their jobs.

The six had lain in bed that night, each in his own home
beside his own wife. A natural arrangement, yet how strange it
seemed to the sleepless men. To be ending the day at midnight
instead of beginning it. To be alone in the dark instead of joking in
the guardhouse with their comrades, sipping coffee, munching
doughnuts and Danish pastries.

What comrades they *were*. For five years they had worked together, but the rapport they shared had required scarcely five days to establish itself. None of them tried to explain the spontaneous bond that had formed. None thought an explanation was needed. They simply had taken a liking to each other, which was explanation enough. In under a week, they had felt thoroughly at ease in each other's presence, discovering a rich vein of common interests that was to prove inexhaustible. In the blending of personalities that had ensued, there was no odd-man-out. All had participated fully in the good-humored fellowship that flowed from one shift to another, the comfortable routine evolving into a way of life they had come to depend on.

So their forced disbandment now was hard to take, harder than a mere loss of employment. Boiling resentments had kept them thrashing under their bedsheets for quite some time after twelve. But sleep eventually came to the members of the gate crew, and with it a dream, at the crossroad of stars.

Hey you bozos, we're flying! . . . *Flying sparklers, who needs lights* . . . *Catch it, Larry. Catch the ball, my man, it's over your head* . . . *Geeziz, what a bunch of bozos* . . . *Ha-Ha-Ha-Ha* . . . *Throw it in to Jimbo, Angie, it's too deep* . . . *Yeah, I can stretch! Like taffy candy. Look how I can stretch myself!* . . . *Now we got it going. Pull, it's easy. Pull together, do it with ease my man, no need to strain; Christ, we're elastic* . . .

Lazily in its own time, instantaneously in the time known to waking consciousness, the gate-crew cosmos was turning outside-in. Understanding came as the transformation progressed. Each of the six came to realize that, in fact, he had not turned into elastic nor was he extending himself through space toward his comrades. Not literally, at any rate, for matter was not being displaced, it was being transcended. This was no stretching of bodies but a softening of boundaries, boundaries that normally kept each "I within" separated from the five external others.

When the sensation of physical extension passed, the process was accelerated. The six now knew that movement was entirely unnecessary, and with the complete suspension of effort, their resonance was dramatically enhanced. Synchronized vibrations increased until each was to the other an incandescent being, then totally transparent—no longer witnessed from an outer perspective but apprehended from his own subjectivity, from inside the window of his soul. Thus locked in phase, every member of the gate crew played consummate host to his mates. All barriers had fallen, acceptance was unconditional, a full and mutual surrendering of identities had occurred. And bliss. Liberation. Infinity encompassed, eternity embraced . . .

Then the gate crew fell back into time, crashing from its penultimate high. Angie opened his eyes to the back of his spouse's head, a massive white kerchief bulging with curlers. Larry sat up in bed, fighting his chronic battle with heartburn. Staggering to their respective bathrooms were Clay and Frank, the latter stubbing his toe on a basket of wash carelessly left in front of the door. And Jimbo and Harris lay quietly, one absently jamming his tongue behind a suspected loose tooth, the other scratching a cluster of fresh mosquito bites.

Later they slept again and dreamed of the plant, of penetrating the walls of the containment building, of passing effortlessly into rooms filled with banks of gauges and cabled panels, switches and flashing lights, high-priced equipment of every variety. Here, a new game was played, but when morning came, all recollection of their nocturnal transactions had faded. When word went out that the turbine had tripped, the men of the gate crew were as surprised as anyone.

But that was not the end of it. Five nights hence, still another communal dream was had, along with another bit of sport with the appliances of Amalgamated Edison. The next afternoon, at 2:45 p.m., the Chairman of the Nuclear Regulatory Commission went on the air to confess to the public that a full-scale meltdown was imminent at the Hackensack power station.

Not four miles from the installation, Colonel Alan Hagger sat in the passenger seat of a black-windowed van, listening impassively to the announcement. Behind the wheel was Franco, his aide, and in the back seat, Peter Lombardy, the Colonel's contact at the plant, the engineer whose report to the Central Intelligence Agency had led to Hagger's early involvement. When the Governor of the state came on the radio with instructions for area residents, Hagger snapped off the receiver and drew the dashboard microphone close to his mouth.

"Max, I want to hear from you. What's going on up there?"

"God oh mighty," said the voice at the other end, "did you hear that news report?"

"Forget it, Max. I want *your* report."

"Well, we're socked in on Cedar at Grove, fender to fender, can't move an inch. And all hell is breaking loose around us."

"I know it, man," shouted Hagger over the blaring horns of panicky motorists. "We've got the same situation back here. But what about our pigeon? Do you still have Kazan in sight?"

"What?" the voice called back over a crackle of static.

Hagger shouted louder. "Do you still see Kazan?"

"Yeah, about a dozen cars up, on the next block—Wait! Is that him? Yeah. He's getting out of his car."

"And . . .?" yelled Hagger.

"And I'm losing him. Too many others. It's pandemonium out there."

"Well, get your butt out after him, and let me know the minute he's spotted. We'll be coming up behind. Ten Four."

"How many blocks have they got on us?" the Colonel snorted to his aide.

"Uh, they're at Grove Street, sir," said Franco, consulting his street map, "which means they're eight blocks east of here."

Grabbing his transceiver, the Colonel said, "Let's get cracking." The three men abandoned the stalled CIA vehicle to the traffic snarl that had enveloped it and proceeded on foot.

"Word sure gets around fast," said Peter Lombardy to Franco, shaking his head at the maze of stacked-up cars choking the town's main road.

"Probably had the word before the Governor," the Colonel's aide replied. "You can't beat word of mouth."

The Colonel himself did not take part in the banter. His mind was fixed on his objective, one Waldo Kazan. This was his prime suspect, and there would be precious little time now to track the bugger down. As the trio strode along Cedar Avenue, Hagger made a conscious effort to compose his thoughts. Oblivious to the gate crew and it's late-night antics, he reviewed the facts as he knew them, the events that had led to this crucial pass . . .

A water pump had malfunctioned. That was the announced cause of the turbine shutdown at the nuclear installation. If water, heated by the atomic reaction in the uranium core, is not pumped, steam cannot be generated. If steam is not generated, pressure in the system cannot be maintained. If pressure is not maintained, the turbine cannot be driven to produce its electricity.

But a shortage of electricity was hardly the primary concern. When pressure had been lost in the circulation loop that drives the turbine, there had been an increase of pressure and temperature in the reactor core. This had triggered the opening of certain valves, allowing radioactive water to leak out onto the floor of the containment building. The loss of water had sent the reactor's temperature even higher.

The plant's engineers had given assurances that a direct threat of nuclear explosion was not a problem. The neutron-absorbing control rods had performed their function faithfully. As soon as the turbine had tripped, the rods had descended into the core to curtail the chain reaction. But while critical mass would not be reached, the core could still become hot enough to burn its way to the bottom of the containment chamber, through the thick concrete base, and deep into the earth, whereupon hitting ground water, it could erupt in a geyser of steam and debris. This "melt-down" could climax by releasing a deadly cloud of radioactivity into the atmosphere.

The Colonel recalled how confident Edison officials had been that it would never come to that. For such a catastrophe to begin, the temperature in the reactor core would have to climb above 3000 degrees Fahrenheit. It was out of the question, he could hear them say. The system was equipped with a fail-safe mechanism programmed to dump thousands of gallons of water on the core, should the temperature rise precipitously.

So went the official explanation. Great pains had been taken to blind the outside world to the true nature of the so-called pump malfunction that had started the crisis. *A hell of a God damn "malfunction,"* thought the Colonel. Somehow the piece of equipment had been pushed right through itself, casehardened metal turned inside-out like a soft leather glove!

This was the sort of thing that only one member of the Edison staff had been trained to recognize and appreciate. In fact, the Agency had placed engineer Lombardy at the installation for that very purpose, and he discharged his duty reliably. The Colonel was summoned at once from his Washington headquarters. Within three hours, he had landed at the Hackensack facility in his Air Force chopper, and with Lombardy at his side, was inspecting the weirdly misshapen piece of equipment. Hagger did not take long to confirm the diagnosis of the pump. It had become a familiar signature in his investigations of psychotronic episodes, though still an enigma to him.

The usual procedures were followed. CIA technicians were brought in to monitor any abnormal atmospheric disturbance or uncommon radiation that might be detected in the vicinity of the plant, while the Colonel launched his own probe of the members of the staff. That was when he discovered to his astonishment that Waldo Kazan was in the employ of Amalgamated Edison . . .

But meanwhile, the managers of the plant had activated the

emergency cooling system, and by the afternoon of the fifth day, the average temperature in the core had dropped to 120 degrees. It was cool enough for a collective sigh of relief to be heaved and for the Colonel to return to the nation's capital for an overnight consultation with his superiors. Yet, in his absence, at three o'clock the following morning by Peter Lombardy's estimate, there was an ominous turn of events. After days of responding predictably to the torrents of emergency coolant, the needles on the temperature gauges had begun to flutter. Within twenty minutes, a trend was discerned in this erratic dance. The indicators appeared to be creeping back up the dials.

It really must have thrown them, thought the Colonel with some grim satisfaction. Of course, they could not have known about Kazan. So the engineers and technicians were completely at a loss, had no explanation to offer. It was not their gauges, that much they knew. One gauge can go awry, but many were employed, each taking independent readings from the various sectors of the containment vessel. On all, the same peculiar pattern had been displayed—a spasmodically deviant indicator, a gradual net rise in temperature.

The one hypothesis that had been seriously considered did not stand up for long. An engineer had suggested that a bubble of hydrogen gas might have formed between the uranium core and the top of its steel housing to block the inflow of coolant. But the system had been designed to permit samplings of the chemistry inside the tank. The connection line from the reactor to the shielded nuclear sampler room was opened and reopened with consistently negative findings. There was water at the top of the tank, not gas.

As Lombardy had described it to the Colonel upon his return from Washington, the mean temperature in the core had ascended to 175 degrees by sunrise, pretty disturbing but still comfortably remote from the 3000-degree meltdown threshold. By 8:30 a.m., it was 225 degrees, by 9:45, 280. When the eleven o'clock reading revealed an average temperature of 315 degrees, upper echelon plant officials met behind closed doors with the on-site representative of the Nuclear Regulatory Commission. From this session Lombardy had been excluded, but he had known full well the issue on the table. Should the telephones be used? They were sealed in a room in a sub-basement, under maximum security. Four steel encased, combination-locked transmitters, earmarked for the region's four state capitals, each a direct line to a chief executive. No one ever expected that the hotline network might have to be activated. It had been installed for an exigency that was virtually impossible: failure of the fail-safe system. But the conferring officials were faced with the fact that the impossible was happening. So it seemed there was no choice, only an obligation to give formal authorization.

Then a reprieve had come. The supervising engineer was buzzed into the conference room with word of a startling development. The trend had halted! With an average reading of 320 degrees, the indicators on the gauges had suddenly ceased their eccentric fluctuations. In fact, they had stopped cold, as if photographic stills had been pasted over all the gauge windows. This paralysis of instruments was a puzzle in its own right to the Edison staff. But they were not about to question the grace they had received. They only prayed it would last, that the gauges would remain stalled, or better yet, begin to give evidence that the reactor's dangerous course was being reversed. At that stage, it did not seem an unreasonable hope. And in the meantime, no grave measures would have to be taken, just continued vigilance.

But at 12:30 p.m., the needles had come alive again. With a sudden jolt they'd leapt forward, swung back for an instant, then steadily begun working their way up the scales. Soon the pace would accelerate. The erratic fluctuations of the morning had come to an end. There was no mistaking the present course of progress.

Twenty four hundred degrees Fahrenheit. That was the

temperature the core had attained just an hour earlier, as Colonel Hagger's helicopter touched down on Edison grounds. His first reaction had been white fury at Lombardy's lame excuses for failing to contact him immediately. When he regained his composure and listened to the engineer's account of the events of the past twelve hours, it was clear that the game of cat and mouse was over with this Waldo Kazan. Kazan was their man, of that the Colonel felt certain.

"Got him!" crackled Max's excited voice over the transceiver.

"*Where?* Spit it out, man."

"He just slipped into a big brick building on the south side of Cedar. Looks like the local high school."

"And the cross street is what?"

"It's Cedar past . . . C-Concord, maybe Concordia."

"Close enough. Okay, listen. I want every exit secured. We're on our way."

The Colonel and his henchmen plunged into the tangled glut of abandoned vehicles and hastily threaded a path to the other side of the road. The throng of surging evacuees had swelled. In the rising tide of panic, Hackensack residents were violating every directive that had been broadcast by the Governor. Fights were breaking out all over, as families struggled to stay together and keep possession of their overstuffed bags of belongings.

Forming themselves into a flying wedge, the CIA men bulled their way down Cedar Street, shoulders and elbows clearing the ground. Through blocks of disoriented mobs they plowed, their charge finally ending at the brick and ivy of Hackensack High. With Hagger in the lead, the three dashed up the concrete steps to Max Arroyo, who was waiting at the main entrance.

"He's in there," said Max.

"Are you sure he didn't give you the slip?" asked a hard-breathing Hagger.

"No way, we've got the building covered on all sides."

The Colonel nodded quick approval and said, "Where's Logan?"

"Back exit," replied Max.

"Pete, get back there and take his place—I need his experience. We're going in."

When Lombardy's replacement arrived, they started for the large brass doors. An elderly man was hastening out. Bald head lowered to an arm full of books, he seemed not to notice them. As they entered the vestibule, another of the staff bustled past, oddly unceremonious in her prim attire. Inside the lobby, not a soul could be found. Hagger's whispered directions echoed faintly in the cavernous hall and the trio fanned out.

Searching independently, they scoured every office and classroom, then converged on the auditorium for a seat-by-seat hunt. Kazan was not on the ground floor.

"Take the basement," Hagger commanded Logan, who was already drawing his pistol. "We'll go up."

Halfway to the second floor, the Colonel and his aide froze in their tracks. A voice could be heard in the corridors above them.

"That him?" breathed Franco.

The Colonel waited and it came again, this time more distinctly. "Emil!" was the plaintive cry. "Where are you, Emil?"

"It's him," Hagger confirmed.

"What's he doing? He must be crazy."

Hagger hissed his subordinate into silence and they continued going up. Reaching the landing, they were inching the stairway door ajar when the plea was heard once more, resounding from the other end of a long passage. The Colonel pressed the shoulder of his aide, the signal to prepare. They unsheathed their weapons and coiled themselves in a crouch. With Kazan's next call, the spring would be released.

"Emil, it's your father!"

Hagger and his assistant leaped into the hall, legs spread, both arms extended, their guns trained squarely on their target.

A dumbstruck Waldo Kazan took one step back, parting his arms in a reflex of surrender. Trembling, he blinked at the approaching pair without comprehension.

"It won't be a problem, Waldo," said the Colonel matter-of-factly. "You only have to cooperate."

The nozzle of Franco's revolver tucked in his armpit, Kazan was ushered into the first open door, a science laboratory. They prodded him past a massive display desk covered with specimens of rocks, past a geological chart, and into the far corner of the room, where he was prompted onto a stool.

As Franco lowered his gun, Kazan made a move to get up but was eased back down by the Colonel.

"I said you will need to *cooperate*," the Colonel intoned, brandishing his pistol in Kazan's face before sheathing it.

"I have seen you somewhere," muttered Kazan, eyes narrowing. "—Look, I do not understand what any of this means, but I must find Emil before—my God, you do not know what is happening?"

"Get this act," said Hagger with scorn, his fists tightening in a murderous impulse to throttle the man. But the Colonel restrained himself. The situation called for finesse. He would play along with Kazan for awhile. "Wait outside for us, Franco, we need a little time alone."

"What *time*? There is no time for anything!" said Kazan, starting up again in panic. "I must find my Emil." Hagger shoved him right back onto the stool.

"Want to tell me who Emil is supposed to be?"

"My son." Kazan's forehead drooped into the palm of his hand. "Troubled. A troubled boy."

"What kind of trouble?"

"He . . . he has a difficulty with . . . with drugs. Every day I must pick him up here, but today—where is my Emil today?!"

"Waldo, look," said Hagger, unimpressed by the histrionics. "You know there's only one way to help your, uh, Emil. And you'd be helping yourself, helping us all. We know all about what you've done."

"What I have done?" Kazan was befuddled.

"Oh come on, man, you don't have to keep on pretending. I told you, we *know*. Just cooperate with us and you won't be sorry. There'll be a quiet deportation for you and your family. No one will get hurt. But first this meltdown has got to be terminated. The process you started will have to be stopped before it's too late for everyone, including your boy."

"*I* started the meltdown? You must be insane! Tell me what this means," Kazan pleaded. "I wish you would tell me. If I only knew what you were insinuating, I am certain I could clear it up."

"You *are* Waldo Kazan?" said Hagger.

"Of course I am Kazan."

"A recent émigré from Czechoslovakia?"

"I am that too. I defected to your Embassy in Paris."

"And you are currently employed at Amalgamated Edison's nuclear power installation, correct?"

"Ah, at the plant," said Kazan, now recognizing his interrogator. "I have seen you at the plant."

Hagger ignored the remark and continued his line of questioning. "Would you care to tell us about your interest in parapsychology—what your countrymen call psychotronics."

"My God, it is that? You don't think that I . . ." Waldo could not complete the sentence. Mutely, he turned his head from side to side in disbelief.

"Then I suppose you were not approached by our government, by *my own agency* for assistance in this field, that you did not flatly reject us, and that you are not still receiving manuscripts from your compatriots."

"I am receiving reprints of scholarly articles. My interest is strictly academic. I am no practitioner."

"And you really expect me to buy that crap," said the Colonel, his composure beginning to slip. "I just don't understand how the idiots in plant security ever gave you clearance. I wonder, Kazan, is it just a psychic gift you have, or did they wire you up or something before you left Brataslava?"

Waldo did not reply.

"Or it could be an *implant*," said Hagger, half to himself and in dark realization. "That would not be so good, my friend. If they planted something inside you, some kind of tuning device they're operating by remote control, then you *couldn't* stop the process, could you? At least not without *my* help."

"You do not really believe this," Kazan implored, his face blanching.

"Too farfetched?" said the Colonel, sounding almost sympathetic. "Maybe so. But I don't have a whole lot of time, Waldo, and the stakes are too high to take the smallest chance."

The Colonel was reaching into his arm holster for his pistol, moving his fingers with steady deliberation, when the sound of running feet came echoing down the corridor. Outside the room, there was excited conversation, then someone rapped on the door and opened it. With pistol in hand, Hagger whirled away from the terror-stricken Kazan and thrust his revolver at the source of the disturbance.

"Whoa, Colonel, please!" shouted Max, jumping back behind the door. "I just came to tell you it's all over. They've got a cool reactor out there and no sign of any meltdown."

Within half an hour, the confused inhabitants of Hackensack were informed that the meltdown process had been contained, that there was no evidence of contamination, no longer a need to evacuate the region. The Nuclear Regulatory Commission did not offer any real explanation. Its official post-mortem included the exhortation to "expect the unexpected in a new line of technology." The public was told that normal activities at the plant were being resumed.

What they were not told was that the reactor had never

actually started reheating on morning six of the crisis. They were unaware that the pressure vessel had never ruptured, that a meltdown had never begun.

Colonel Hagger ordered the plant sealed off. A second barbed wire fence was thrown up around the installation and the 24-hour military guard was doubled. No one was permitted to enter or leave the grounds without going through the Colonel's office, getting his personal authorization. On the steel portals of the plant's control room, a boldly lettered sign warned "DANGER! NO ADMITTANCE!" Those who had already seen the condition of the temperature gauges behind these doors were being detained indefinitely; those who had not, never would. They would never be permitted to see that the indicator needles on all the gauges had been twisted grotesquely out of shape, a few contorted into knots, and that each and every needle was protruding *outside of* the display windows that had encased them, with not a trace of broken glass to be found.

Waldo Kazan was being held in a basement isolation cell under continuous watch. But the Colonel had serious doubts now about the émigré's involvement. They had virtually demolished the man's apartment yet could turn up nothing save the load of books and periodicals they had expected. Nor were any special devices found on his person or in the microscan of his body. Moreover, Kazan had withstood their most effective means of persuasion, had passed the tests of polygraph and pentothol with flying colors. His story had held firm.

But if Kazan was not responsible, who was? the Colonel wondered. In the dragnet of the plant and its environs, only three additional leads had materialized, three cases where a motive for sabotage could conceivably exist. There was the senior janitor of the facility, an old-timer whose parents had been Bolsheviks in the Twenties, and secondly, Hackensack's resident rabble rouser, a big-mouthed peacenik who had organized the local resistance to nuclear power. The first two suspects were not proving out. For one thing, they had ironclad alibis. Of course, the game of psychotronic chess did not necessarily require the pawns to be physically present at the scene of the treachery. More important were the profiles of their personalities, their activity patterns. Hagger's vast experience with conspiratorial types told him this wasn't a match.

The Colonel was even less optimistic about the third possibility. The members of the plant's gate crew had been sacked around the time the incident had begun, so the motive for hostile action was there. But these simple souls were patriots to a man, and they had never even seen the inside of the containment building.

Even if a Hackensack operative were apprehended, it was clear to the Colonel that the events in Hackensack did not originate there. The mayhem had a distant source, and Hagger was sure he knew what it was. But how had they done it, if *not* with the aid of a local accomplice? By some sort of wave? His specialists had been unable to detect any unusual electromagnetic signals in the area. Perhaps there was something they were missing. Maybe the enemy was further along than anyone dreamed. Had Hackensack been the testing ground for some subtle form of radiant transmission covertly developed? Not that the Colonel could see how a wave of any kind could produce such effects. The damage seemed too selective to result from the action of a wave front, and much too perverse. What kind of wave could make matter pass through matter without a surface being broken? This was a question that would have to be answered.

So many questions and so few answers, thought the Colonel, feeling oppressed. He was no high-powered theoretician. He really did not have the head for this sort of thing. Assistance would be required.

Kazan seemed the natural place to start, given his interest in this psychotronic business, that and the plain fact that the man was at their disposal. In the effort to enlist his cooperation, they had allowed a visit from his wife. It had been a mistake. In the brief encounter with his spouse, Kazan discovered that his son had expired on an overdose of Angel Dust. The émigré was now in the throes of a profound depression and was flagrantly suicidal. It was not likely that Kazan could have given the Colonel the answers he needed, in any case. Another, richer vein would have to be tapped. Some withdrawals would have to be made from the Agency's mind-bank.

 **9**

The Wavelength of the Soul

SUPERVISOR VLADIMIR MALEK OF THE KGB's
Section for Advanced Analysis and Strategic Design sat in the
Moscow State Theater. Beside him was his wife, Ludmila,
absorbed in the second movement of "The Firebird Suite."
Uncrossing his legs, Malek pushed down on the sides of his seat to
straighten his posture. His discomfort was increasing. Discretely,
he shifted his position once more, not wishing to draw attention to
himself. Now Malek's head started forward, a slight involuntary
movement he immediately checked. Somewhere at the back of
his temples, the sensation he dreaded was forming, a diffuse
flickering of muted lights. The penumbra was beginning to
spread. Soon the pain would follow, then the nausea. Closing his
eyes, he tightly pressed the bridge of his nose with thumb and
forefinger, as if to subdue the strains of Stravinsky that pounded in
his skull.

Tart, Targ, Putoff, Rao, Rauscher, Ryzl . . . The names swam before him, blurred as his vision was blurring, seemingly tinted by the aura of his impending migraine onslaught. American "*parapsychologists*," thought Malek, curling his lip at such a vaguely metaphysical term. It was so *typically* American. And in the research they conducted, it appeared to be every man for himself, as the Westerners would say. Was this chaotic state of affairs merely the outcome of their highly vaunted system of "private enterprise," or was it an intentional ploy to confuse their opponents? What *was* the nature of the research being done, the true nature? How was it being funded? By university? Industry? Government? Yes, surely their government was involved. But just which government agencies were providing support—CIA, DIA, Department of State, Army, Navy?—and to which research centers? How *much* aid was being given to the various laboratories that were scattered across the North American continent? The facts that he possessed had come slowly, bits and pieces ferreted out at great cost, at tremendous risk to his operatives. But Malek was convinced there was an underlying pattern, and it was this he needed to decipher. It was imperative for the defense of the motherland that a coherent picture be brought to light. Yet thus far, his efforts had failed. The picture had eluded him. All his attempts to make sense of the American initiate in the field of psychoenergetics had come to naught.

The matter was further complicated by the vocal community of alleged skeptics in the United States. How stridently outspoken was their so-called Committee for Sense and Sanity, with its Forrest Reynolds, Paul Krantz, and Martin Gradine. What contempt these critics had shown for the "New Nonsense," as they called it. Did they protest too loudly? Was this another crude ploy designed for the benefit of Supervisor Malek and his KGB associates, so as to throw them off their guard?

As the orchestra began its transition to Ludmila's favorite passage from "The Firebird," she brushed her husband's sleeve with her fingertips, casting a pleased glance in his direction. Vladimir smiled back, concealing his mounting anguish. His thoughts remained fixed on the problem that plagued him. There had to be a pattern in the data his department had amassed, a thread that wove through the patchwork of psychoenergetic activities in which American researchers were engaged. Perhaps there was a central bureau, an office or agency that directed all projects, masterminded all strategy in the area? Certainly it would be shrouded in the utmost secrecy, but Malek believed that no secret was beyond his reckoning. He had always found a way . . .

The pain from his headache was blinding him now, and it fragmented his train of thought into disconnected details. The names scrolled before him again as they had in countless computer readouts, along with locations of laboratories by city and state, letter codes for types of experiments, serial numbers identifying instrumentation, figures of budgets estimated in rubles. Details. They had always been his forte. *Was the key to the pattern of American treachery still to be teased from the details?* wondered Malek, dizzied by the fierceness of his migraine assault. *Or was there no coherent pattern after all?* As the Moscow Symphony Orchestra reached a crescendo, his sense of decorum was flooded by a wave of nausea. Malek suddenly rose and staggered to the washroom.

Nearing the brink of mental exhaustion, Colonel Hagger was engaged in his fifth consultation of the day. The theoretician who sat across the desk from him had been summoned to CIA headquarters from the Hudson Institute, a world-class think tank endowed by the Agency through an indirect arrangement. Attired in a rumpled khaki suit a size too large for his lanky frame, the young man's uncombed hair billowed up in a frizzy mass. Though barely out of his twenties, he wore goggle-like spectacles and carried a cane. The prodigy was losing his vision to a degenerative disease.

"Give it to me again, and this time a little more slowly," said the Colonel.

"We are speaking of a vast reservoir of energy that cannot be directly observed."

"Yet you're sure it is there."

"According to the theory, there is very little doubt."

"But if it's just a theory . . ."

"Yes, but by 'theory,' I don't mean a casual guess. Years of effort went into developing it. Agreement is fairly strong."

"And the reason you can't observe this energy—what did you call it—?"

"Paraphysical."

"—This paraphysical energy can't be observed because . . .?"

"There are built-in limits to what we can observe."

"That much I gathered. But *what* limits?"

"It is a question of scale. Below a certain scale, a certain minimal length defined by Planck's constant, direct measurement is impossible."

"Are you talking about atoms, the length of an atom?"

"Smaller. Much smaller than that."

"Then where is all the energy coming from?"

"Think, Colonel Hagger, of Hiroshima and Nagasaki. That was done by splitting the atom."

"The smaller the space, the hotter the blast," commented Hagger.

"True, in a sense that is true," said the theoretician, "but in paraphysical 'space,' the *amount* of energy is not the critical factor."

"What is?"

"You see, within this minimal length I'm speaking of, any-thing is possible, *literally* anything, because space-time restrictions cease to operate."

The Colonel sighed in audible exasperation.

"Listen, Colonel Hagger," said the nearsighted prodigy, lean-

ing toward his host, "space and time impose *limits* on what you
can do, but inside the Planck length these limitations disappear."

"So you've gone beyond space and time?"

"Yes, that is a fair statement. Ordinarily, your ability to affect
your environment requires you to *transmit* energy over a given
distance—through space, in other words—and this takes a
definite amount of time. In the process, the energy dissipates, you
lose it, and you need to pump more in to keep the process going.
So space is a kind of impediment or obstacle to the free, undimin-
ished flow of physical energy."

"But for *para*physical energy the rules don't apply?"

"That is the general idea. Within the Planck length, it is *space*
that dissipates, physical space blinks out, along with all the restrictions on energy flow."

"Space 'blinks out.' Okay," said the Colonel, shrugging his
shoulders indifferently, "let's say I take that on faith. But it's time
for us to get practical. I need to hear you tell me about
applications."

"I was afraid we would be getting to that," the theoretician
smiled ruefully. He removed his glasses and polished their heavy
lenses with a handkerchief drawn from a pocket of his pants.
"Well, the results could be quite spectacular, if the paraphysical
reservoir could be tapped. Extraordinary effects could be produced anywhere in space instantaneously."

"What kind of effects?" the Colonel asked impatiently.

"Physical, psychical . . . the possibilities are endless," said the
theoretician, sounding almost regretful. "Telepathic appropria-
tion of state secrets, the minds of scientists and government officials molded at a distance, whole weather systems manipulated
. . ."

"You can do this?"

"There is the potential."

"But nothing actual has been done yet?"

"Not yet. We *have* been working with certain mathematical

programs, special anti-gravity solutions to Einstein's field equations . . ."

"What *is* that?" the Colonel cut in. "Is that anything tangible?"

"In time, it could be. It is a question of learning to channel the energy, to direct it to specifically selected targets without being engulfed by it ourselves."

"So you have nothing concrete to show me?"

The theoretician shook his head in the negative.

"Well, I have something to show *you*. Franco, do the honors."

The aide went to the steel filing cabinet in the far corner of the room, and crouching in front of the lower drawer, spun the dial on the combination lock. A sharp-cornered bulging sack was produced and lugged to the Colonel's desk. Franco loosened the drawstring and peeled back the mouth of the bag to reveal its contents.

"What is it?" asked the theoretician.

"A water pump," Hagger replied, motioning to his aide. The pump was laid before their nearly-blind visitor for close inspection. "It's standard fare in the nuclear energy business. They use it for generating steam. This particular item was taken from a Hackensack power plant after it tripped a turbine."

"And created a bit of a meltdown scare, as I recall from media reports." Hunched over the piece of equipment as he spoke, the prodigy was probing its surfaces with palms and fingers. "There is something peculiar about this, but I am not sure what."

" 'Peculiar' is a damned good word. Know what the men in the physics lab said?"

There was no response.

"They said this thing is impossible. But there it is," the Colonel remarked. "You're holding the son-of-a-bitch in your hands. It's circumverted, pushed right through itself, turned inside out like a glove. Matter through matter, and according to microscopic analysis, not a single cut was made in the metal.

"Put your fingers into the open end of the cylindrical elbow,"

Hagger instructed. "Do you feel the raised lettering? It's the Edison imprint. Once that label was on the *outside* of the pump. Notice anything unusual about the letters?"

"My God, they are mirror reversed!" exclaimed the stunned theoretician. "How did you do it?"

"How did *we* do it?" Hagger echoed sardonically. "If *we* could do it, there'd be no point to this meeting, would there? . . . You can *feel* it, man," said Hagger, reaching across his desk to squeeze a tubular section of the queerly transfigured pump. "This is no mathematical formula. It's a hard result."

The theoretician's face was flushed with excitement, and in his voice was a note of admiration. "So my Eastern European colleagues have gone this far already."

"Don't sound so happy about it. They seem to have succeeded where you have failed. Could your, er, 'paraphysical energy' create such an effect?"

"In theory, yes," said the theoretician. Speaking distractedly now, he gazed toward the window through sightless eyes. "As I already said, virtually anything would be possible if you could tap into the Planck length. Space-time restrictions would melt away."

"But for the Russians, it's not 'would' or 'could,' is it?"

"What did you say?"

"Forget about it."

"I'm sorry, Colonel, my mind wandered . . . Did you ever read 'The Plattner Story'? I read it at the ripe age of seven. By H. G. Wells, it is about a fellow named Plattner who is blown into the fourth dimension. When he comes back, everything is inside-out and reversed—he is left-handed, his heart is on the right side and he can only write in mirror script."

"The pump was blown into the fourth dimension?"

"Hmm? Oh yes, you might be able to put it that way." The theoretician was still absorbed in his own thoughts. "Actually," he said, more to himself than to the Colonel, "I am wondering whether the effect can be expressed in the equation as a chirality

operator using the hypernumber epsilon for the spin component."
Colonel Hagger got up abruptly. "Well, it's been very illumi-
nating and we'll have to do this again sometime. Franco, would
you show our guest out?"

"What horseshit!" the Colonel snarled, when his aide
returned. "I need hard results and they send me a cross-eyed whiz
kid with 'chirality operators.' There's no more time for this egg-
headed crap. *Action*—that's what we've got to have, and it better
be damned soon."

That evening, the Colonel sat alone in his office, reflecting on
the matter. How much simpler action would have been, had he
been able to find a local accomplice in the Hackensack affair.
Actually, the investigation was not quite complete. He had put it
on the back burner when his only suspects turned out to be such
duds. Still, their cases had not been closed. Colonel Hagger
decided it was time to reorder his priorities. Before taking on any
more hot-shot theoreticians, he would press his inquest to its
conclusion. His chances were slim, but maybe something would
materialize.

Three days after Hagger's return to Hackensack, the plant
janitor and the anti-nuclear agitator had been re-interviewed, their
stories double-checked, their files reviewed with a fine tooth
comb for the slightest trace of an inconsistency. The net result was
zero. Now, following up on his only remaining lead, the Colonel
sat in the sun-baked stands of the Hackensack Park athletic field.
His aide was at his side, along with Peter Lombardy. They were
observing a practice session.

"C'mon, you bozos," yelled Jimbo Archibald, lofting the
football high over the heads of his comrades, "run under it, turn on
the heat—stretch it out, Larry—great catch, my man!"

Trotting back to the bench on the sideline, the hard-breathing
five staggered all over their coach in feigned exhaustion. "Get
serious, bozos," said a grinning Jimbo as he was buffeted about.

"We're gonna try the stutter step." Playfully, he patted heads and rear ends, relieving Larry of the football. "It's dance, freeze, and go. Let's have Clay lead it off, and Angie, you block. Dance-freeze-and-go. Got it?"

Jimbo took his hands from the shoulders of the pair designated for the next action sequence and smacked his palms together to cue the start of the play. The two men set out, Clay weaving an erratic path down field, shadowed by Angie. "Dance, you bozos!" shouted Jimbo, his arm coiled back to unleash the ball.

"Now freeze it cold," Jimbo bellowed, "—and *go!*" The pass fell short of the intended receiver. "You didn't stop," Jimbo blandly chided, when a breathless Clay returned to the bench. "You gotta freeze like a picture postcard, then take off!

"Harris and Frank go next . . ."

There were few enjoyments in Colonel Hagger's life, but he enjoyed watching the sport of the former members of the gate crew. These were his kind of men, sharing a morning of free-spirited fellowship, American style. How long it had been since he had known a carefree summer day like this. His adversaries had seen to that. But wasn't this what he was fighting for, thought the Colonel—that other Americans might have what for him was no longer possible.

Their workout concluded, the company marched off the field to the shade of an oversized beach umbrella they had planted in the grass. The Colonel and his associates followed. Climbing out of the bleachers, they approached the perspiring cronies, who by now were languidly sprawled on a large white bedspread around a cooler of beer. Each of the six held an open can in his hand.

"Hey, look who's here," said Larry to his companions, "our buddies from the plant."

"We saw ya' sittin' up there, but we didn't recognize ya'," Harris remarked.

"Yeah," said a smiling Jimbo, "we thought you were scouting

us out for an NFL contract, or something."

"You boys do look pretty professional," said the Colonel.

"No shit? Well, Jimbo's too shy to admit it," said Angie, "but he actually had this football scholarship they gave him at Rutgers, ya' know?"

"Right," said Jimbo, "I had it for a whole two months, before they gave me the boot." Everyone laughed.

"Well lately, my boy," added a jovial Clay, wrapping his arm around Jimbo, "we *all* felt that boot, didn't we?" The second round of laughter was louder than the first, but Hagger did not join the merriment.

"It was a damn shame the Edison people had to let you all go," said the Colonel.

"Aw, no sweat," Jimbo said, waving his indifference, and Frank injected philosophically, "Ain't that the way the cookie crumbles."

"So what are you men doing now?"

"My friend, you're lookin' at it." Jimbo grinned, opening his arms to their surroundings.

"And it isn't half bad, but, I mean, do any of you have jobs yet?"

"Jobs? What are those?" said Clay to his mates, still in good humor.

"Actually," Jimbo said, "Angie and Frank are in job retraining—"

"—What a pain in the butt *that* is—" inserted Angie.

"—And the rest of us get an odd piece of work here and there, enough for us to manage."

"Yeah, *we're* doin' pretty good . . ." said Harris.

"Uh, you guys want a beer or something?" Larry asked the Colonel. "We got plenty a' room here—stretch your bones and join us for a beer."

"No. No thanks," said Hagger. "We're fine. We're gonna be leaving Hackensack in a day or two, and we just wanted to touch base with you on that meltdown business. One more time around, just for our records. That okay with you?"

Four hours later, Colonel Hagger was back in his motel room. Stripped to his undershirt and shorts, he stood above a suitcase which lay open on the bed. He was packing in preparation for his departure from Hackensack.

"I don't know about this," said Peter Lombardy, expressing misgivings from a chair in the corner.

"Well, I know," Hagger replied hostilely, before disappearing into the closet.

"But leaving now could be a big mistake," Lombardy called out.

The Colonel returned with a handful of shirts and confronted his colleague. "What is it, Lombardy? What's your gripe against them?"

"I . . .I can't really say."

"Right. So I'm supposed to hang around here in beautiful downtown Hackensack, the armpit of the East, until you find your tongue."

"There's something just not right." The apprehensive Lombardy was shaking his head.

"God damn it, I need more than that," said Hagger, throwing his shirts on the bed. "Look, those guys are about as capable of espionage as my old aunt Tilly. They're solid red-white-and-blue, and even if they weren't, they wouldn't have the smarts."

"I know, but . . ."

"But *what?*" Hagger gritted his teeth. "If there's any 'but,' you better spit it out fast, because I'm on my way South already." He grabbed a leather case that sat on top of the bureau and started for the bathroom.

"You'll think it's crazy," Lombardy said, raising his voice nervously, "but you didn't see those gauges."

"All right, man," said the Colonel, glaring back over his

shoulder. "I don't know what the fuck you're talking about, but I'm going in for a five-minute shave. You've got five minutes to say what's on your mind."

Lombardy sat for a moment without moving, then propelled himself from his chair and approached the open bathroom door. Hagger was lathering up.

"Colonel, this is hard to explain. Maybe it *is* crazy, just a crazy hunch, but it keeps on replaying in my head."

Without taking his eyes from his own mirror image, Hagger laid down the lather brush and lifted the razor to his chin.

"It was . . . that routine they did with the football," said Lombardy to Hagger's back, forcing out his words. "Y'know that dance, freeze and go bit?"

"So?"

"Well, I can't help thinking of those screwed up gauges. Damnedest uncanny thing. I mean, those needles—dance, freeze and go—just like their football routine!"

"Interesting, Lombardy. You said your last vacation was when . . .?"

"You didn't see those gauges," Lombardy loudly protested.

"No. Thanks to your ineptitude, I didn't."

"I told you why I couldn't call Washington that day—they were watching me like hawks."

Hagger gave no reply.

"I'm just saying you had to see those gauges to know what I'm talking about."

The Colonel interrupted his shave and turned to face Lombardy. "What in the hell *are* you talking about?" he glowered.

"I'm . . . not sure," Lombardy said quietly. "Just that the pattern seemed so close, like the needles had *their* trademark on them or something. So I thought maybe those guys could have . . ." His voice trailed off and he left the bathroom.

A few minutes later, Hagger was drying his cheeks. When he

turned off the water in the bathroom sink, he could hear the sound of whirring and mechanical squawking from the other room. Dropping his towel on the toilet seat, he returned to the bedroom to find Lombardy back in his chair, the Agency tape recorder balanced in his lap.

"Jesus Christ, you're not giving up on them, are you?"

"One more thing came back to me. Just one more thing, and you gotta listen." Lombardy snapped down a button on the small machine, producing the voice of Jimbo Archibald.

". . .yeah, we're pretty good sleepers," Jimbo was saying, "slept right through the whole deal."

"Well, we had Angie's birthday party the night before," the voice of Larry explained.

"Never miss a chance to party," cackled Clay.

"Boy, were we looped," Jimbo said. "Out cold the whole night. Morning, too. Slept right around the clock."

"I didn't hear nothin' till my wife came in screechin' about the Governor and all," added Angie.

"Yeah," came Clay's gravelly voice, "it's a shame we missed all that meltdown razzle dazzle. Musta' been some scene in there, all our old buddies runnin' around like chickens without heads, hardware all fouled up, pointers dancin' all over the place . . ."

Lombardy punched the stop button on the tape recorder and stared at Hagger expectantly. "What do you think?"

"I think I've had enough of your crap." Turning away, the Colonel pulled a pair of socks from the bureau top, sat down on the edge of the bed and began rolling them on.

"You didn't hear it?" asked Lombardy in disbelief. He put the recorder in reverse. A brief whir and click was followed by a replay of Clay's last few phrases. ". . .runnin' around like chickens without heads, hardware all fouled up, pointers dancin' all over the place . . ."

"Colonel Hagger, how did he know?"

"Know what?" the Colonel muttered imperviously. He was

reaching for the shirt and tie he had draped on a hook beneath the air-conditioning vent.

"That the needles were *dancing around.*"

"It's just his manner of talking," said Hagger, after a moment's pause. But he lowered his hand from the hook without removing his clothes.

"His manner of talking?" Lombardy was incredulous.

"Needles can dance around."

"Not ordinarily," the engineer answered.

"You call what happened ordinary?" said Hagger, meeting Lombardy's eyes.

"Colonel, that's not the point. I mean, the needles could have done anything. But he said they *danced.* How did he know they danced?"

"In all likelihood, he didn't," said Hagger, now assuming an indulgent air. "What you've got here is an innocent coincidence."

"Maybe so, but it only strengthens my feeling about them."

"Oh come on, Pete, those boys are perfect pussy cats. I told you, they've been double and triple checked and check out the color of the flag. You can see it just by looking at them."

"Okay, Colonel, so humor me. Keep a stake out on them a few more days. What have you got to lose?"

Nothing really, thought Hagger. He had no other concrete leads and did not relish the idea of the interviews he would have to conduct with the last of the abstract heads who were waiting for him in Washington. The Colonel decided to extend his surveillance of the former gate crew for seventy-two hours. He was not taking Lombardy seriously, not expecting that likeable bunch to be incriminated in any way. A few more days in Hackensack could be a respite. Maybe he would get to watch another practice session, even join in the action himself. *A morning of football in the park,* thought the Colonel, once again feeling nostalgia for that great American custom.

The crystal goblet enclosed in the bell jar shattered into countless fragments, while the jar itself remained intact. It was an impressive demonstration, and Supervisor Vladimir Malek turned to the white-coated scientist who had conducted it. But Robodny was attending his equipment.

Adjoining the laboratory table on which the bell jar stood was a steel cabinet bedecked with instrument panels and a display scope sprouting thick cable leads. Its lower section was level with the table top, and from it protruded a funnel-shaped nozzle aimed at the jar. Operating a row of toggle switches mounted in the side of the console, Professor Nicholai Robodny was realigning the nozzle, altering its pitch, widening the diameter of its mouth. After making the necessary adjustments, he regarded the luminous wave pattern displayed on the electronic monitor built into the upper portion of the cabinet. Just below the oscilloscope screen were several rows of labeled knobs and switches. Robodny deftly manipulated the controls and the flickering curve on the monitor changed its shape. Now he instructed Malek to stand away from the table and raise the protective goggles he had been issued. When the two were a safe distance from the bell jar, Robodny pressed the remote control button held in his hand. With a violent shudder, the jar disintegrated.

Malek brought his palms emphatically together. "That is excellent, Professor. My compliments. I am eager to have your explanation of this."

Professor Robodny's response was polite. Showing his guest to a chair at his desk, he measured out a smile. When the scientist spoke, it was in a tone of precision. "As I am sure you are aware, Supervisor Malek, we live in a pulsating universe. Every physical system vibrates. That bell jar . . ." Robodny said, pointing to the shards of glass on the table, "or an oil refinery, a missile silo, a human brain."

"Quite so," replied Malek, gazing at his host intently.

From a delicate porcelain pot warming on a trivet, Robodny

poured tea for himself and his visitor. "Yet most systems pulsate in an asynchronous manner."

"By that you mean. . .?"

"That they are 'noisy,' so to speak. They emit many different frequencies simultaneously, frequencies that compete with and cancel one another."

The KGB official bobbed his head, signaling Robodny to continue. "But for each kind of system, there is a certain character-istic band of frequencies. If one were to isolate this band, rein-force it selectively, any system in the particular class could be brought into synchronous pulsation, made to vibrate coherently."

"As you have demonstrated."

Nodding, Robodny gestured toward the steel console with a flourish. "Our transmitter first was tuned to the synchronization band of the goblet, then to the bell jar. The result should be the same for *any* target system so modulated. Irradiate it continuously at its characteristic frequency, and its vibratory energy will increase without limit, since you have eliminated interference from competing frequencies. When the process is carried to con-clusion . . . well, the outcome speaks for itself."

"Yes, yes," said Malek, musing aloud. "Any system, at any distance from the transmitter . . . Of course, this line of research is not new, and there is reason to believe our adversaries are dili-gently pursuing it. But you have refined it to a remarkable degree."

"Perhaps," Robodny acknowledged, screwing his lips in a semblance of a smile, "but not *enough*. If a system could be made to vibrate coherently *enough*, it could be brought into a unique state of attunement before its destruction. Naturally, the irradia-tion period would need to be kept sufficiently brief."

"Unique state of attunement?"

Robodny disregarded the query. "We need to eliminate *all* noise from the system, tune it to a fineness approaching perfec-tion. This means that the narrow band of frequencies characteris-tic of a class of systems would have to be made narrower still.

Every *member* of a class should have its own particular synchronization frequency, and this is the level of refinement that would have to be achieved."

"To what end?" Malek pressed. "What is this singular state of attunement?"

Robodny sighed. "Unless you are familiar with the subtleties of quantum mechanics—"

"—I am not, but explain yourself anyway." Malek was beginning to feel some antagonism for his host.

"In practical terms, transmitting a signal at the specific synchronization frequency of a system would not merely increase its rate of vibration. An extraordinary channel of influence would open. The target would be utterly at one's disposal, for access would be gained to its innermost structure. You may imagine the implications of this for a *human* target system."

"Controlling its actions, manipulating its thoughts?"

"Anything we wished," Robodny answered, "there would be virtually no restrictions on what we could accomplish."

"Then two questions must be asked. Firstly," said Malek, enumerating with his index finger, "how close are you to achieving your goal? And second, in your estimation, how close is our opposition?"

Robodny snickered. "The opposition? I am afraid that matter is more in your province than in mine. We are kept in blissful ignorance of the progress of our colleagues in the West.

"But concerning our own progress here, I can say I believe we are close, quite close indeed."

"Can you say any more?"

"Better than that, Supervisor, there is more I can *show*. But first, a further word of explanation, since I wish you to comprehend what you are shortly to see.

"It seems that opening the psychoenergetic channel, as we call it, is not sufficient. There must also be a means of inserting the desired information."

Robodny told Malek of past research involving the attempted use of *initiation systems.*

"Initiation systems?" the Supervisor queried.

"A system under the immediate control of the experimenter, one that matches the target in every dimension, is a faithful facsimile. In principle, whatever would be input to such a system would be transmitted to the target, regardless of distance."

"As in the West Indian practice of voodoo," Malek observed.

"Just so," laughed Robodny, though Malek had intended no humor. "But these recent practitioners have not done very much to modernize the ritual, make it technically efficacious."

"And their results?"

"Equivocal. Oh, their efforts are not entirely lacking in sophistication. Some of our Czechoslovakian comrades, for example, have done experiments on disease transmission between cell cultures derived from the same sample."

"So the cultures would be matched genetically," said the Supervisor.

"Precisely. It is a far cry from casting spells with jujus, and yet it falls short of what is required. If the psychoenergetic channel is to be opened between systems, the initiation system must be matched to the *specific synchronization frequency* of the target, tuned so finely to the target that it could literally be placed on the identical wave length."

"Then?"

"Then," said Robodny, his eyes shining, "with both systems primed at the given frequency, any influence brought to bear on one—gross or subtle, simple or complex—would be felt instantaneously by the other."

"This effect would be reliable?" asked Malek.

"There would be no possibility of error, Comrade Malek. You see, the procedure would annul the separation of systems. In effect, the initiator would *become* the target, though the target might be thousands of kilometers away."

"Hmm. An intriguing prospect," Malek remarked. "Of

course, a complex biological system is not a cell culture. If each system has a synchronization frequency unique to its own specific brain morphology and there are vast differences in the fine structures of any two brains, how do you propose achieving the match? Identical twins? Surely *they* would have highly similar configurations, but we could hardly expect that a target requiring our attention would happen to have a twin."

"Not identical twins," said Robodny, shaking his head in mild amusement. "The possibility of cloning has also been eliminated."

"I can see why," Malek commented. "Acquiring a cell sample from a hostile target would be a dangerous proposition."

"Technically impracticable, as well," added Robodny. "No," he said regretfully, "there is no convenient short cut."

Professor Robodny now was ready to give the graphic presentation he had promised. He emphasized that the research still was in its infancy, that development had been stunted by insufficient government funds. "Nevertheless, we have managed to progress quite a bit beyond what you have already seen."

Robodny unlocked a drawer of his desk and removed a videotape cassette. Climbing from his chair, he escorted Malek to a television monitor bracketed to the laboratory wall. As he inserted the cassette in the slot beneath the screen, the scientist prepared his visitor for what he was about to view. "The first segment demonstrates the tuning of the human brain to a considerably finer degree than earlier thought possible."

The machinery was activated and the screen came alive with a stark admonition, bold black letters proclaiming SECRET/ SENSITIVE: DISCRETION IMPERATIVE. An exotically coded listing of mandated security clearances next appeared — CADRE, TUNDRA XV, Q.R., GORKY COMMAND . . . and after additional seconds of blank tape, a dull metallic bulkhead marked "Emissions Modulation Unit" was shown.

A sweep of the chamber's interior pictured a range of techni-

cal paraphernalia similar to that of Robodny's laboratory —
equipment consoles, a variety of instrument panels, electronic
display devices, and wires and cables twining out in every direction. The brief visual sequence ended with a tight shot of what
Malek recognized as the same type of transmitter used to break
the goblet, but here the funnel-shaped nozzle was snugly screwed
into a brass-rimmed orifice appearing halfway up the wall.

Next, a windowless compartment was projected on the
screen. From an overhead angle a subject was seen, a swarthy,
black-bearded man sitting at the edge of a cot. In Malek's estimation, the fellow was likely a native of one of the southern Republics
or possibly an Afghan. He was plugged into the wall on a long,
slack braid of multicolored wire strands gathered in a ring at the
crown of his head and originating from electrode placements
about his scalp, face and upper torso. Shoulders sloped forward,
arms dangling between open legs, his index fingers were in fluid
motion above the featureless floor. He seemed to be tracing out
spirals.

A neat row of ciphers appeared on the monitor, superimposed below the image of the man. The luminous digits began
registering the passage of time.

00 04:49

The subject straightened his posture without getting up and
began flexing the muscles of his neck.

00 19:16

The subject slumped to one side, his left elbow dropping to
the surface of the cot, his cheek propped on the palm of his hand.
With the fingers of his other hand, he jabbed at his right temple,
stiffly pushing and pulling at the flesh. His eyes squeezed shut.

Rolling onto his back, the subject now vigorously massaged
both temples. An increase in stress was apparent.

00 34:51

The subject lurched from the cot, staggering against the wall.
Proceeding unsteadily, he made his way to the chemical toilet in
the rear of the compartment. The tremor in his hands was marked.

Falling to one knee above the mouth of the toilet, he vomited into the bowl.

"This is the standard effect," Robodny pointed out, as the segment ended.

The emissions unit was momentarily reshown for the disclosure of a previously unseen apparatus. Issuing from within the floor was a duct whose stout girth was belted with white enameled ridges. It snaked upward through a framework of metal ribs, stays, burnished support clamps, and terminated in a nose cone laterally oriented toward the wall. A helix of transparent tubing wound around the cone, straightening near the tip and extending somewhat beyond. From the tapered muzzle of the end tube, a filament-bearing needle jutted out.

00 00:00

The bearded subject lolled astride the toilet. His eyes were closed and caked with viscous matter. Traces of spittle appeared at the corners of his mouth, mucous draining from his nostrils.

00 03:14

The subject's head snapped back. A violent twitching of his arms and legs commenced.

00 11:49

The subject toppled to the padded base of the toilet, convulsions unabating.

"What you have witnessed here are the results of experimental micro-modulation," Robodny explained to Malek. "The hyper-masing device housed below the Emissions Unit allowed us to narrow the transmission bandwidth substantially, tailor it to the specific vibratory pattern of our subject."

"But had the man fully recovered from the earlier session?" asked Malek.

"Despite his appearance, Supervisor, I assure you his normal brain rhythm had been restored. Yet with our advanced device, he was brought within a hair's breath of termination in a fraction of the time.

"Impressively lethal, perhaps," said Robodny, "but this is not really what interests us. It is the *special influence channel* we intended to open—alas, without success."

"Can you be certain of that?"

"There is no question. Had the psychoenergetic channel opened, the signal would have been fed back to the transmitter instantaneously, producing a sizeable surge of power. But the critical surge has not been detected. Evidently, we must learn the knack of delivering a still more coherent signal, and at a shorter exposure time, so as not to lose our subject prematurely."

"This learning process," said Malek, his thoughts returning to the enemies of the Soviet Union and the parallel program of research they assuredly were conducting, "how much longer must we wait for it? Days, weeks, months? I need a clearer assessment, Robodny. Our policy critically depends on the factor of time."

"No doubt," Robodny smiled condescendingly, "but a timetable cannot be given for the act of scientific discovery. I can say no more than I have said—that I believe we are very close . . . In any case, Supervisor Malek, you have not yet seen all of what we *have* accomplished."

The video equipment again was activated and Professor Robodny himself now appeared on the tape, stiltedly posing with a group of white-coated colleagues before the portals of a bleak gray building. Robodny identified his companions as his surgical team. The plaque over the entrance at which they stood was engraved, IVAN PETROVITCH PAVLOV INSTITUTE FOR ADVANCED BIOENGINEERING.

With an abrupt flicker that told Malek the tape had been spliced, the scene changed and for the third time, the subject was shown in his cell, his head now swarthed in bandages. *But was it the same person?* Malek wondered.

He lay on his cot, sprawling listlessly on his side. The clothes of the black-bearded man were the same, baggy overalls and a rumpled shirt. The size and shape of his body, the proportions of limbs, torso, head all seemed the same. *His face though . . . what was it about his face?* pondered Malek. Anticipating the viewer's puzzlement, Robodny stopped the tape and played it back to a previous segment, holding on a close shot of the subject. "You see the difference," he said, before returning Malek to the present. The contrast was accented by the appearance of a fresh close-up which Supervisor Malek scrutinized.

Beyond the loss of tension in the jaws, anxious concern in the eyes, the deadening of nearly every trace of human responsiveness, there was another difference Malek noticed, something structural. In a subtle manner, the entire expression had been altered as if the relations of all the muscles had been slightly realigned.

The digital count began and Robodny narrated.

"He is being irradiated at the modulation that almost killed him before. Nothing like that will happen now . . .

"Headache again. . .

"Nausea, dizziness, his coordination gone. . .

"The standard effect you already observed, developing over approximately the same span of time. . ."

With the dark-bearded man draped over the toilet mouth in a state of collapse, the image dissolved.

"We have come to the final session with this subject," said Robodny. "The purified signal from our hyper-maser has been remodulated to his post-operative neural configuration. Incidentally, the censor sends his regrets for editing out the surgery segment. Apparently, you did not have the necessary clearance for that. The results will bear eloquent testimony, however."

At 00 09:17, the subject's brain exploded.

" 'OPENED FOR POSTAL INSPECTION' my ass!" hissed

Colonel Hagger, when he saw the notice stamped on the mail his aide had delivered. He threw the parcel against the wall of his motel room.

Who the fuck do they think I am, some petty bureaucrat they can harass with impunity?

It was a big mistake to remain in Hackensack, Hagger thought. Twenty-four hours of extended surveillance had passed. The former members of the gate crew had been staked out continuously, trailed all over town—to the movies, the ball field, to the Pizza Hut and the local beer hall—with nothing to show for it. And that was the way it would continue to be, Hagger knew. He knew those boys just did not have it in them to be involved in any treasonous acts.

He should never have allowed that bloody paranoid to talk him into staying in the first place. Lombardy with his "dance-freeze-and-go" obsession. *Where was the man's judgment?* thought Hagger. *How could he take an innocent coincidence and blow it out of all proportion?* It was worse than grasping at straws. This connection Lombardy saw between maneuvers on a football field and the behavior of gauges inside an instrument panel was out-and-out lunacy.

That's it, the Colonel resolved. *I'm cutting it short, going back to Washington tonight.* The first thing in the morning, he intended to be camped in the Postmaster General's office. His mail had been opened one time too many, and he vowed to get to the bottom of it, find the culprits who were harassing him and straighten them out.

"So you surgically altered the structure of his brain," said Supervisor Malek to Professor Robodny.

"Yes, and this shifted the specific frequency at which it could be fine tuned. But you have yet to see the *coup de grâce*."

Turning off the tape player, Robodny gestured politely toward the laboratory exit. On their way out of the room, he picked up a sealed envelope that had been sitting on top of the filing cabinet next to his desk.

Without conversing, they walked down the long hallway to the other end of the building. The pair took an elevator to the basement and entered an anteroom where they were confronted by a uniformed sentry guarding a pylon. The security arch stood before a bolted iron door. Moving under the canopy of the scanning apparatus, their identities were confirmed by computer, the door clicked open, and they proceeded into a narrow corridor. On both sides of the passageway were a number of locked compartments patrolled by several additional sentries. Leading Malek to a compartment on the right, Robodny raised a small metal flap hinged to the door at eye level and invited his guest to look inside.

The cell was similar to the one Malek had seen in the videotape. Its occupant lay sleeping, stubbled jaws agape, gaunt visage drained of color. He had been treated in the special way, Malek surmised.

"The neural reconstruction of subject one—our unfortunate Afghan—was by no means a random modification," said Professor Robodny. "You are looking at the *template.*"

"You mean the Afghan's brain was rebuilt to match. . ."

"To match the brain of the individual you now are viewing," Robodny said. "Virtually speaking, his entire cerebral cortex is stored in our Luria 1000. Every centimeter of it has been scanned holographically at fine resolution, the bits of information being pieced back together in their proper relations to simulate the whole."

"And you were able to restructure the Afghan's brain to correlate with this, this whole?" Malek was awed.

"Ugh," said Robodny, shaking his head, "I can think of no system less malleable than the human nervous system. The recon-

struction process was truly a grueling affair involving many delicate stages of successive approximation. Here a slight realignment
of synaptic patterning, there a minor adjustment of dendritic
geometry, and after each procedure, two days at least for the
Afghan to recover. The better part of three months was required
to achieve our results."

"Which were, to put the Afghan on the same specific frequency. . .," said Malek.

"—On the same specific synchronization frequency as our
template," said Robodny. "Yet actually, I'm afraid it was not *quite*
the same. The match was not complete, though our, uh, final
transmission to the Afghan *was* in the template's refined frequency band."

"And, as you have said," observed Malek, "no *special* channel
of influence was opened between them."

"Evidently not," replied Robodny, "yet there was an experiment we had planned to conduct that might have borne out my
contention that we are on the very brink of success. A pity the
Afghan did not have a stronger constitution."

"An experiment in thought transference?" Malek conjectured.

"Precisely so. When the psychoenergetic channel linking
matched systems is ready to open, a dramatic increase in telepathic rapport should be observable.

"But have no fear, Comrade Malek, we have not been procrastinating. Surgical reconstruction already is in progress on a
second subject—this time, a heartier one. In a matter of weeks,
perhaps even days, we may be able to perform the crucial
experiment.

"In the meantime," Robodny continued, now smiling slyly, "I
would like to have your impression. Did you notice anything
interesting about the appearance of our template?"

"Interesting? Only that he seems to have sustained the effects
of your advanced masing procedure."

Producing a razor blade from the pocket of his lab coat,

Robodny made a neat incision across the top of the envelope he had brought and removed two glossy black-and-white photographs. Supervisor Malek recognized both as pictures of the deceased Afghan, and both bore the same identification number, but the caption on one read "Before Surgical Modification," while that on the other was labeled "After."

Malek recalled his reaction to the contrast when he had encountered it on the videotape. The post-operative appearance of the subject was uncannily different. He peered through the spy hole again, then reexamined the photographs. It had not occurred to him on his first glimpse into the cubicle, but there was an unmistakable likeness between the man inside and the Afghan. He supposed that subjects had been selected for this project on the basis of anatomical similarity in the hope of minimizing the reconstructive effort that would be necessary. So Malek was not especially surprised by the pre-operative comparison. Unquestionably, a resemblance of a global sort existed, more in the general shape of the head and face than any specific parameter.

The *post*-surgical likeness was another matter. Within the constraints imposed by the bone structure of his face, the features of the Afghan had been perceptibly standardized, forced into subtly mask-like alignment with those of the man who lay sleeping in the cell.

10

Eyes Watching Eyes

THE FURY FELT IN THE AFTERNOON HAD cooled considerably. Colonel Hagger still intended to leave Hackensack two days earlier than planned, that very night, in fact. What was the point of continuing surveillance over a group of individuals who obviously were guiltless, when the outrageous matter of his compromised mail demanded his presence in Washington? But the Colonel had decided that before returning, he would allow himself a few additional hours of diversion after all. So for the second time in as many days, he sat in a grandstand watching a football game, yet now his aide and he were surrounded by 70,000 screaming fans in a massive steel oval of the Meadowlands Sports Complex. The New Jersey Generals were on the verge of winning the championship game of the United States Football League.

After the final whistle blew to signal the Generals' triumph, bedlam erupted all around Hagger and Franco. Hemmed in on both sides by ecstatic, pennant-flapping celebrants, they could barely climb out of their seats. When an errant gob of beer foam grazed his cheek, Hagger took the bull by the horns. Pushing past the line of revelers in his row, he forced his way to the aisle, then plowed down the steps through a cluster of devotees who had taken up the chant of "we're number one." With Franco struggling to keep pace, they made their way to the concourse under the stands and onto a crowded escalator that led to the parking lot.

"I think I've had my fill of Hackensack," the Colonel sourly remarked to his aide. But as the escalator descended, he noticed some familiar faces waiting at the landing. The six men were smiling up at him, gesturing their greetings.

"Didn't you see us in the stands?" a convivial Jimbo Archibald asked the Colonel, as the group stepped away from the escalator. "We were sitting in the next section waving to you."

"No kidding. I don't know how you picked us out in a mob scene like that. You lads must have the eyes of eagles.

"And how did you get down here so bloody fast?"

" 'Cause we know Giants' Stadium like the back of our palms," said Clay.

"So Colonel, what did you think of the game?" asked Jimbo.

"Some fuckin' fantastic game!" Angie echoed tipsily, and Harris added two choruses of "we're number one."

"I enjoyed it," said Hagger. "Your fans are a little intense, but I haven't done this sort of thing in a month of Sundays."

"Well then, how 'bout topping it off with a nightcap?" Jimbo asked.

"Sorry, but we're on our way out of town."

"You leaving Hackensack?"

" 'Fraid so."

"Then you *gotta* stop over for a farewell toast," said Jimbo.

"And t'toast the fuckin' Generals," Angie chimed in, prompting still another victory chorus from Harris.

"It's at my place," Larry said, "just ten minutes up the road, and we'd be real delighted if you'd come over."

"What do you think?" said Hagger to his aide. "Do we have time for a final fling before we get back to the grind?"

"Well, the shuttles run till eleven o'clock," said Franco, consulting his watch, "so it looks like an extra hour or so wouldn't do any harm."

The Stadium parking lot was clogged with departing motorists trumpeting their tribute to their team as they jockied for the best path of convergence on the exit. Finally clearing the bottleneck, the Agency van pulled up behind the gate crew's waiting jalopy. Franco followed the beat-up old Ford down a series of side roads, past long rows of substantial tudors and colonials with neatly manicured lawns, and into a seedier section of town. They stopped in front of a ramshackle bungalow, Larry leading the way into his kitchen through a screen door that was falling off its hinges.

"Hey, Dora, you got it on ice?" Larry called out.

"Stick ya' head in it." The peevish reply was shouted over the blaring of the television in the adjacent room.

His face flushing, Larry smiled at the Colonel apologetically. "Pull up some seats," he said to the group. Hastily setting an example, he opened a bridge chair that was resting against the wall and shoved it under the circular table that filled the small dining space. Then he ducked his head into the living room for a muffled exchange with his wife, and the television music was lowered.

"Voilà!" said Larry, moving to the refrigerator and throwing open the door. Save for a single container of milk, an apple and a few unwrapped slices of american cheese, the shelves were brimming with beer.

"It's time to refresh!" proclaimed Clay, and as Larry bent into the box to unload the six-packs, Angie, who already had consumed his share of brew that night, tottered to his assistance.

With all eight men settled in around the table and their beer cans unsnapped, Jimbo raised his. "To our Jersey Generals and our Colonel — not necessarily in that order!"

Hagger spoke above loud applause and exuberant whistles. "Gentlemen, gentlemen, I am greatly honored."

"Well, when you came here, Hackensack was in pretty bad

shape with that meltdown and all, and now we're all straightened out," said Jimbo. "So we just wanna say thanks — thanks to the good old U.S. Government."

"I'll drink to that," said Clay, in his gravelly voice. "We sure hope you guys got that meltdown thing all sorted out."

"So, my friends," said Hagger, changing the subject, "are you planning any more football scrimmages in the park?"

"Nah, not till September," said Frank.

"That's when the New York Giants begin *their* season," Jimbo explained.

"The *who*?" said Frank in a menacing tone.

"Oh, right. Sorry, man. The New *Jersey* Giants."

"You betta believe it!"

"Then who is it you fellas support," asked Hagger, "the Generals or the Giants?"

"No need to choose, 'cause we got 'em both." Jimbo's reply brought cheers to the table.

"But wouldn't it be fantastic," Harris said wistfully, "if there was a playoff or somethin'? Generals versus Giants."

"Fan-fuckin'-tastic!" Angie enthused.

"Hey bozo," Clay said to Harris, "how do you figure that one? You got two separate leagues there."

"I'm just sayin' *if*."

"And who knows what could happen in the future," said Jimbo, siding with Harris. "Couldn't the leagues merge? It wouldn't be the first time."

"Speaking of the future," said the Colonel, "I wanted you to know that before I closed my office at the plant, I had a chat with the head of personnel. Now he made no promises, but I can tell you something just might be cooking over there for the lot of you." The revelation brought a fresh burst of applause.

"I guess you guys must miss your old job pretty badly."

The Colonel's remark was followed by silence. Fingering their beer cans with downcast eyes, Harris and Frank shifted in their chairs. Whimsically, Clay began blowing a bubble of foam around the tip of his finger, and Larry got up to put a bag of potato chips on the table. The mood was broken when Angie burped out loud. The first one to speak was Jimbo.

"We miss it, Colonel Hagger. Guess there's no use trying to deny it meant something special, 'cause it did. Harris tells me he's even dreamed about the place."

"Yeah," said Harris with a somber nod. 'Playin' ball in there and stuff."

"Hey, me too!" said Frank. "Harry, you never told me about no dreams like that. Playin' touch tackle in that container house, that's my dream."

"He means the containment building," said Jimbo to Hagger, whose only response was a stiff nod.

"Damn it, I know what I mean," burped Frank. "—Is that like *your* dream, Harry? Like a game a' touch tackle in the container house?"

"Somethin' like that," Harris replied.

"For Chrissakes, I think I had the same God damn dream!" Larry was rising halfway out of his chair.

"When was that?" asked Jimbo.

"I don't know. It didn't come back to me right away."

"Me neither," said Frank, "like my memory on it was delayed or somethin.' "

"Anyway," Larry continued, "there were bright lights, fire-crackers, like the Fourth of July, like we were flyin' or somethin.' Then we were messin' around down in the plant."

Colonel Hagger's mouth opened, but it was not to speak. The color had drained from his face.

"I believe you jokers are flyin' right now," said Clay, "— one step away from good buddy, Angie, over here." Clay poured the remaining drops of his beer can on the head of his companion, who lay slumped on the table. Snoring lightly, Angie did not stir.

"You might've had the dream too, buddy boy," said Frank to

Clay. "You just don't remember your dreams."

"But I'm holdin' my beer," Clay shot back, "and you clowns are provin' you ain't."

Jimbo now offered an impression of his own. "Weirdest damn thing, but *I* get an echo of it now, as if the dream is right on the tip of my tongue."

"Bah!" waved Clay in disgust, "what a bunch of weak-bellied flakes."

Signaling to Franco, Colonel Hagger stood up. "It's been a real pleasure, gentlemen, but it's time for us to take our leave."

"You just got here," Larry protested.

"Maybe so, but we've had your generous toast, and duty calls."

"What's the story, Franco?" asked Hagger.

"Sir, five more minutes, ten tops."

Turning to the window, Hagger gazed through his own reflection at the cars they were passing on the New Jersey Turnpike. *It can't be,* he thought, as they sped toward Newark Airport.

Hagger had been shaken by the odd correspondence of the gate crew's dream to Lombardy's hunch, so unnerved by it that it had driven him from Larry's bungalow. But already he had begun to rationalize.

It just can't be any more than another coincidence, the Colonel thought. Was it so surprising that men who have just been fired will dream of their work place and dream of it in connection with a game that was their passion? But the episode at Amalgamated Edison, that was no dream, Hagger reasoned, and it could not be caused by one. It was a hard reality, part of a definite pattern of sabotage and treachery the Colonel felt he yet would come to understand fully. As for the identity of the perpetrators, the gate crew was out of the question. Plainly, these simple men could not be responsible. He closed his mind once and for all to the possibility that they were involved in any way. The villains could be none other than the enemies of America whom he had suspected all along. His definition of himself and his valorous mission depended on it.

The following morning, the Colonel met in Washington with the Postmaster General, an interview that turned out to be less than satisfactory. In Hagger's estimation, the man was a liar. Effusively apologetic, he claimed he had no idea that Hagger's mail had been tampered with, gave emphatic but vague assurances that the matter would be investigated, then had the gall to terminate the meeting before Hagger could question him further. This son-of-a-bitch would not get away so easily, the Colonel swore. A mental note was made to contact the Internal Revenue Service, an agency with which he had considerable influence.

On his way out of the Postmaster's office, insult was added to injury. Hagger saw one of the vans again, its dark-tinted windshield gleaming enigmatically as it cruised down the block.

Who in the hell are they? Hagger asked himself, sitting in the chair of his Bethesda dentist several hours later. He assumed he had been under surveillance for at least a week, for he had first begun noticing the drab brown vehicles before his return to Hackensack. They did not even have the good sense to change their license plates.

Well, he was not about to be intimidated. He had no intention of yielding passively to such tactics. His own charcoal gray vans, even more anonymous in appearance than those of his trackers, were out now doing their job. Eyes watching eyes. Before long, he would know enough for decisive action to be taken.

"Open," said the dentist.

The Colonel absently opened his mouth.

"A little wider, please."

Jesus, does he want to tear my jaw? thought Hagger. But he complied.

Did the mystery of the so-called postal inspections stem from the same source as the mysterious brown vans? That would mean a powerful antagonist. On the other hand, a single opponent might be easier to deal with. No matter. Whoever they were, the Colonel was confident that *he* would prevail in the end.

"It's a deep one, sir. We'll be drilling close to the nerve. Will you take the nitrous oxide?"

His mouth crowded with hardware, he managed an "uh huh."

Hagger had been the subject of harassment before. It was an occupational hazard in the CIA. With his recent presidential appointment as Special Projects Coordinator for Advanced Military Research, it had become an occupational inevitability. Harassment and perhaps more, thought the Colonel. God only knew all the machinations that were likely to be hatching, with *his* office, *himself*, as their target. Undoubtedly, some would spring from petty domestic rivalries. Others might have more insidious roots.

The Colonel was prepared for any eventuality. No incursion would be tolerated, no intrusion in his sphere of operations, for he saw the larger danger to the country and believed he was among the few who understood the nature of the remedy. The sense of purpose and responsibility this created made personal considerations wholly irrelevant.

Clear and present danger, he was thinking, and as the gas took effect, the thought seemed to stretch to infinity.

The insipid strains of radio music that had been droning in the background somehow dissolved into a voice reporting the weather. "One o'clock . . . readings. . . at Dulles International. . . temperature. . . seventy-eight. . . degrees. . . humidity. . . "

At his mouth, fingers were interminably at work, an achingly endless repetition of details of movements convincing him that the eventfulness of his life was an illusion, that in fact he had always been in that chair under these ministrations. A kind of bitterness overtook him, a gnawing sense of having been betrayed. He closed his eyes and listened to the radio.

". . .and at . . . the top . . . of the news . . . *is the White House announcement that a clear and present danger exists, resulting from the bombardment of government buildings in the capital with a highly potent, paraphysical ray believed capable of turning matter inside out. The President has declared a state of national emergency and put our strategic forces on global alert. In rebuking what he termed "an intolerable incursion that amounts to an act of war," he has issued an ultimatum. If the treachery does not cease and desist within the twenty-four hour period just begun, decisive action will be taken whose consequences he would disavow."*

Arms flailing, the patient struggled up from the dental apparatus encumbering him.

"Sir, what's the matter?"

"Didn't you hear? . . . No, you didn't, did you," said the Colonel, falling back.

"Hear what?"

Getting no reply, the dentist stooped to retrieve his equipment. His patient's eyes were upon him.

"*What* was that chemical you gave me, Doc?"

"You mean for the pain?"

"Right."

"Why, nitrous oxide. What else?"

The Colonel had serious misgivings.

In Professor Robodny's laboratory, a panel in the wall rolled down to expose two blank-screened video monitors. The letters imprinted over the first read "INITIATION SYSTEM," while the second was captioned "TARGET."

Returning from the washroom where he had taken a precau-

tionary headache tablet, Supervisor Malek went to the side of his
host. The white-coated scientist stood before the receivers, a
clipboard in his hand.

"If you are ready. . ." said Robodny, punching a control
button.

At once the monitors blinked on. On each appeared a live
picture of a man in a large reclining chair, wrists bound loosely to
arm rests, ankles to leg supports. The men lay still, their bodies
limp, their ears encased in bulky headphones. Mounted on a
tripod, a viewing screen was positioned in front of the subject
designated as the initiator. Coiling from under the bandages that
swarthed his head, and from every extremity on his body, were
multicolored wires that fed into a terminal box installed on the
back of his chair. Except for the absence of bandages, the target
subject was identically wired.

"Each chamber is acoustically and electromagnetically
shielded," explained Robodny. "No radiation of any kind can
enter to influence them — that is, none but the specific, highly
coherent signal we have been transmitting."

The screens blinked again and close-ups were shown of the
subjects. Malek had seen the target before. It was his brain that
had served as the template for reconstructing the brains of the
initiators. Turning his attention to the other subject, the Supervisor
noticed that this new initiator appeared more robust than the
deceased Afghan, as Robodny had assured he would. And the
features of the fellow's face had their distinct character. Yet Malek
marveled once more at the eerie uniformity that apparently had
resulted from the neurosurgery. Like his predecessor, the countenance of the bigger man evidently had been transfigured, the
muscles realigned to create a subtle resemblance to the target.

The door to the laboratory now opened. From the threshold,
a stethoscoped, white-clad young woman motioned to Robodny
with a raised pencil.

"The physician has pronounced them sufficiently fit," said Robodny. "We can proceed to the first trial."

Moving his hand to the control panel below the monitors, the Professor placed his index finger over a red button. "I am about to give the initiator his cue, a single tone sent through the earpiece. This will prepare him for the stimulus that will appear on his viewer in precisely five seconds. A short time after that, irradiation will commence. Both subjects will be hyper-mased on the common frequency."

"What kind of stimulus is to be shown? How *much* time will elapse before masing? You must give me all the details, Professor Robodny." Malek was sensing the onset of the migraine attack. The pill he had ingested had not yet taken effect.

"Exactly three seconds — that is the interval in question, if you really need to know. As for the nature of the stimulus, any visual image is possible," Robodny shrugged. "The computer will randomly select a picture or symbol from the large pool of alternatives stored in its memory, and project it to the initiator."

"After irradiation, what happens then?" inquired Malek.

"The target is required to give his immediate impressions of what he believes his counterpart has been viewing. You will notice the microphone clipped to the pocket of his shirt. It is for recording his responses and," said Robodny, tapping the circular grill of a speaker built into the monitor, "for broadcasting them to us."

"And because the target will be mased at the same specific frequency," said Malek, "you are expecting his mental associations to match the picture."

"Correct. The hope is that we will achieve an appreciable match. As I already explained, this would serve to validate our approach. It would be the crucial indication that the psychoenergetic channel between them was close to being opened."

"Why could it not simply *open?*"

"It could," confirmed Robodny, "today, perhaps it could.

Our frequency band is still not sufficiently narrow. But we will be attempting a further refinement this very day. In fact . . ." Robodny said, pausing to consult his clipboard, "the new modulation is scheduled for trial four. Comrade, you well may be a witness to a singular moment in the history of science."

The aura from his headache beginning to form, Malek smiled quirkily. "Are you certain the subjects will cooperate? The initiator could decline to attend to the stimulus."

"As you know, Supervisor, they are —"

"—Yes. Prisoners from the labor camps who have been led to believe they may reduce their sentences."

"So there is no question that they are adequately motivated. Can we proceed now with the first trial?" asked Robodny, showing signs of impatience. With Malek nodding assent, the Professor purposefully lowered his finger to the signal button and depressed it.

The initiator instantly grew agitated. In anticipation of what was to come, he squirmed and thrashed under his restraints. Presently, a serene image was projected on his viewing screen, the silhouettes of a mother and child standing in a wading pool beneath a setting sun. Moments later, the heads of both subjects violently snapped back, their limbs twitching spasmodically. Then, just as suddenly, they slumped in their chairs. The brief irradiation period had come to an end.

At his control panel, Robodny pressed additional buttons. The speaker was activated and the target cued to give his responses. But seconds went by and the only sound that could be heard from the isolation cell was the rasp of uneven breathing. Several more times Robodny jabbed the cuing button. Finally, a reaction was evoked.

". . .Uh. . .I s-see. . .f-flowers," the subject stammered in a hoarse whisper. "And, uh . . . b-books, s-shelves of books . . ."

For fifteen minutes, the chain of stuttered responses drawled on. Malek was unimpressed. He could see no meaningful correspondence between the subject's associations and the picture being viewed by the initiator. For his part, Robodny was showing no concern. The scientist crisply proceeded to trial two.

The new stimulus was a farm scene, cows being milked by kerchiefed peasant women who sat astride stools. In their separate chambers, the men were jolted again, and the target was cued to respond.

". . .F-flashing colors," the subject croaked. "Inside my h-head. . .f-flashing lights. . .Seeing d-double. . .v-vision g-getting blurry. . .It's aching, oh, it h-hurts. . .p-pressure inside my h-head getting bad. . ."

This is very curious, thought Malek uneasily. The associations were completely unrelated to the scene on the initiator's viewer but closely attuned to what he, Vladimir Malek, was experiencing as his migraine headache grew worse.

For the third time, a stimulus was projected and the subjects irradiated. Now the voice that came through the speaker seemed weakened, the stutter more pronounced.

". . .Ooohh. . .s-such p-p-pain. . .p-pill isn't w-w-wor-k-king. . .w-wrong p-pills. . .L-lud-m-mila. . .s-she g-gave wr-r-ong b-b-bottle. . ."

"We are losing him," said Robodny, jamming the cuing button in disgust. "The fool is free-associating, not responding to the stimulus." Looking away from the screen, Robodny saw his colleague leaning against the wall, his hand held out for support. Malek's face was the color of ash.

"There is some kind of a problem, Supervisor Malek?"

"I. . .I am afraid so. A touch of indigestion. I am afraid I will need to use your washroom again."

When Malek returned to the laboratory, his complexion had barely improved, but he insisted he was ready to continue. Despite the questionable condition of the subjects, Robodny had decided to proceed to the critical trial. The attempt would be made to open the psychoenergetic channel. "What have we to lose," Robodny reasoned.

A fresh stimulus was projected on the initiator's viewer and the volunteers were irradiated at the newly-refined modulation. Like synchronized marionettes, they danced grotesquely, literally lifting out of their chairs. And together they dropped in a motionless heap when the masing was finished.

Robodny pressed the cuing button but got no response. He pressed it again. Still nothing. In a state of utter collapse, the target seemed unconscious.

The physician now entered the laboratory to report that the life sign displays on her physiological monitor were completely flat. She was on her way in to examine the subjects, but felt there would be little she could do. Apparently, they had expired.

"You will have to be patient with us," said a tight-lipped Robodny to Supervisor Malek. "Our work here requires the utmost —" Abruptly, he broke off his sentence, for a distinctly audible sound had come over the speaker.

Robodny's hand shot to the control panel, his index finger to a switch that brought a close-up of the target to the screen. The subject's eyelids were fluttering open. Oddly, his face appeared relaxed now, in fact, almost blissful. As he spoke, not a trace of his stutter was in evidence.

". . .So beautiful. . .a beautiful glow. . .Ah, so *warm*. . . It is Love," the man murmured, a hint of a smile playing at the corners of his cracked lips. "I am going inside it. . .It is inside *me*, Love is inside me. . ."

The subject closed his eyes and said no more.

Sixty stories above the bedrock of Manhattan turned a brightly lit crystal carousel. *Renard Picault's* perched in pristine elegance atop the Westinghouse Building, its transparent hull open to the night. It was New York's newest cafe of distinction.

Colonel Hagger was led up a steel spiral stairway into a white-on-white setting of post-Bauhaus space-age design. The sleek lines, low silvered surfaces and polished tubularity reminded him of scenes from *2001*. Yet filmmaker Stanley Kubrick's hi tech interiors *were* interiors, thought the Colonel, and this seemed anything but. The curved outer wall was all window, the ceiling a skylight cupola. *Renard Picault's* lay bare to its surroundings, and Hagger felt apprehension.

In the center of the cabaret, a columnar stage rose halfway into the dome and upon it, a slinkily-gowned vocalist played at a baby grand. Encasing the slowly turning pillar on which she performed was a smoke-tinted mirror whose rotation captured multiple changing images of the city. *It's a God damn fun house*, Hagger thought, as he was ushered to a table at the glass perimeter.

Van Castle sat waiting. Towering beside the government executive was a square-shouldered matron in a man-tailored suit. She was introduced as a "White House observer," but from her Amazonian proportions, Hagger supposed she might just as well be Van Castle's bodyguard.

"They picked a funny place to conduct business," the Colonel commented, when standard salutations had been exchanged. Van Castle replied with a shrug. "Ours is not to reason why."

Martinis were ordered and promptly served.

"Well, I'm ready for my *debriefing*," said Hagger sarcastically, after taking a sip of his drink.

The Assistant Director of the Defense Intelligence Agency chuckled at this petulant opening. "There's really no need for this. You're in the Big Leagues, Al. At our level of operations, close surveillance is S.O.P. I watch you, you watch me, everyone watches everyone else. That's how we keep each other in line, checks and balances. . . it's the democratic way."

"I was not informed."

"Did you have to be?"

"Let's just say I'm naive that way."

"Then you are hereby so informed," said Van Castle.

"And that's that?"

"I'm here to answer your questions. Feel flattered. If you weren't thought of so highly, I wouldn't be doing it."

Van Castle proved evasive in the dialogue that followed. Specific queries were answered in terms the Colonel found too vague, and when he pressed, he was told that the delicate balance of privileged information could not be further jeopardized. Colonel Hagger well understood the technique. In fact, he admired the professional artistry with which it was being applied. At the same time, he was bound and determined to make the most of his opportunity, to arm himself by learning whatever he possibly could.

The Colonel persisted, and genuine progress actually began to be made, more than he expected. *More than should have been allowed?* he started wondering. Should he have been permitted to know how the Labor Department got FBI undercover agents hired for inside bugging operations? Why had he been given details on the latest model of telescopic lens used for long-range surveillance by Van Castle's own agency? Was Van Castle slipping? Was the second martini having an effect? That was unlikely. Maybe the Colonel was merely getting his due, information to which he was entitled. Or was information deliberately being *planted?*

As the Colonel's malaise intensified, he realized that something else was contributing to it. It was the room. Something had changed in the room.

"Do you feel it?" asked Hagger.

"What?"

"The room."

The Assistant Director looked befuddled.

"It is *moving*," asserted the Colonel.

"No kidding," Van Castle replied with a sidelong glance at his hulking companion.

"Cut the crap, man, you know what I mean. It's turning *faster*."

Van Castle took a moment for appraisal. "Holy shit, I think you're right."

The politely subdued, uniform drone of conversation in the cabaret was now giving way to audible expressions of alarm. The speed of rotation further increased and the clatter and clank of sliding plates and silverware could be heard all around. Metallic crash and breakage fed the din as the missiles unleashed grew more formidable — a tumbling bar stool, two empty chairs skidding out of control, a tray-bearing waiter sent reeling into a gathering of patrons. Yet a semblance of order was preserved.

Then all at once, *Renard Picault's* started jittering. Like a tire come off its rim, it began bumping erratically up and down. Rising above the general pandemonium, microphone-amplified shrieks came from the elevated stage. The panicked singer on top of the dais frantically clung to the only solid object at her disposal, her piano. Each time the cabaret shuddered, the piano shifted closer to the unprotected edge of the platform.

"You! It is you!" the Colonel suddenly shouted at his companions. But they stood transfixed, gaping at the agonizing progress of the piano toward the precipice. Neither responded to the crazed accusation.

"Stop your fuckin' game right now!" Hagger roared. In the flash of dazzling clarity that comes with a paranoid break, he knew that *they* were behind the event that was unfolding, that it was all an elaborate set-up that would end with his assassination. *I do not have a choice*, thought the Colonel, drawing his revolver.

He was not surprised to see the Amazon react first. Snarling, she reached for the bulge in her jacket. This monstrosity was playing the Judas' stooge, as he had suspected. Hagger blew her away. Judas himself had time for little more than a dumbfounded stare before being dispatched. The Colonel then retrieved Gretta Kellog's weapon and turned it on himself.

His shoulder exploded. Dropping to his knees above the

outstretched form of his vanquished opponent, he was quickly losing consciousness. But in a triumph of will, Hagger summoned the strength to grasp Kellog's clenched right palm and forcibly pry it open. With the gun returned to the hand of its owner, trigger finger properly in place, the Colonel could surrender to oblivion.

 **11**

False Starts

TONIGHT IT WAS GOOD. SANDY AND PHIL WERE easy with each other, holding, hugging, being together.

Later, in the semi-dark, they embraced, pressed in urgent contact. With the sweetly swelling passion was mingled a yearning, a nostalgia for the moment they had lost.

This was not the way back, they knew. Sandy and Phil had learned it was not enough by itself. Yet they could *pretend* and in the game find a lesser ecstasy that would sustain them for the present.

By touching you I become *you.* That was the game's single rule. *Touching your arm, I define it as my own. Stroking it, caressing every part of it, it becomes more deeply and inwardly mine . . . arms, shoulders, neck and cheeks, eyes, lips . . . I can sense these now from within myself, feel them* become *my self.*

So the game was played — perhaps not the key to the merger they sought, but potent enough, nonetheless, for a limited enactment. And as Phil reached his climax, he erupted in laughter.

"Why do you always do that?" asked Sandy, not in reproach.
"It's the reflection. We're right in the middle of one another
—no words or thoughts, no distance at all, just acting and connect-
ing, and it's so real. Then I'm *reflecting* on the reality, but not in a
way that spoils it. I'm detached, I can see what we're doing, yet
somehow *not* detached, *not* cut off from the doing, and that
combination is unbeatable, a hilarious joy!"

But Phil dropped rapidly from the high. When Sandy slipped
her palm into his to restart the game, he was no longer with her.
His mind had gone back to the events that followed the night of
the blackout. Everything had changed after that, thought Phil.
Changed, yet remained the same. . .

They had taken a quantum leap which neither could explain.
Only once did they make the attempt, on the subsequent morning.
They could merely confirm that it had happened, that it could not
have been an hallucination, that their "mutual OBE" or "communion" or whatever it was—was important, needed to happen again,
be reexperienced, in some way expanded on.

They needed to be together. Phil moved into Sandy's flat
later that day and their first encounter was a staggering event.
Fewer than twenty-four hours had passed and, carnally triggered,
it *was* happening again, or so it seemed. Their sensual upheaval
seemed to move the earth, and so to jolt them from their familiar
selves, as they had been jolted the night before. They went out of
their bodies again, then went to the core of each other, fully
possessing each other. That is how it had appeared to them right
afterwards, so much did they want to believe.

But the spell soon was broken. As they lay face to face, their
wordless understanding was that it had *not* been the same. An
awesome transaction it certainly was, a sublime sexual exchange,
exhilarating, inspiring, but not the same.

They were encouraged, though, for this was just their first try and considering the results, they felt sure they had come close. Who knew how close they had come on only their first attempt? Neither had to say there would be others.

They resumed early the next morning, a mind-shattering sunrise ritual carried out before the curtain-drawn window. Afternoon and evening sessions followed and were nearly as intense, magnificent couplings that transported them, although still of the *corporeal* kind. The transcendence was only metaphoric and there was no transformation. Yet realistically, could they expect more? The process had just begun, they told each other, confidently vowing to be patient.

Then Monday intruded. That did not prevent a superlative start to the day, but Sandy was depleted by her hours as the new cashier for a local bookstore, and Phil was drained just as much by his academic duties at Franklin College, chores that kept him on campus well into the evening. They met for coffee after Sandy's late Psychology and Law class, camouflaging the loss of luster as best they could. The remainder of the night was something of a masquerade half-heartedly acted to a less than spectacular climax.

It went no better on Tuesday, and Wednesday was worse, traces of their old animosity beginning to show. On Thursday night they talked. Little probing seemed needed to pinpoint the problem. They were holding back, making a partial commitment when a total one was called for. Friday the path was cleared. Sandy quit her job at the bookstore, Phil cancelled his classes, putting himself on indefinite leave. The major distractions were eliminated and they were ready to go all out, mount a decisive drive toward their dimly perceived but strongly intuited goal.

It did not happen. Two weeks together without interruption, days on end of unobstructed physical closeness, and no progress was made. In the initial stage, they *knew* they were on the verge, that it was imminent, that metamorphosis would be occurring at any instant, and it electrified them. They were raised to a level of

sexual excitation and fulfillment that paralleled the greatest
moments of the weekend past. But that *special* rapture was not
forthcoming. Of course not, they reasoned in stage two. They were forcing
a process that could not be forced. They needed to be more yogic
—yoga was what they needed to do. The asanas were performed.
For long hours they stretched, sometimes together with Sandy
assisting, sometimes alone. With open palms, they sat in lotus,
breathed in tandem, their conviction holding firm for a number of
days. Conviction then gave way to doubt.

Maybe it had been an elaborate hallucination after all, a *foliè
a deux*. Or was it just that they were screwing it up, botching the
chance they had been given, Phil asked himself in agitation. He
decided that that must be it. They were going about this in the
wrong way. A more aggressive approach was required, a syste-
matic, full-scale mobilization of their potency. He constructed a
schedule that would be adhered to religiously. Before every meal
and again, late in the evening, they would sexually engage, with
the option for a fifth encounter at bedtime, assuming they still had
the fortitude. Periods between sessions would be given over to
complete relaxation. They would spend the time listening to his
audio tapes of chamber music classics, and Sandy could provide
an exercise or two from her repertoire of yoga, just to help loosen
them up. Aside from that, there would be no deviation from his
plan of attack. Its implementation would commence the following morning.

Phil's eyes came open at daybreak, but he lay motionless as
minutes passed uncountably and the room brightened. Curiously,
a great inertia was in his bones. It oozed through his limbs, creating
a kind of paralysis whose grip was broken finally by the nagging
of his bladder.

The face in the bathroom mirror was an object of distaste
—so crudely, concretely there. Slack jaw, stubbled beard, cheeks

pale and drawn, eyes so empty of life. The visage was hollow, present in only the most trivial sense. Hardly a candidate for metamorphosis. But Phil composed what there was and went ahead.

He lowered himself gingerly, sitting on the edge of the bed beside her fetally curled form. "Time to get going, baby," Phil nudged with tenderness. She did not stir.

Turning away, he spoke half to himself, not expecting a reply. "Are we gonna get started?" he muttered. Phil could feel the heaviness again. Never completely dispelled, it was quickly re-establishing itself. For many moments more he sat, elbows propped on knees, head inclined to the floor. Then, feebly, a rally was attempted. He was struggling for words, at least for the strength to utter the word that was her name. And he was just about to achieve his small success when abruptly, Sandy sat up.

She moved past him, out of bed and hastily into the bathroom. Phil was grateful. No longer faced with the burden of arousing her, it would be easier for him to rouse himself. Already he felt more alive, more equal to the commitment he had made for them.

The toilet flushed, a signal he must marshal his reserves. The bathroom door clicked open and his expectations rose. But she did not return. Instead Phil heard the water running in the kitchen sink.

"What are you doing?" he called.

"What do you want for breakfast?" she called back.

"Breakfast?" cried Phil, rushing into the kitchen. "It's got to happen *before* breakfast. I *told* you that."

"Not today."

"What do you mean?"

"It isn't going to happen today."

"Then *when*? I don't understand."

"I'll need a few days."

"Bullshit, Sandy, you're crapping out. If it's too much for you to handle, why don't you just tell me that?"

"Scrambled or poached?" she asked, as she scoured the frying pan.

Phil's conflict and frustration gave way to rage. "I said *admit* it," he growled, grabbing her wrist, twisting it hard.

She dropped the pan in the sink and lurched back, her eyes ablaze. "I got my period today, you asshole!"

Shoving the dripping wad of steel wool into his face, Sandy ran out of the room. . .

Lord, what a jackass I was, thought Phil, recalling how they had laughed about it later. The very next day, they'd returned to the world, for it had dawned on them that whatever had been gained the night of the "leap" had not been theirs exclusively to reclaim and develop. They felt certain there were others who must have taken their own "quantum leaps." They realized that in some way, they would need to involve themselves with others.

"No . . . it was *never* ours alone," he whispered to her now, though from the rhythm of her breathing, he knew she had given up their game of pretend and fallen asleep.

They were groping, casting about for a lead, a meaningful direction to pursue. The books on out-of-the-body and "astral" projections were many in number, and Sandy and Phil went through them together, as Sandy had once done alone. There were fascinating volumes, intriguing accounts of personal experiences, investigations in the laboratory, books on "How To." The relevance of the material to their own experience was undeniable. Yet in a sense deeply felt, it left them cold.

They broadened their involvement, began attending lectures and seminars and spending weekend afternoons at the libraries of the American Society for Psychical Research, the Anthroposophical Society, the Eastern Studies Institute. A wide-ranging exploration of the subject of consciousness was opened—its states, levels, potentials for transformation. They heard one authority argue that the mind was naught but a microprocessor, proving his point with long strings of squiggles, the language of symbolic logic. In an address on brain evolution, a speaker portrayed human consciousness as a magnificent accident, the improbable outcome of a genetic mutation graced by natural selection to survive and flourish. Sandy and Phil found especially chilling a lecture on the military applications of psi phenomena, the presenter intimating that top secret research was already in progress in laboratories around the world.

In other presentations, much was made of energies, ethers, plasmas and fields of every variety. Hidden dimensions, spaceless spaces and timeless times liberally were invoked, or volumes were taken to say that consciousness was unsayable. And there was the metaphor. Consciousness is a stream, an ocean of vibrations or a bottomless pit. It is the inner screen upon which the movies of the mind are continuously shown, the Eye of the Creator, or an infinitely porous Cosmic Sponge.

They were enjoying themselves. In a one-day conference at the C. G. Jung Institute, they happened upon Arthur Rosenberg and Mindy Harris, Sandy's former parapsychology classmates. Now living together, Mindy and Arthur had embarked on a quest of their own, and the four spent the rest of that afternoon discussing Arthur's concerns over the dangers of misunderstanding psi. It could not be manipulated for political advantage, Arthur insisted. He felt that if human beings tried to use it for that kind of gain, it was bound to backfire, for Arthur had come to view psi events as an indication that something spontaneous was happening, that human consciousness spontaneously was changing. Sandy and Phil found themselves agreeing with the student's intuition, and when Sandy remarked that it reminded her of the views of their parapsychology professor, Arthur acknowledged Noel Innerman's recent and substantial influence on his thinking.

In the days that followed, Sandy and Phil met other seekers along the way, formed new relationships through which ideas were exchanged, encouragement given. In the vestibules of lecture halls and out on the street, in Greenwich Village pubs and East Side cafes, the dialogue unfolded. Earnest deliberations went late into the night, running debates on the mysteries of psi and the nature of consciousness. And there was commiseration, too, on their status as intellectual outcasts. More than the formal discourse, the fellowship, the mutual support was a welcome source of satisfaction.

But it was all still so pale, Sandy and Phil felt—faint outlines wispily stroked when no mere picture should suffice. They needed to *leave* the canvas, engage the living reality, as once they had done.

It was for this reason that Sandy had disclosed their experience to a certain acquaintance, though in all their transactions with their fellow pilgrims, it had never been mentioned. She made her confession to Phil with the hope he would not feel betrayed, that he could be made to understand about Jenine.

A long friendship with the girl had not been required. From their first meeting in the bookstore the day Sandy had returned to her job, she believed she knew this person. "You've never seen such openness. Amazing sensitivity. She must be some kind of genius at it, Phil, because when I told her about us, she seemed to get it right away, like she'd been *with* us. But honey, you can see for yourself. Let's invite her over."

The young woman who entered their apartment was not under twenty years old, but Phil immediately was struck by her bewitchingly childlike quality. Jenine was wearing slightly baggy white denim overalls and a polo shirt with the emblem of a rainbow brightly embossed across the front. Except for a single, well-formed braid arranged on her shoulder, her titian hair was sleekly drawn back over petite heart-shaped ears, revealing the whole neat contour of her delicate jaw.

Everything about her seemed fresh and kinetic to Phil—rich skin tones of copper and rose vibrantly blending, guileless wide-open smile wickedly framed by sensuous lips. One instant her dark-lashed, almond-shaped eyes were large with expectation; the next they were sparkling in a spirit of warm-natured play. When Jenine said hello, she appeared to be smiling at him with the whole of her body, both hands extended to his, shoulders angled forward expressively.

"Will you join us for tea?" asked Sandy. The girl declined, but admiring the coziness of their layout, she trailed her hostess into the kitchen. When Sandy opened the refrigerator for a lemon, the guest said, "I wouldn't mind an orange."

Jenine preferred the floor to the sofa. She dropped to her knees across from Sandy and Phil, spreading the napkin for her orange on the open side of the coffee table at which they sat. Then, in a sinuous motion Phil wanted replayed, she swiveled into a comfortable cross-legged position, knees projecting under the table, elbows resting lightly upon it.

At once her eyelids fluttered closed, the features of her face growing smoother than they naturally were, smoother than possible, thought Phil, as if they might disappear. Unself-consciously, she raised the orange before her like a sacramental object, her head inclined to it. A kind of chant now commenced, a single resonant syllable intoned from deep in the cavity of her chest.

"It helps you digest it," Jenine grinned brightly, her eyes abruptly popping open. Sandy nodded emphatic affirmation, returning her grin, and Phil too was smiling, though with the color rising fast around his ears.

Lifting the skin from her fruit, the guest spoke again. "Before anything else is said, I need to say thanks. Sandra Peterson, thank you for your dynamite mind! Phil, she's been making my days at the bookstore since the day she arrived."

Sandy reached over the table and the girls squeezed hands.

"How long have *you* been at the bookstore?" Phil inquired.

"Mmmm. . . a year or so, I guess."

"And before that?"

"A bunch of bad stuff."

"School?"

"No, just running around, scratching around to survive."

"What about prior to *that*?"

"It was worse. I was living at home."

"Not in New York?" asked Sandy.

"St. Louis, with my father. A very ugly scene. He, uh, started doing things to me after my mother died, and, uh. . ."

"You don't have to say," Phil interjected.

"No, it's okay. It was bad abuse, mostly sexual things, you know. And, uh, he would always apologize for it later when he'd sobered up. He'd get real sheepish, bring me breakfast in bed or money for jeans or something. That's when I hated him most, when I wasn't afraid, you know?"

"So how did you get out?"

"By screaming the house down," smiled Jenine. "One night he really went out of his head, started using his belt and all. I started screaming. I wasn't scared any more. I was beyond that. Dad kept shouting at me to stop. He tried hitting me harder, at first tried to cover my mouth with his hands, with a pillow, but I kicked at him, squirmed away and ran out of the room, screaming louder than ever. When the police arrived, I was still yelling. I saw them open the door to his room, saw him standing on his bed with his belt around his neck. He was fumbling with the long end, drunkenly trying to tie it around the ceiling fixture. How I loathed him at that moment."

"I can understand," whispered Sandy.

"No, honey," said Jenine, "*I didn't* understand. The man was *possessed*. Something had hold of him, like some kind of demon. He really could not help himself."

"What happened?" Phil softly pursued.

"They gave me a medical and that was it. He was, uh, put away, and I went out on my own."

A heavy silence was broken by Jenine herself. "But can you

believe it turned out to be a *blessing?*" she prettily beamed. "I'm really stronger for it. And good things have been happening lately—"

"Like Renewal?" Sandy cut in.

"—Yes, things are really getting sorted out. I feel more whole now than I ever was, maybe than I ever could have been."

"We can *see* it, Jenine. It's something you radiate," said Phil.

"Really? That's wonderful to hear. What about you guys? Are you a parapsychologist, Phil?"

"Not exactly," he laughed. "Just an interested observer. Sandy and I find the subject intriguing."

"More than that, from what your lady tells me. You sound pretty intent on getting to the bottom of it all."

"We haven't been too successful though. Not yet, anyway," added Sandy.

"But the 'trip' you two took, that was just super."

"You make it sound like you were there," Phil said.

"Didn't you ever hear this woman of yours describe it? Outrageous! Besides. . .I didn't tell you yet Sandy, but we tried it ourselves and . . . *zounds!*" Shutting her eyes, Jenine heaved her shoulders in rapture. Her shoulders again—that's what was getting him most, Phil realized. They were so infectiously animated, so charged with spontaneity. But what did she mean by "we"?

He inquired, and suddenly she was reticent. Coyly, Jenine looked to Sandy.

"Jenny's involved with a great group of people—Renewal Unlimited, isn't it?"

The girl nodded.

"That's what you meant by 'Renewal'?" asked Phil.

"Uh huh," said Jenine.

"And. . .?"

"And we're doing astonishing things."

"Like what?"

"Like what you've been looking for, maybe."

"Terrific," Phil said, "but you're not telling me anything, Jenny."

Jenine glanced to Sandy again.

"They're a little sensitive about talking out of context, afraid of being misunderstood. They feel Renewal needs to be *experienced*. Jenny wants us to give it a try."

"Just for a weekend if you can. I'd really love to have you," Jenine said to Phil.

12

At the Threshold, On the Brink . . .

SUPERVISOR VLADIMIR MALEK WATCHED THE image of the Soviet leader on the bulkhead screen of the military aircraft. He studied Premier Provokin's darkly impassive face, the calculated movement of thickset lips intoning an admonition:

"The courageous Soviet peoples have come too far in their struggle of liberation to permit their hard-won accomplishments to be imperiled. Aggression will be halted whatever its form, be it overt or insidious, and we will employ every means at our disposal to do this. Let the burden of responsibility fall on the shoulders of those who, in their cynicism and arrogance, indulge themselves in the folly of believing they can. . ."

Malek was listening to the Premier's address, but the words were not being heard as much as the actual meaning he knew to be behind them. The colleague at his side nudged him from brooding contemplation.

"That's Vasil'kov, I believe," said Colonel Brumel, nodding to the porthole. "From this height, the picture of serenity, eh?"

"Hmm," the Supervisor murmured, with little appetite for the banality of his psychiatrist associate. When Brumel was not being boring, he was being contentious, and Malek was glad that this was the last leg of their investigative tour.

In the towns of Vasil'kov to the West, Rasskazovo to the East and Krasnador to the South, a curious epidemic had erupted. Three well-separated population centers simultaneously had been infected with a mysterious disorder. The official diagnosis was mass hysteria, but of its origin, nothing was said. Yet suspicions existed, and these had not been dispelled by the evidence so far collected. Malek therefore was led to think the unthinkable—that the psychoenergetic channel had been opened by the enemies of the motherland.

From the airport in Kiev, it was a 35 kilometer drive to the psychiatric unit that hastily had been set up outside Vasil'kov. It consisted of rows of prefabricated boxes the size of small hangars located in a barren field enclosed by barbed wire.

Malek and Brumel took half an hour to settle themselves in their spartan accommodations, then joined the staff in the central office.

"Of course you are familiar with the general procedure," the chief administrator said to Malek. "Each new case is immediately brought in for quarantine and examination. After nine days of operations, our count has risen to 147."

"What was the initial intake?"

"Nearly 100."

"And a handful each day thereafter?"

"Correct."

"May I assume you have made adequate provisions for keeping them isolated?" Malek asked.

"We have done what we could with partitions and surveillance, but I am sure you can appreciate our difficulties in this makeshift facility."

Hesitating for a moment, Malek requested the overall psychiatric profile and was told what he had fervently hoped he would not hear. As at the other two locations in the South Soviet triangle, Vasil'kov had been the scene of a collective hallucination. In the primary outbreak, individuals by the score reported the same delusion. They experienced leaving their bodies, merging to form a common identity and accelerating through a "long dark tunnel" at the end of which was encountered a "being of light." Reputedly, this had been followed by sensations of "warmth", "joy", "connectedness. . ."

Malek looked at Brumel. The expected confirmation was given with a nod and a shrug of the shoulders. It could not even be said that a *similar* pattern existed. Plainly, the pattern was *identical.*

The medical officer's account required little elaboration. All tests simply had proven negative. From a physical standpoint, there was apparently no pathology. In fact, an unusual number of the stricken showed excellent health, their life signs uncannily vibrant.

The biochemical specialist was called on next and again, not much could be said. Samples of body tissue and organic fluids had been subjected to careful scrutiny without the smallest trace of anomalous reaction or foreign substance being found. Nor could the environmental analyst claim any evidence of contamination in the air or water supply. In short, not a single sign of intervention had been discovered, yet it was clear to Malek that intervention had occurred.

"No, not sleeping. As I told you earlier, I was in bed but had been listening to symphonic selections on the radio."

"Yes. Well, that is all. Thank you for coming in."

Shaking his head, Brumel stopped the tape recorder. "Astonishingly consistent," he remarked when Malek stepped back into the room. "As if a mass rehearsal of the story had been staged in advance. Uh. . .I suppose that possibility has been explored."

"We are dealing with impressionable people, dear Brumel. They've had ample time to discuss their experience and that alone could assure convergence."

"To the degree we have been observing it? And what of Krasnodar, Rasskazovo? The fantasies alleged there were substantially the same, were they not?"

Malek did not reply. It was undesirable for the psychiatrist to know with certainty that the conspiracy hypothesis indeed had been investigated. The idea of an organized, politically motivated effort to embarass the Government actually had been the first to be considered. But the KGB, renowned for its thoroughness in such matters, had detected no indication whatever of political intrigue.

After conferring on particular portions of the testimony, Malek left the cubicle and the tape was restarted. Brumel spoke into the microphone. "Subject eleven. . .Constantin Nesor. . .35 years of age."

A brawny young man with still-freckled forehead and wavy auburn hair was shown in and seated across the desk from Brumel. The long silence contrived by the psychiatrist did not appear to ruffle him. Brumel's steady, searching smile seemed placidly accepted.

"Constantin Nesor. Age 35. Unmarried and living alone. A postal worker for 14 years."

Nesor inclined his head in affirmation.

"Would you please give me the year, the republic in which you live, and the name of its capital city."

Grinning, the young man complied.

"Tell me about your work, Mr. Nesor. Are you satisfied?"

"I've made the necessary adjustment."

"Your records show an aptitude for language."

"Mınn."

"And you qualified on the state examination for academy instructor, then promptly declined the position that was offered. A problem with curriculum, perhaps?"

"Let us say a problem with temperament."

"Sorting letters better suits your temperament?"

Nesor gave a good-natured shrug.

"Living alone as you do cannot always be easy. Do you consider yourself a lonely man?"

"It is a lonely time for all of us, I believe. Yet I cannot complain. My days are well filled."

"With what in particular, outside of your work?"

"Football, mainly. Our coach is relentless. Three hours of practice each night for a two-hour game on Tuesday. The team will frequently travel."

"What else, Constantin? Music? You must do some reading?"

"Certainly, when there is time."

"What sort of books are of interest?"

"Football, in fact, but also some literature and art."

"Mr. Nesor, have you ever read the Christian Bible?"

"I have never *seen* a bible."

"Then your parents had no religious convictions?"

"I was raised in a State orphanage."

"What about your own convictions? Do you believe in a supreme being?"

Nesor did not answer.

"This is a difficult question?" persisted Brumel.

"It would be far easier to list the ways I do *not* believe."

"Which means that you *believe*, at least in a sense."

"Yes, in a sense. And to be honest, it is not unrelated to the reason I am here."

Brumel poured two cups of water from the pitcher on his desk. "Tell me from the beginning. Exactly what was your experience."

Almost a minute passed before the subject began to speak.

"In the morning I run. At least half an hour each dawn, something I depend on to set a rhythm for the day.

"I will reach a point of balance when motion seems to stop,

like the blade of a fast-turning fan or the wheels of a train—the motion of my limbs, my thoughts, seems to freeze into a blur. But there is no lack of clarity. The 'blur' is actually a unity, or should I say *harmony*, of feeling and thinking.

"That is how it started, in this state of 'suspended animation' I have grown accustomed to in my running. Then there was a . . . a what? A vision? I do not know. Like a dream, but not a dream. I felt movement again, yet not like the pumping of arms and legs —a smooth, flowing movement. I was coasting along on a sled in a field of drifting snow. It was very cold but somehow comfortably *warm*, I think because the snow was so radiant. It seemed to be generating its own energy, piping it up from within, sending it out to saturate the atmosphere, myself included.

"The sled was lifting now, I thought, and in the next instant realized that it was *I* who was lifting, rising into the air, leaving my gliding—or running?—body below.

"I sensed there were others. I knew they were doing the same, and with this knowledge another change occurred, as if I was being yanked or twisted around into a strange new position. I could see myself from the 'eyes' of the others, from the viewpoint of their larger identity.

"As I—or we—continued going up, we were sucked into a tube or some sort of funnel that flattened our trajectory. Far ahead of us at first, then suddenly much nearer and more intense, was a *light*. We were inching toward it now, and the closer we came, the more unbearable it was, like pressure building up inside, getting ready to explode."

Nesor began smiling.

"What is it?" asked Brumel.

"No, no. It is nothing important. Just that I realized, in telling it again, that the experience was more akin to a conception than to a birth."

"A conception? This you will have to explain," said the puzzled psychiatrist.

"Well, I had been thinking about the happening as a kind of a birth, the moving through a narrow passage toward light, the increase in pressure, and so forth. But birth ends in separation. The fetus is divided from its mother. It just dawned on me that *our* experience was quite the opposite—not so much a fission as a *fusion.*"

"Fusion?"

"A bonding," Nesor said gleefully, "a melding with that light."

"Describe this 'melding'."

The young athlete apologetically opened his palms. "I am running out of words."

"Nevertheless, I want you to make an attempt."

"But I told you I —"

"I said an *attempt.*"

"If that is what you want, should I begin by confessing that the 'light' was not really a light?"

"Begin, Mr. Nesor. Just begin." Colonel Brumel poured another cup of water. "What was it if not a light?"

"What can I call it?" Nesor questioned himself. "An *awareness. . .*? Perhaps an infinite awareness, because it appeared to have a life and consciousness of its own, one without limits.

"It did seem to be out there in front of us before we or it made contact. It seemed to have definite boundaries, a definite position in space. But then it was everywhere, and inside of *us*, at the core of us the instant of touching. We understood too that it had *always* been there. That was the third transformation, as if looking in a mirror, seeing the inner core of our being in an outward reflection. . ."

"How long did the experience last?"

Nesor was unable to say. "In a sense, it did not 'last' but was happening and happening and happening. Time was not a factor. Somehow time simply did not matter."

"Simply?" echoed Brumel, his voice betraying exasperation. Sighing resignedly, he asked the postal worker to finish his account.

"It would be pointless to continue," the young man replied. "You are *missing* the point, Mr. Nesor. We do not have an option. Every detail of what you think you experienced is required for our records."

"Very well," said Nesor, shaking his head with a cautionary smile, "but I'm afraid this will be even less comprehensible than what I told you already.

"In a way, we and that light encompassed everything, but it was clear to us too that we were only a *seed*. We could feel ourselves starting to grow in an undreamed-of direction. Like the first embryo of some new species, we were shaping and extending ourselves, creating a dimension of experience we were barely beginning to grasp."

To the final draft of the Malek report, a brief document was appended. Close monitoring in the area of the three cities had revealed no unusual wave transmission patterns of any kind. Of course, conventional irradiation might have occurred *prior* to the erection of the special stations around Vasil'kov, Krasnodar and Rasskozovo. But considering the dramatic effect on these communities, had there been such emissions, most likely they would have been detected in the permanent observation network that operated continuously across the country.

Moreover, Malek disclosed that only two weeks before the general outbreak, he personally had observed the same hallucinatory pattern in an environment that no conventional wave transmission could penetrate. In the laboratory of Professor Nicholai Robodny, a labor colony volunteer had spoken of seeing a warm glow, of going inside it, of it being inside him. The dying words of Robodny's subject closely matched the language later used by many of the citizens in the afflicted region, too closely to be written off as a mere coincidence. In Malek's judgment, the laboratory incident had been covertly engineered by agents of the West as a trial run. The enemy had dared to use an installation of the KGB as its proving ground!

The gravity of these developments was obvious to every member of the special committee that had been called into urgent session in the Kremlin. These were the secret architects of the nation's experimental weapons program, each the top ranking expert in his own field of psychoenergetic research. It was evident to them now from this latest episode that the enemy had managed success where they had been thwarted. There seemed little choice but to conclude that the psychoenergetic channel indeed had been opened, that direct manipulation of thoughts at a distance had been accomplished. Incoming signals could not be detected because none were being sent, not in the usual sense of being spread through ordinary space. By working through *psychoenergetic* space, Western scientists apparently had succeeded in bypassing their entire detection system.

After all the theorizing and speculation, a concrete proposal for action finally would need to be made. Until then, the recommendation they were considering—beyond being a flat admission of failure—had been inconceivable. So resistance to it was indulged in and tolerated for quite a while. Yes, it would be an onerous responsibility, the Committee concurred. Yes, the consequences well might be catastrophic. Further additional checks on the Malek report and related incidents certainly would be made. Might there not still be some time for a breakthrough in their own psychoenergetics program. . .?

No. The predominant feeling was that, in all likelihood, time had run out. It appeared that the machinery for a massive preemptive assault would have to be set in motion. When some of the Committee members began to rationalize, halfheartedly arguing that the global repercussions might be held to a minimum if not completely averted, all knew the die was cast. They would make their recommendation. At least the *ultimate* decision would be out of their hands.

"Gentlemen, they're doing it to us, hitting us where we live, and it can't be permitted to continue."

In a darkened conference room of the Executive Office Building, Major General Alan Hagger was addressing a small gathering of government officials. He stood before a wall screen, bathed above his waist in the light from an overhead projector. Scenes of the wreckage at the Havinghurst electonics plant were being shown, each of the simultaneously displayed frames detailing the destruction at the facility from a different perspective.

Hagger had made great strides since the night of bloodshed at *Renard Picault's.* Once the administration had become convinced that the slayings at the posh restaurant were the result of a conflict within the government's intelligence community, its chief concern was the pursuit of silence. With an election coming up, a violent family feud had been less intolerable than an open scandal.

Hagger's version of the murderous affair was that a power-envious Gretta Kellog had come unglued. He claimed that she had shot her superior, Van Castle, through the head, and had shattered Hagger's shoulder before he could stop her. Investigation of his account was deferred, and meanwhile, partly to assure his co-operation, Hagger was promoted and given a key position on the National Security Council.

"This is not an accident," General Hagger now was saying as he snaked his pointer along the twisted metal contours shown in one frame, the peculiar deformations of massive concrete blocks pictured in another. "There's a recognizable pattern here that can't be explained by anything you might find in a textbook. I've seen it in Colorado Springs, in Calcutta, in Hackensack, New Jersey, had it studied by an army of metallurgists, engineers, physical chemists and by our leading theoreticians.

"We think we know what's been happening and the news is not good. We know what the enemy has been up to because we have been up to the same thing, or at least we've made an effort in that direction. Frankly, I've never been optimistic about our chances. Just being taken seriously by the men who hold the purse strings was a major accomplishment for us, and the support that finally came was tentative, gentlemen, luke warm at best. Well, it seems the Soviets have made their breakthrough, solved a fundamental problem in space-time engineering.

"To begin to understand what you're seeing on this screen, you'd have to throw out all standard volumes on matter and energy, cause and effect. What it amounts to in practical terms is an influence capacity that's potentially unlimited. Much sooner than we think, we should be open to them, at their disposal—our documents, equipment, personnel—the very thoughts we think may be theirs to shape. And there'll be no way to stop them, no barrier to build, no effective obstacle to put in their path.

"In short, they'll have us by the balls. Every indication tells us that's what's happening, that they're tunneling through to us, getting ready to put us away in their pockets. If there's any option still available, I'm afraid it's the ultimate one: Hit them as hard as we can with whatever we can, hit them immediately, and pray that it works."

Mute moments were followed by a question from the floor, posed by a bureaucrat. "Isn't it a fairly big leap from damage at some physical installations to total mind control?"

"I haven't succeeded in making my point," replied Hagger, pitching his response to the whole group. "The significant factor here is not so much the physical damage itself but the *nature* of this damage and its correspondence with what we already know from our own research."

His head bowed, Hagger paced a few steps away from the screen as if preparing to go deeper into the subject. Instead, he called for the lights. "There'll be enough time for in-depth analysis in Wednesday's follow-up briefing. Details will be provided, specific questions answered by me and by the experts. Today I only want to broach the issue, open it up for your broad consideration. "I ask you to bear with me for the time being. Accept the fact that our specialists are on top of this. They've computer checked the data a thousand times—I wouldn't be up here if they hadn't.

"However stupefying the conclusion reached, however much we'd like to resist it, push it from our thoughts, it is *there* and *real* and it will not go away. We believe the enemy is achieving control at a level of nature where space and time do not seem to *mean* anything, where mind can't be separated from matter. We're convinced the incident at Havinghurst and the others reported were merely pilot runs, the prelude to an all-out assault."

A government official asked when this assault was expected and was told that six months was likely a generous estimate.

"Wouldn't such an engineering coup make their defenses impregnable?" a uniformed participant inquired.

"Maybe," replied Hagger. "Maybe even probably. But it becomes more and more a *certainty* with every unacted-on second."

General Hagger's bolt from the blue met with further expressions of incredulity. He responded by requesting only that they begin to think about the matter, keeping an open mind until Wednesday's session.

"And that's supposed to get us to set off a global holocaust?" came a remark from a civilian conferee.

"I understand the 'no winner' philosophy of the '60s and '70s is on the way out," Hagger retorted. "But I'm not the expert on that, not like some of you present in this room.

"*My* only reason for being here is to discharge my duty, alert you to the critical development. Our judgment is that an ominous threshold has been crossed, and we seem left with no other option but to strike while we can —unless you consider outright surrender an option."

After another period of silence, there was a comment from a member of the military contingent. "Well, he's got a point about the changing philosophy. Nowadays it's even conceivable that the first strike could be the only strike."

"Whoa, George, whoa!" reproved a second man in Army dress. "That's going a bit too far. I'll grant there've been impressive advances in guidance and delivery, but as I think you know, our counterforce capability still has limitations. Every footprint can't be covered, especially not from mobile targets like their submarines. You can bet they'll get some of their re-entrant vehicles up, and a certain proportion of these are going to come in."

"Maybe. Maybe so," the first Army officer responded. "But it's got to be seen in *relative* terms. Any losses we might sustain from a counter strike should look like cuts and bruises compared to what the Russians lose—damn it, this is *armed conflict* we're talking about, not some damned cricket match. If the game is played out, I say there *can* be a winner and that has got to be *us*. We can take losses if we have to, when the only other choice is losing everything."

Speaking for the first time, a bureaucrat raised a point of information. "Do we have a projection on the *order* of losses we'd absorb?"

"It depends on how thorough we are in the initial foray," the second Army officer replied. "But assuming the Soviets muster *some* sort of response, we'd need to expect a measure of economic and social disruption because we're talking megatons here. The exact extent of the problem we'd have is anyone's guess. Too many unknowns to account for. Too many variables for a reliable profile of costs."

"Is there any estimate of the human cost?" asked the bureaucrat.

"Guesswork again. But all right. Let's suppose we interdict, say, eighty-five per cent of their second-strike force, and their counter-strike programming is not too vindictive. Let's further assume that our civil defense command manages a reasonable shuffle of civilian populations—here we couldn't ask for too much, given the short preparation time they'd have and the limitations in our shelter and evacuation programs. In this scenario, we get eight figures as our best rough estimate. We should be able to keep the number down to the low eight figures.

"Now, that is a monstrous number—maybe twenty to thirty million. But if a conflict is inevitable, it's probably the best we're going to do. In such a disaster, it's true that ten per cent of the glass would be emptied but also a fact that *ninety* per cent would still be full. Ninety per cent of the population left to rebuild and regenerate."

One government administrator had difficulty accepting the Army officer's assumption of minimal vindictiveness in a counter-strike action. "They're going to want to turn the screws on us."

"What would they gain from it?"

"You can't be serious, man! In those circumstances, we could count on human nature to do its worst. They'd ground-burst their filthiest, highest-yield devices upwind of our largest population centers and go out gloating over visions of wholesale slaughter from the radiation."

The first Army officer responded to this, saying they would simply have to trust that a determined initial strike would limit the enemy's opportunities.

"I'm buying the conjecture of eighty-five per cent on that. Allowing we're that efficient," pressed the civilian administrator, "what happens to the counter-strike casualty figure if the Russians want to fuck us as badly as they can?"

"It would have to go up," said the second officer, "but—"

"As high as nine figures?"

"We don't *know* it would be that bad."

"We know we'd *survive*," the first officer interjected. "That's the bottom line—to guarantee survival for our own kind, preserve our way of life. A preemptive strike clearly would accomplish that for us. Hardships might have to be faced, but our survival would be assured."

A participant wearing Air Force blue reminded those assembled that another scenario was possible. The Soviets might be adopting a *launch-on-warning* posture. "They don't wait for us to hit the motherland. They empty their silos when the first word is given from their satellites and radars that we're on the way."

"So our warheads home in on empty holes!" a bureaucrat declared.

"Exactly. The strategy is designed to nullify the first-strike advantage. It's a blueprint for mutual annihilation that will not fail to work, if used."

"Is either side doing it?" the bureaucrat inquired.

"We know *we're* not, not yet, anyway. The Russian policy on this is still pretty much a mystery."

"I don't believe the Russians have the guts," asserted the first Army officer. "If they were in a launch-on-warning mode, there's a good chance we'd find out about it sooner or later. They *know* that. They know that once we knew, *we* would be obliged to adopt the same posture. And the Russians have a long memory. They haven't forgotten the 'Market Street' episode of '73, for example."

"The computer snafu?"

The second Army officer recounted the incident for the group. An American early-warning satellite had detected the launching of a missile from a base in the Ural Mountains. The computer system of the North American Air Defense Command generated a prediction of the re-entrant vehicle's trajectory and probable site of impact: downtown San Francisco. Only after the Strategic Air Command had sprung into high alert and American missile combat officers all over the world had inserted launching keys in their consoles, was it revealed that the computer had miscalculated.

"If we'd been in launch-on-warning in '73, who knows. . ." the first Army officer commented. "Today there might *be* no Communist threat."

"Still and all," said the Air Force chief who had introduced the issue, "the enemy may feel compelled to take the risk. We need to understand Soviet thinking on command and control. It is a highly centralized affair for them. Their field commanders are given very little latitude to act on their own. So they should be especially sensitive to the prospect of 'decapitation'—a preemptive strike that would smash the chain of communications linking their political and military heads to the battlefield.

"If the Russians *are* obsessed with the idea of being caught unprepared, if they're worried sick that in an effective first strike there'd be no way to order retaliation, they may well take their chances with launch-on-warning. Whatever other dangers it might involve, it does seem to neutralize the possibility of decapitation."

"Very nice analysis," the first Army officer commended. "Very insightful. But listen, if *we* are under the gun, we may be forced to take some chances of our own, maybe the ultimate chance."

"It may be," agreed the second Army officer, "it just may come to that. If it's true the Russians are at the point where they actually might be able to gain control of our. . .

"General Hagger, in Wednesday's follow-up briefing, you'll have Professors Tully and Morgan with you—am I right?"

Hagger nodded assent.

The first Army officer now rose with a grave admonition for his colleagues. "Gentlemen, if the General turns out to be correct, we're going to have to forget our war-games mentality and do that very fast. He's telling us we are already in the field of combat, whether we like it or not. In combat you don't just play head games with options, you make a commitment to *action*. It's not an easy transition, especially when the action called for is monumental. Maybe the battlefield is the last place we want to be right now, but if the Russians have us out there, we'd damn well better recognize it and behave accordingly."

"Come on baby, up s'daisy. Come up for Mama," Maggie said. Hagger did not react.

He was close to his objective now, so close the darkness within him was almost perceptible. Yet it was exultation he thought he was feeling, for he believed a solemn privilege would be his after all.

"Oh baby, what's wrong tonight?" asked Maggie, working more determinedly between the thighs of her client. "You all worn out?"

A few remaining obstacles stood in his way, some weak sisters pissing in their pants over the prospect of a true confrontation, one or two boneheaded skeptics still unable to accept the reality of what the Soviets had accomplished. Tully, Morgan, Kaminsky—they would take care of that. The weight these scientists carried, the force of their influence on the nation's strategic policies could not be resisted. Then he, Hagger, would ascend to his rightful position. A War of Redemption was to be fought, a battle of purification fated to be waged on the scale of the myths. And he had been favored by destiny as leader of the faithful. His would be the Avenging Hand.

"Whew!" cried Maggie, leaning back. "I must be doing *something* wrong."

Hagger rose past her without a word. He pulled on his clothes and moved to the door, dropping a hundred dollar bill on the floor as he went out.

13

Renewal Unlimited

ON A FRIDAY MORNING AT 6 A.M., A BATTERED old station wagon pulled up in front of Sandy and Phil's apartment house. Still half asleep and moving mechanically, Phil lifted their bags from the sidewalk. The driver got out and came around to them. He was a trim young man, wholesomely attired in a light sweater and jeans, his blond hair neatly clipped across his forehead. To the groggy Phil, it seemed the fellow was reaching for their bags. It was Phil for whom he reached. The lad took him into a bear-hug welcome that jarred Phil so that he dropped the luggage.

With their belongings secured, Sandy and Phil were crammed into the back seat of the car, he on one side of the assembled crew, she on the other. They were greeted warmly by friendly young faces, eager hands playfully pawing hello, spirits elevated all around. Lord, they're so awake, thought Phil, feeling dead to the world.

Turning to him from the front was the rainbow-shirted

Jenine. "Can you sense this energy?" she enthused. Phil smiled thinly in assent but *he* could only sense *matter*—thighs, elbows, hips—pressing close against him. Was the Old Phil blocking his perception? he wondered.

The youth of Renewal Unlimited continued celebrating the presence of Sandy and Phil as the car lurched forward, swerved steeply around and proceeded uptown in the direction of the Cross Bronx Expressway. Everyone was being congratulated. A top-notch college professor was now in their ranks—a really dynamite omen for The Movement. And Sandy was so adorable, no one could get over her. When were they converted, the group wanted to know. Where? How? How did it affect them, their working, their living, their loving?

For the start-and-stop half-hour drive up through city streets, Phil and Sandy remained the focus of attention. Then they came onto the ramp for the highway, ascended and moved out on the open road, and the company's attention shifted. There were moments of silence, followed by Jenine's sweet soprano trilling the first stanza of a familiar folk tune from the nineteen sixties. A full-voiced chorus replied, intoning a slightly altered version of "Michael, Row the Boat Ashore." "Michael" became "Brother Vincent," and "Sister" was made "Sister Margaret."

All grinning, the young people loosely linked arms, Sandy's and Phil's included, and began clapping to augment the rhythm for the next round of verses. Another stanza was provided and another, their exuberance building with each repetition. They were stamping the floor of the car now, both feet in tempo, totally immersed, caught up more in themselves than each other, it seemed to Phil. And with every round, a different verse was given, as on it went.

Phil was trying for a fixed view of Sandy. Without exerting himself in an obvious way, he could only get fleeting glimpses of her through the undulating forms. But he could see that she was singing and clapping with them, that her cheeks were flushed like theirs. And God, the look in her eyes was *their* look of ecstatic involvement. Apparently, she had surrendered already.

For his part, Phil kept up a front of benign observer, not actively engaging in the ritual, but allowing himself to be carried along, the veneer of an amiable smile concealing his misery.

Finally, it stopped. They cheered themselves, hugged each other exultantly, embraced their new recruits.

"You see how beautiful it can be," Jenine said with earnest intensity, curving her neck back toward Phil once again. Not waiting for his reply, she held her palms out before her and smacked them together. A second time, a third, a fourth time, Jenine struck the new beat:

This land is your land,
This land is my land,
From California,
To the New York high—

"Hey you guys, hold on a second." Phil was nearly shouting. "Old age must be creeping up on me. I'm afraid I need to make a stop. The sign we just passed said two miles to the next comfort station."

"Well, how about right here," the driver cheerfully responded. He pulled the station wagon onto a shoulder of the road adjacent to a cluster of bushes. "I bet we can all use some instant relief—old and young alike."

Tires crunched on gravel, sun-heated dust swirled up through open windows, as they turned past the hand-lettered sign for "Renewal Unlimited!" onto a bumpy dirt road. Coughing, Phil dabbed his sweaty face with the remains of an already half-saturated tissue. *Jesus*, he thought, *I'm walking into this madness with my eyes wide open!* He was astounded at himself.

Maybe an article will come out of it, Phil momentarily reasoned—"The Phenomenology of Cult Life", "Children 'Reborn' ," or some such title. Of course it would never happen. That wasn't why he was here. Feeling depressed, he cast a glance down the columns of corn stalks flanking both sides of the road almost to the horizon. Damned "Yellow Brick Road," thought Phil, whimsically associating to *The Wizard of Oz*. Then he shifted his attention to Jenine. This day, she had arranged her braid in a pertly mounted ponytail. It bounced with the choppy motion of the car, jerking and twitching with every pit and furrow in their roller coaster ride to the campsite.

At the end of the cornfield, the road curved sharply to the left and a group of buildings could be seen up ahead, gathered at the foot of a grassy incline. Approaching, they saw six or seven structures, each a different size but of similar design, slope-rooved, wood-planked rustic affairs, with disproportionately large windows and doorsteads minus doors. The larger of the units looked rather like barns.

Pointing to his left, the driver identified the first doorless shack they passed as the infirmary. "That's the mess hall beyond, and on the right, printing, public address and administration." Not a living soul was in evidence.

"Way over there," said the driver, gesturing to the open area behind the administration office, "our picnic and meeting grounds begin. We've got volley ball, badminton, a nature trail and there's Lake Cornucopia."

The station wagon slowed to a crawl as notice was directed to the last and biggest building in the cluster. "That's where we all turn in, our hall of residence." Phil thought they would stop to unload their belongings, but they accelerated up the hillside instead.

Over the crest, a sprawling version of the basic barnhouse came into view, along with what appeared to be a welcoming committee. Waving and smiling, a squadron of bright-faced young people dashed to meet the car. Even before the travellers could disembark, hands were being pumped, shoulders squeezed, kisses exchanged. Sandy and Phil were greeted no less extravagantly. Treated as returning compatriots, they were solicitously encircled, showered with expressions of warm good will. The circle then divided for the short walk to the meetinghouse, the newcomers being separately attended.

They entered the auditorium at opposite ends and were hustled down the aisles to a scattering of applause— like a fancy Jewish wedding, Phil mused. Abreast the speaker's platform on both sides, empty chairs were waiting, but they were not intended for immediate use. Their escorts turned Sandy and Phil to face the audience and the cheers began to mount.

Presently, a white-panted figure with an open white shirt strode upstage from the rear, arms outstretched and pointing to the new arrivals. The demonstrators audibly responded. Brother Bob put his hands above his head now, his palms to the ceiling, and the house shook with approval. Just as promptly, the reception died away when the signal for order was given. All those assembled took their seats, save for Sandy and Phil whose errant movements toward their chairs were gently corrected.

"In the name of Brother Vincent and Sister Margaret, we welcome two new seekers, Philip and Sandra, into our midst. Our hearts are open to them!"

There was a fresh round of applause, fervent but decorous, after which the beaming, flaxen-haired dynamo on the dias nodded to his left, then his right. The recruits at last could get off their feet.

A sudden look of serenity settled on the face of Brother Bob. He bowed his head, a lock of yellow hair falling innocently across his brow. Closing his eyes, Bob murmured two words into the microphone: "White Light." And again, somnambulistically, he said, "White Light." The morning meditation commenced.

They weren't *all* adolescents, Phil observed, scanning the rows of the faithful, his eyes cast low. A few older couples could be counted among them, though their presence did seem incongruous. In Phil's estimation, Brother Bob himself was roughly his contemporary. Yet the leader managed, through his animated bearing and high-noted musical voice, to project an almost child-like image of himself. At the same time, there was never any question of who was in command.

The long silence was broken by the electronically-amplified rustling of papers at the lectern. Brother Bob was removing the contents of an envelope.

"It's from you know who!" Bob exclaimed, holding the letter on high. Yet another surge of excitement swept the hall. The leader grinned indulgently, waiting for the reaction to subside. Then he began to read:

" 'Dear Brothers and Sisters, Can you feel us reaching out to you?' " The auditorium exploded in affirmation.

" 'We are a thousand miles away, doing the work of Renewal. But where you are is where we want to be, *can* be—you just need to feel our energy pouring over the miles.' "

Apparently, they could feel it.

" 'It is *your* energy, Sisters and Brothers, that keeps us going wherever we go. Every bit of it is needed to meet Renewal's great challenge, and we love every one of you for your unselfish giving.

" 'The city we are in is old. Most of its citizens walk in their sleep, dreaming petty dreams of getting and keeping, paranoid over what is privately theirs, obsessed with protecting their turf, completely shut off from each other.

" 'We nudge them. With gentle persistence, we try to stir them from their slumber, whisper in their ears the message of Renewal so that *they* may be renewed. Our words are simple. They were spoken and well understood before the first flame was lit, the first wheel and weapon cut crudely from stone. . .' "

"You can't sleep here, Phil," one of his escorts whispered in his ear. Phil struggled from his languor, forcing himself to sit erect. The next moment, he felt himself slipping back. The day was proving too much for him.

" '. . .the children are here, but where is the magic of childhood, the wide-open wonder that makes true growing possible?
They know so much in this city, are so worldly wise, so sophisti-
cated, and this knowledge is choking them. They are caught in a
tangle of technology, lost in a hardware jungle of cold, shining
surfaces, gadgets and contrivances of every size, shape and purpose, multi-channelled cable TVs, home computer systems that
do everything but wipe their noses. . .and when. . .if they would
only. . .because it is obvious that. . .' "

"Please Professor, please. Let's try and get with it."

"Sorry," Phil muttered, straightening his posture once more.

After that he fought to keep awake, though the words of
Vincent and Margaret were now without content, sounds strung in
droning succession. Time and again through the agony, his hope
for a merciful climax was raised by Brother Bob's lyrical render-
ing, only to be dashed with the production of a new page from the
bounteous missive.

It could not go on forever. He could not continue the battle to
stay conscious. He was surrendering, letting sleep take hold, allowing himself to drift off again. Renewal be damned, he would gain
his own renewal. But just as he fell away, Phil was rudely jolted by
shouts of jubilation. It was over at last.

Outside the assembly hall, Phil and Sandy were briefly re-
united. The station wagon had vanished, leaving their belongings
on the road, and they were permitted to retrieve them unaccom-
panied. While lifting the larger of the suitcases, Phil asked her if
she'd had enough. She declared with a sigh that the weekend
wasn't over. As he was about to tell her how ghastly she looked,
their respective entourages arrived on the scene, cheerful and
solicitous as ever.

Lugging his bag down the steep road to the hall of residence,
Phil had more than a little trouble maintaining his footing, and
each time he stumbled, the loose dry earth rose in a cloud to set
him coughing and sneezing. He was scarcely heartened by the

attendants' stout strains of "This Land Was Made For You and
Me," even ungrateful when they grabbed his arms to prevent a
headlong tumble down the hill. Their promise of a cold shower at
his destination *was* of definite interest.

There were no beds in the oversized barn upon which everyone converged, just scores of mattresses, sheeted, blanketed or
bare, somewhat haphazardly arrayed over the floor's full expanse.
Beneath the large rainbow murals splashed high on opposite walls
of the enclosure, a vast assortment of personal effects were draped
upon hooks or lain on open shelves. Members of the community
who had already arrived were in the process of disrobing, some
milling about in various stages of undress.

Phil and Sandy were each handed a blanket, sheet and towel
and directed to their separate accommodations at the far ends of
the room. Unceremoniously, Phil dropped his bag on the mattress
they gave him and squatting, unzipped it to search for his
bathrobe. "It's in the other case," he grumbled, then said curtly to
his hosts, "My friend and I will have to make an exchange."

"What do you need?"

"What difference does it make?" replied Phil.

"Well, whatever it is, you two can sort things out later. Right
now we want you to join us for our High Sun Awakener."

"How about the shower?"

"Yes, that's what we mean," said one of the genial youths. "It's
a blessing we joyfully share."

After the communal watering, there was to be a period of
meditation before lunch. Wordlessly, the faithful streamed back
into the hall of residence, each returning to his or her space where
at once a cross-legged or lotus position was assumed.

Phil had a different agenda. His first order of business was a
simple interchange with Sandy. He pulled several of her essentials
from the bag, and without consulting his companions, whose bed
mats encircled his own, he started across the room through the
maze of unwrapped meditators. Naturally, his attendants were in
close pursuit.

Sandy had fallen out of the proper devotional posture into a fetal crouch and was fast asleep. A team of three was attempting to correct the situation as Phil arrived. He said, "Why don't you leave her *alone*," and wedging himself into their midst, forceably shouldered them back. Paying no heed to the unctious explanations they offered as they withdrew, he reached for the towel that lay at her side and used it to cover her rump. Next he turned to the suitcase she had carried and dug out his robe and jeans, a shirt and some underwear. The items brought for Sandy were left inside on top.

Back at the square assigned him, Phil spread his sheet on the coarse-grained mattress and stretched out. In short order, he was drifting, and in this state of reverie, he had a vision of someone familiar approaching him. Was it Sandy? Jenine? Perhaps someone older. Her lips were moving as she came near, her voice filled with plaintive emotion. But she was speaking too softly. He could not make out the words.

"Awaken refreshed, Brothers and Sisters," the P.A. system crackled. "It's time for the mid-day meal!"

Lunch was less than a gourmet's delight, in Phil's estimation. The main and only course was bean stew served on a gummy mound of rice. Evidently, there was more in the concoction than beans, but all the ingredients were the uniform dun of the gravy, and all had the same soggy consistency and flavor. With a stalish slice of whole wheat bread and cup of pulpy juice rounding out the meal, Phil amused himself with the thought that the diners at least could be confident that it was free of additives and preservatives. After lightly sampling the food against his better judgment, he declined everything but the unsweetened liquid. That, he sought more of, and was sent all around the room only to return to his table with lukewarm water in his cup.

At the end of the hour, the call for quiet was sounded in the mess hall, and Brother Bob appeared on the platform in the center of the room. Not unexpectedly, his theme was Renewal. In the present rendition, special emphasis was placed on the benefits accruing to those who chose the path of selflessness. "—When you work for Renewal, dear Sisters and Brothers, Renewal works for *you*." In fact, Renewal would be working for them again in the very next period of activity. They were to be given the opportunity to continue the community project of raising a new hall of residence. Was there a better sign of Renewal's vitality than the need for more housing? observed Brother Bob. Was there a better way for them to strengthen themselves than by making it possible for their number to increase, their kind to multiply and flourish?

The construction site was a tract of half-cleared land a little way up the hill from the existing residence hall. Phil arrived to find a number of enthusiasts already at work in the hot sun, shirts off and chopping through vegetation, or laboring at the tailboard of a fenderless pick-up truck, dropping large wooden planks into an unruly heap.

"Ready for action, Brother Phil?" said a member of his team, handing him a rusty-bladed scythe. Phil shook his head, politely but firmly refusing. "You have to be patient with us members of the older generation. We don't have your stamina."

He sat on the sidelines for the next activity, as well, a mass volley ball event that was more a ritual of free-form movement than an organized game. But Phil did not go unattended through his period of non-participation. Ever at his side, ever exuding a loving concern for his enlightenment, were his appointed companions.

The afternoon program ended as did the morning one, with a cooling and cleansing of body and spirit. Emerging from the baptismal waters of Lake Cornucopia, the children of Renewal formed themselves into five great circles for guided meditation. In the center of Phil's ring was the rainbow-shirted, lithesome Jenine, her head to the sky. In a gesture poetically graceful, she raised her upturned palms high above her, then closed them, drawing them down to her brow as if gathering to herself an unseen essence. On repeating the motion, she exhorted the lotus-postured, closed-eyed participants to feel the inpouring of golden vibrations.

"Now imagine a time at the *beginning* of time," Jenine intoned, "a morning of mornings. We drift through a mist on a still sea, are at rest on the deck of a barge marked with ageless engravings. Listen. Can you hear the water lapping at the hull? Do you hear its quiet rhythm?"

Phil could hear nothing. Again he had fallen asleep.

Save for a carrot cake dessert that Phil could swear smelled of fish, dinner was indistinguishable from lunch. But he had not really eaten since sunup and was in no condition to be finicky. He ingested what was given him, then rose from the table.

"Where are you going, Brother Phil?"

"I'll be back."

"But we're almost finished here. We'll be starting up the hill for our evening celebration."

"That's just fine. I'll meet you there."

"You can't do that," a team member said, sounding mildly alarmed. "It's dark out there and you don't know the grounds." Another attendant swiveled his knees to block Phil's path.

"I just want to change to long sleeves. Can't you feel the temperature dropping?"

"Hey, you know he's right," a third youth exclaimed. "I think I will join you, Brother Phil."

The evening service in the hall of assembly was a marathon hootenanny with Brother Bob on guitar and the taped harmonies of Brother Vincent and Sister Margaret singing the message of Renewal through the altered lyrics of uncountable folk tunes and hymns. It was simply impossible for Phil to stay awake, nor was he permitted to sleep. Each time he dozed off, he was jarringly aroused by a friendly elbow or affectionate squeeze of the shoulder. As the battering of his sensibilities continued at length, Phil slipped into a stupor and was only dimly aware of the songfest ending, of being led back down the hill to the shore of the lake.

There, in the blaze of a dozen campfires, he made a partial recovery.

Waiting for him beside a lakefront tree were Jenine and the other members of the small pack over which she now presided.

Midway through the after-dinner musicale, Sandy had stopped singing. She no longer had the stomach even to pretend. The spell had been broken hours before, but she had allowed herself to be carried along in the spirit of Renewal, partly out of inertia and fear, partly because she had not wanted to give up hoping that something authentic might still be possible, in spite of what she was experiencing.

Following Brother Bob's lunchtime sermon on serving Renewal, Sandy and a few other young women had been singled out for a special tour of duty. Brother Bob himself drove them miles away to a busy bus depot where the work of Renewal was in progress—the sale of art prints each inscribed on the back with the wisdom of Vincent and Margaret. Bob's car was their observation post and they were told to study the techniques of their compatriots, instructed on how likely prospects were spotted and approached. Then one by one, the initiates were sent into the field to try for themselves.

Much of the afternoon had been spent in this endeavor, and on the trip home, the girls were praised for their freehearted efforts. In fact, a reward was in store. They were to have the privilege of bathing in Vincent and Margaret's own sanctuary. There at poolside, Brother Bob, who was quartered in the tree-hidden mansion on the far shore of the lake, would personally guide their meditation.

Bob was truly a master of visual narrative, and as he wove magical images, each young woman was given his individual attention. The spine must be straight for proper communion, head held erect, shoulders square but relaxed, thighs, knees, and calves correctly infolded. Brother Bob took great pains with every participant to assure that all was harmoniously aligned.

When the others had been dismissed for the evening repast, Sandy was invited to remain and partake with the master. He wanted her to know how impressed he had been with the dedication she had shown and more importantly, with her unmistakable aptitude for transformation and growth. Speaking earnestly of the great significance of The Movement for the whole of humanity and of the meaningful role she might play in its mission, he approached her, closed his hands on her waist.

She stepped out of reach. His kind comments and offer to dine were very flattering, declared Sandy, but she had given her promise to help in the mess hall. Bob remarked that she was dedicated to a *fault*, and she did not dispute him. Smiling regretfully, Sandy hurried to the trail she had seen her sisters take minutes before.

"Maybe some other time—," she stammered, departing in haste. . .

Now, moving through the firelit field, she followed the lead of her attendants, but in a manner detached and mechanical. She was riding out the day.

Phil was in the circle of cross-legged votaries to which Sandy was escorted. On seeing her, he got up and she started in his direction. But before the gap could be closed, Jenine was between them, greeting Sandy with an affectionate hug, draping her arms around both.

"Tonight, these two are our main attraction—remarkable human beings!" waxed Jenine, squeezing their shoulders. Then she took Phil's wrist in one hand, Sandy's in her other, and raised their arms high before the gathering. A burst of applause was triggered.

"Here's proof that Renewal lives!" Jenine proclaimed, undaunted by the fact that both Sandy and Phil had wriggled out of her grasp. "We're a going, growing concern and getting stronger all the time—Brother Vincent said it would happen and it is. Now look who we have among us, this man and this woman, a distinguished college professor, a master of psychology. They're with us because they feel what *we* feel, our need to be reborn in the One. And we are with *them!*"

Amidst cheers from the small band of devotees, Jenine ushered Sandy and Phil to the center of the ring, pressed down on their shoulders to cue them to sit, then squatted beside them.

"You two have had a dynamite awakening," Jenine said publically to Sandy and Phil, "and we want to make that our focus tonight.

"We've all heard the news. From Sandy's great description of the experience, some of *us* have tried it, and has it worked out for us?" The group rhapsodically affirmed that it had. "But this is *their* night," Jenine said to the faithful. "We're going to pool our energies for them, so they can get back into their incredible space."

Jenine turned to the couple, and hugging them once more, urged them to relax. "Just be yourselves," she said, moving her fingertips to their cheeks, "be one with each other like you were that special time, and we'll be one with *you*."

"Yes, but it didn't happen in a crowd," said Phil, getting up from the ground.

"This is no crowd," replied Jenine in dismay. "We want to be *part* of you, Phil."

"I understand that. I'm only saying that if it's going to be just like it was, we'll need to be alone."

"And I'm saying to *you*, Brother, that opening yourself to us, our field of energy, will help make it just like it was."

"There's no argument here," added Sandy, rising to join Phil. "Why can't we be open to the group without being physically right in the middle of it? Phil simply means it will be easier for us to get started if we have the same kind of *physical* situation we had before. He's probably right."

With some reluctance, Jenine accepted their condition. "There's a private place behind the tree. We'll stay right here and plug in, but take a good last look at us before you leave, look into our eyes and hearts, feel our vibrations and keep on feeling them, so we can be there with you when you need us."

When the couple was gone, the band reformed itself at Jenine's direction, closing ranks around the fire, kneeling thigh to thigh with arms entwined, eyes fixed on the flame. The young people sat in the manner prescribed for minutes on end, striking a pose of reverent contemplation.

"Let the light in," Jenine finally whispered from above them. "Can you feel it pass inside you, a warm glow moving in back of your eyes, inside your head.

"I can see it moving down, down into your throats, your lungs, all the way down, lighting up every part of you, cleaning you out from the inside.

"How does it *feel?*"

"Hmmmmn," was the blissful collective reply.

"Oh, and I see *them* now, lying against the tree. Can you see them too? If you close your eyes you can make out their auras.

"Brother Phil is a dullish green and he looks so miserable. Sandy's a washed-out yellow. Look at them try to make contact. They're trying *so* hard but they can't seem to reach each other.

"Let's not wait. We have what they need and we're willing and able to share it. Brothers and Sisters, send them your light."

After just a few seconds of silence, Jenine said, "Hey, are you really trying? You need to try harder because nothing is happening. Poor Sandy and Phil are still far apart, still looking pretty anemic. You've *got* the light, *send it*. Concentrate on sending them your energy. Concentrate. . .

". . .*Concentrate*," Jenine pressed, "they're waiting for *you*, counting on *you*, so *concentrate*. . ."

One youth jumped up, pointing high above the tree. "What's that up there? Isn't that them?"

"Not yet, Brother Hank, but don't stop trying," Jenine softly coaxed, guiding him back into place. "Let's *all* keep making the effort to plug ourselves into them so they can plug into each other."

Moments later, another child cried in excitement, "I think they're getting it! Do they have it now?"

There was a pause. "Dear Father, I believe you're right," Jenine said joyously, "because the auras *are* getting brighter, moving closer together. And look at that! The boundary is melting! It's a white hot fusion of souls!"

The votaries erupted. Surging in jubilation, they broke their circle to celebrate the triumph of innocent spirit renewed. It was the Garden of Eden again, and this time the Serpent was vanquished, they knew. Their joy was unrestrained, their gleeful commingling played out to the full.

The only thing left was the simple confirmation. Sister Jenine called her breathless charges to order, then led them on tiptoes to the place behind the tree.

But no one was there. Not a trace of Sandy and Phil was in evidence!

Had they dematerialized? Had their ecstasy been so profound that it had caused them literally to vanish? A few of the youth seemed to feel it was so, but most only stood in blinking uncomprehension. It did not occur to the children of Renewal that Sandy and Phil had simply slipped away, gone back to the empty hall of residence, packed their belongings and walked out of the camp.

They were on the road, hiking by moonlight, arms around waists, bags skimming gravel and earth. They leaned to each other as they moved and were giddy, peculiarly gay. He staggered, she swooned, burlesquing their total exhaustion. They reflected on their folly as they traipsed through the night, and peals of sweet laughter rang out.

PART III

FIGUREGROUND MELD

14

Cave Without Walls

THE ISSUE OF THEIR TRANSFORMATION DID not arise in the weeks that followed the episode at Renewal. Sandy and Phil were together, and that was all that mattered. They were more than happy to resume their routine, pick up the threads of their comfortable way of relating. But it was not to continue. Sandy had started leaving her body again.

She knew what had set it off but was not sure why. They had been browsing through Soho one rainy Sunday morning, leisurely making the rounds of shops and boutiques. In a gallery on Ninth Street, Phil had engaged the proprietor in a discussion of framing techniques, a subject in which he had never shown the slightest interest. Puzzling over his sudden fascination with the topic, Sandy wandered to the back of the store to a display of contemporary European works. She was scanning the rows of prints with a casual eye, not really paying attention, when she came upon an op art rendition of a boy in a twisted room gazing at twisted pictures. *Like those queer mirrors they have at carnivals*, she thought, and in the next instant, she was out of her body.

Immediately, Sandy willed herself back and was at Phil's shoulder a moment later, letting him know she was ready to leave, a cosmetic smile concealing her emotions.

Phil had not been told about the unscheduled flight, nor of the excursions out of body that had come after. Once it had happened in the bathtub as she was drowsily recuperating from a day of scraping wallpaper. At a Mendelsohn concert, it had threatened again, and Sandy had to fight to suppress it. On two other occasions, she had experienced the separation while falling asleep. Now, on her way back from the supermarket, it was occurring once more, this time out in the open with no walls or ceilings to contain her. Waiting on line at a bus stop, she had just bent down to relieve her arms of her grocery bags and was straightening up when suddenly her whole body was vibrating and she was *aloft*.

Sandy surprised herself. Though panic was close at hand, she delayed the command to go back, maintained her bizarre perspective above the heads of the queued up travelers for a few seconds longer. From this vantage point, a familiar face was seen in a shop window down the block.

"Professor Innerman?" said Sandy, reaching the door of the dry cleaning store as he was stepping outside.

"Sandy Peterson! Would you believe that just this minute I happened to be thinking about you?"

"Really?" she laughed, feeling a little flustered. "What were you thinking?"

"Oh, about the drawing you did last semester, your prize-winning lovers. You were the premiere artist of my parapsychology class!"

"And probably your very first student—remember how I cornered you months before your class even began?"

"Didn't it have to do with an OBE project?"

"Uh huh."

"Ever make any progress with it?"

"Well uh, this is a little awkward, but do you think we could . . ."

"Want to talk?"

"Oh, I'd love that," she said. "When will you have the time?"

Innerman heard the tremor in her voice, saw the pallor of her cheeks and said, "Now?"

"Sure, but what about these?" She lowered her chin to the over-stuffed bags she was barely managing to support.

"There's a coffee shop right across the street," said Noel, taking charge of one load. "If there's nothing here that will spoil, let's bring them with us and go in for a drink."

They slid into the back booth of the tiny lunchroom. Noel ordered half a cantaloupe for himself and a glass of juice for Sandy.

"Feel all right?" he asked, and she nodded in assurance.

"So tell me how it's going at Franklin. Are you pretty close to getting your degree?"

"Not that close," she grinned. "I'm waiting for your next parapsych course."

"Then you won't have long to wait. I'll be doing another one in the spring."

"Fantastic! You can count me in. I was so glad you decided to continue at the College."

"Why shouldn't I?"

"Uh, the grad student grapevine is very efficient. We heard about all the harassment and that Bert Biggs thing."

"Oh, that. Didn't you think that was funny?"

"In an excruciating kind of way."

"Yeah, at the time I guess it was. But I leave myself open for that sort of thing. I've got to learn to grin and bear it."

"Professor Innerman, what about that novel you were working on? Are you at liberty to talk about it?"

"I'd really rather talk about you," Noel said. "I'd like to know what's been happening."

"I n-never got back to you about my . . .my special interest."

"I noticed."

"Remember how we left it?" said Sandy. "It was a question of learning to *control* the OBEs. You suggested yoga."

"It's a good discipline."

"Right, and that's what I got involved with, so much so that the separation experience itself no longer seemed to matter. I wasn't having OBEs at that point anyway. And then, uh . . . something . . . something happened . . ."

She was trembling visibly. Noel reached across the table and lightly grasped her shoulders. "We can save it for another time."

"*No*," was her reply. "I want to tell it now."

Sandy told him everything. She spoke first of her early relationship with Phil, of what a disaster it had been. Then she described that impossible day which, in fact, was the day of the Bert Biggs fiasco. The confession was made that she had been in the audience suffering through every indignity during those dreadful proceedings, and that when it was over, images of the debacle had lingered on painfully. She had been unable to stop thinking of Noel.

That was also the day of the big blackout, and for Sandy and Phil, it was a night of sheer insanity that altered their lives.

"At first I thought it was *you*, that *you* were in my bed, taking my form, merging with me. *Was* it you at first?" Sandy asked Noel.

"*I*? Was I part of your communion with Phil? I'm not aware of it —not at *this* level of consciousness, anyway," said Noel with a smile.

Continuing her account, Sandy described how she and Phil had tried so desperately to regain their lost moment, how it had not worked, how weeks of intimate relations were to no avail. She spoke of the efforts made later to *understand* their experience. "We felt we needed some sort of concept or theory, that an accurate map of the territory we'd glimpsed might help us find our way back."

"I know what you mean," nodded Noel. "Symbolizing or modeling the experience can help you recapture it. A good authentic map might even be necessary for doing it right, though it may not work completely like magic."

"Well anyway," Sandy said, "we never did find a suitable concept. In the end, we wound up spending a day with a group called 'Renewal Unlimited'. " Noel smiled with her as she related the episode. He was not unfamiliar with that kind of organized self-deception.

"The problem," said Sandy, "is that when we got out of there and back to the real world, when everything seemed to be returning to normal and we were accepting it, were happy with it, I . . . s-started going out of my body again, all on my own."

"Just like that?" Noel inquired.

"Uh uh. It was something I *saw.*"

Innerman waited for futher explanation, but she could not find her voice. "Would you like another glass of juice?" he asked, noticing that she had begun to tremble again.

"It was a picture," Sandy blurted out.

"Of . . .?"

She did not answer.

"Was it something familiar?"

"No. Well. . .maybe. I don't know," she said in distress. "I just thought you might be able to go over to that gallery and look at it."

"And *you?*"

"I'd rather not."

"Which I can understand. But Sandy, I think you need to be there. Phil too. Has he been told about any of this?"

She shook her head in the negative.

"I think he should be, because he'd be part of what might be happening."

"What might be happening?" came a tremulous echo.

"I'm not really sure," said Noel, taking her hands in his. "Look, you've just told me about a mind-shattering out-of-the-body merger with Phil. You tried valiantly to recapture it but didn't succeed. Yet now, all of a sudden, you're going out of your body again, caught up in a whole new series of OBEs you think was triggered by this picture."

"—I *know* it was the picture. But Professor Innerman, where's the comparison? What happened with Phil was totally different."

"Totally?" he asked.

"Well, maybe that's too strong a word," conceded Sandy.

"What I want to know," Noel gently said, "is why you never told Phil."

"I didn't want to upset him."

"Him, or the comfortable routine you two have resumed? Don't you see what not telling him may be doing? It may be *keeping* your OBEs a private affair, locking him out, blocking the chance the two of you finally might be getting."

She stayed in contact with his searching eyes for a moment more, then sighed and looked away. "Always so perceptive, Dr. Innerman. But maybe Phil and I are happy with where we are now. Maybe we're no longer interested in transformation."

"If that's really true . . ." said Noel.

"It's true. *Part* of it is, because I guess we're scared. But for the most part," said Sandy, her eyes returning to his, "it's a lie."

"Then I'd like the three of us to meet in the gallery where you saw that picture. The picture is clue number one. It might even turn out to be a kind of map.

"Is tommorow evening too soon?" asked Noel.

In the morning, sitting before his word processor, Innerman was working on the closing chapters of his novel, his vision of the near future. *But it has got to be* more *than a novel*, he told himself. *Somehow, the gap between fiction and fact has got to be bridged.*

It **was happening**, wrote Noel, **the planet was**

going mad, its foremost species rehearsing for suicide. But as this world turned inside out, as old images and familiar shapes deformed and collapsed on themselves, a more deeply familiar contour began to be noticed. The shape was also a process, a process of linking and healing, of creative change, of evolving.

"Not exactly gentle on the eye," said Phil, his arm wrapped around Sandy. Innerman stood on her other side. The threesome was gazing at the picture.

" 'Print Gallery' by M.C. Escher," Noel read aloud from the caption.

"I don't think I like it," Phil said. "That's a nasty asymmetry, as if the artist put a screwdriver in the middle and gave it a turn."

"Some turn it gave *me*," Sandy laughed shakily, her eyes misting over.

Phil tightened his protective embrace and asked how she was feeling at the moment.

"Maybe a little unsteady, but not like *flying*, if that's what you mean."

"So what is it supposed to *be*?" said Phil, directing his query at Innerman.

"A conceptual mystery, from what I know of Escher. You've got to find the right way to look at it."

"Okay then," Phil responded, eying the composition, "what do we have here? Along the bottom is a picture gallery, two rows of prints hanging on a wall."

"But you can only get in from the right," said Sandy, gaining her composure. "See the open archway in the lower right-hand corner?"

"It's some kind of circular progression," Phil concluded. "You enter on the right, move left along the rows of pictures, and they get bigger as you advance."

"*Everything* gets bigger," Sandy noticed. "Going up the circle on the left, the head of the boy is almost twice as big as his shoulders."

"Oh, I love this," said Noel in delight. "Look what happens right above him. Do you see what happens to the print the boy is viewing just above his head?"

"It's becoming enormous," Phil observed.

"It's twisting around," added Sandy. "And the houses are growing three-dimensional—like what happens in your Moebius twist."

"Yes, but look further, follow the rotation of the print *all* the way around, just like the boy who's viewing it does."

". . .His eyes are tracing the clockwise expansion of the houses," Sandy said, "and they come around to—is that possible?"

"It's the roof of the gallery he's standing in!" Phil exclaimed. "A hell of a trick. The picture starts out in the gallery, but the gallery winds up in the picture."

"The *boy* winds up in the picture," murmured Sandy.

They asked her to repeat her remark.

"The boy winds up seeing *himself* in the picture he is viewing."

"Jesus, she's right!" said Phil. "He should be able to view himself the way *we* can view him."

"He's come outside the print," Sandy continued, "outside of himself. He can look back on his other self still inside." She had turned the color of chalk.

"It's a complete blueprint for getting out of your body," said Phil. Squeezing Sandy closer, his face also was blanched. "Yet we're still intact. Why is that? If it worked the first time, if it was potent enough to trigger Sandy's OBE, why not now?"

"Because it's not sheer magic," Noel replied, "not like 'abracadabra' or 'Open Sesame'—it doesn't automatically open the door every time it's used."

"There shouldn't be *any* magic," said Phil, protesting the

whole situation. "I don't *believe* in magic. And yet. . ." He looked
at the artwork and shook his head in chagrin.

"Well, let's not call it magic," Noel suggested. "The Moebius
twisted 'Print Gallery' may be an example of what a modern
alchemist would call an *archetype.*"

"A symbol with the power to transform," said Sandy, her eyes
staying fixed on the graphic composition.

"Right, but not like abracadabra," Noel remarked. "It isn't
mechanical. You've got to *want* the change, consciously work at it."

"*Evolve* to it?" offered Sandy.

"Yes," said Noel, "or it won't take steady hold. It's as if a safety
feature were built into Nature to prevent power from being
abused."

"Then we're speaking about a catalyst," said Phil, "more than
a sure-fire cause."

"Good way to put it," Noel responded. "Not a mechanical
cause."

"How about a *map*?" Sandy added.

"Okay," replied Noel, "but if this map is an archetype, it
wouldn't just abstractly *represent* the territory—it also would *be*
the territory. That much magic it would have."

"Are we back to magic?" said Phil in dismay.

"Well, *white* magic, anyway," Noel laughed, "not simply
self-serving, but working through a deeper Self to help nurture a
creative potential."

When they left the shop, the wrapped "Print Gallery" went
with them.

Early in the morning, Noel was staring again at the blinking
cursor on the monitor of his personal computer. The screen was
blank.

How do I get the reader to understand about my book? he
wondered. *It is not a factual account, and not just science fiction,*

but something in between . . . between what actually is, and an imaginative guess about what might be, between what has already happened and what is yet to occur. What I am writing about is happen-ing. Now, as I sit here in my office, I believe it is happening.

His fingers moved to the keyboard and he began to work.

. . .This morning Khomo Bandrinko has returned from the **cave without walls**. She lies in her Nairobi hospital bed and is serene, yet filled with a sense of commitment greater than any she had ever known as a director of the Pan African Relief Fund or with Amnesty International. Khomo has suffered a massive coronary, traveled to the threshold of death and come back with a vision of Life. They will say she has regressed, reverted to her "primitive origins," the "tribal unconscious." In a limited sense, they may be right, but at least as well wrong.

The cave had at first been a lightless tomb. She had been unable to breathe, was suffocating. Then, without leaving her place, she was moving through the enclosure in a curious way—as if her body had gone plastic, were elongating, stretching lengthwise forward. As Khomo expanded through the cave, her breathing grew easier, her environment brighter. She was sensing no light at the end of this tunnel. The brightness was coming from the walls. **Could these walls be getting thinner**? Khomo had thought. No, they simply had become less enclosing, though inexplicably, she remained completely within.

In a pre-dawn glimmer, she saw the village of her childhood, heard the echo of the drums pulsing affirmation that hearts were beating together, the wordless, perfect intimacy. But it was only an echo. Lost, never to be regained. Then what was she experiencing as she continued to expand, as the light grew more intense? Other villages, larger communities, cities, the entire continent, the planet itself—was all the Earth pulsing to the living rhythm of her childhood?

No, it was not the wholeness of her childhood she had witnessed, she understands this morning. To that dim, unwitting innocence, those shadows, that rapturous magic, there can be no going back. Had the brightness of the cave meant a **new** kind of wholeness? **Can we go "back" to wholeness by going** forward **from our present fragmentation**? Khomo asks herself.

It is a mystery. A great puzzle. At the same time, the promise of the **cave without walls** is so clear to Khomo that she knows it will shape the remainder of her life. From this moment on, in whatever she undertakes, the rhythm of possible wholeness, of an Earth that is healed and made one, will be working within her. She is planning to undertake much. Let them call her a primitive.

. . .This morning the Director wrestles again with his cinematic problem. For seven years, he has been working with a radically new technique. Holography, it is called, and through it he can produce moving three-dimensional images so much like life that when projected into an audience, the impact is profound, viewers are drawn deeply into the action. The premiere of his first holographic film had shown how potent the experience could be, and the Director had been pleased about that. But the effect had proven negative, an intrusion that had disturbed his audience, upset them so badly that many had been driven from the theater. How can he touch his patrons without intruding on them?

He thinks now of the property behind those powerful images, the striking characteristic of the record captured on the the photographic plate when laser light has been properly reflected. Mapped into any given segment of a hologram, however small, is **all** the information from the holographed object—the image of the whole is enfolded in each and every part of the record! This also means that parts are enfolded in each other, intimately interrelated.

In the showing of his first film, the **audience** apparently had become enfolded. An artist needs to engage his audience, but the more effective he is at it, the greater is his responsiblity. Then perhaps in the art of holocinema, the viewers can no longer be encouraged simply to surrender themselves to the artist's product, identify completely with the moving images, for images are no longer flattened and confined to a screen that is safely remote. Identification can be too intense. And yet, meaningful contact demands identification.

Suppose viewers were made conscious not only of the holographed images created but of the creation **process**? Suppose they were to identify fully with the content of the film yet at the same time be deprogrammed, made aware of what lay **behind** this content, its production and projection? If the feat could be carried off, viewers would be operating on two levels simultaneously: caught up **in** the action, and **outside** of the action as well.

The Director suddenly knows the subject of his next holographic drama—the holographic drama itself. He will dramatize the premiere of his inaugural film. The holographic images with which his audience will identify will be of an audience enfolded by holographic images, and of the holographers who have cast the spell.

The image-maker sees **himself** projected before his audience, emerging from the cover of his images, contacting his viewers directly so they might better share his perspective, participate in the process of creation.

. . .This morning cosmonaut Marissa Vlatkin rides above the rim of the Earth. Her official period of rest has commenced. But she lingers at the spacecraft's port, peering at the white, blue and green pastel colossus. How insignificant she feels, how incomplete confronting such fullness.

Then a sudden shift in perspective is triggered by the sight of her reflection superimposed on the looming plenum. It **is I**, Marissa recognizes with exhilaration, **I am this whole, a part of it and somehow, also the entirety.**

For a moment, it seems she is viewing the spheroid from an angle so wide that none of its surface is hidden. A moment later, she realizes that her vantage point is from **within**, that the planetary body is her own.

Marissa feels the pain now from every tortured cell fighting its own transformation, preferring madness and death to its own evolution. **I am not yet a body**, she understands, **not yet an organic whole.** It is the challenge she resolves she will meet. . . .

Sandy and Phil had been at it since 10 a.m., he sprawled over cushions on the living room floor, she in the bedroom sitting cross-legged on their bed. Sundays were for viewing. Each was watching a videotape of the other.

Noel had called it *mutual electronic yoga.* "You each make a tape of yourselves," he had explained, "a personal statement of who you are. There is no restriction on the content. It just has to be authentic, as open and spontaneous as you can bear. When both of you feel ready, the tapes are exchanged, you view one another, try to absorb one another."

For the past ten days, Sandy and Phil had poured themselves out onto hours of tape, each working alone with a video recorder mounted on a tripod. They were intent on telling and seeing the truth, and the pain was considerable.

Presently, their concentration was broken by the sound of someone at the front door. The images on their screens commanded their attention for several seconds more, then they snapped their respective playback buttons to stop. Coming in with a rain-dampened bag from the Japanese restaurant, Noel called out greetings and went through to the kitchen. By the time the others joined him, he had set the table and laid out the food.

"You two hungry?" he asked.

"Starved," Sandy said, but in a voice that was distant. Phil said nothing. The couple seated themselves at oblique angles on opposite sides of Noel. A silence quickly set in.

"I don't know how much longer I can put up with it," Noel blurted out.

"With what?" replied an irritated Phil.

"Us?" Sandy asked, smiling crookedly.

Noel reminded them of a problem of his that he had mentioned before. He lived in a second-story apartment overlooking the street. City officials had decided that the sidewalk just below his windows was in need of extensive repairs. They had sent in a battalion of workers equipped to the hilt, and now his rooms quaked and rattled in tune with their pneumatic drills. "The place is barely liveable," Noel complained, "to say nothing of workable."

What was he going to do? They spent the meal discussing alternatives.

Afterward, Noel brightened. He had brought something he wanted them to see, an old videotape of a classroom lecture. He clicked his cassette into the living room tape player and they settled down before the monitor. The screen flickered on, revealing an image of the teacher in profile framed by a blackboard and addressing four rows of young men and women.

For a short while, the trio watched without comment, then Phil asked, "Wouldn't it help for us to hear what you're saying?"

"Not now," replied Noel, "at the moment, that's not what I'm after."

A few seconds later, he suddenly said, "Look at my jaw." Sandy and Phil turned around.

"Not over here, on the *screen*," Noel directed. They laughed and complied.

"Can you see the tension? See the mouth, how mechanically my lips are moving? Look at the way the muscles of my face are grouped. Rigid sets of muscles, almost no mobility, especially around the eyes and brow. Naturally, it's because I'm terrified. The students and camera are watching me, *judging* me, I believe, and I'm judging myself. Acceptance is out of the question.

"Can I accept you now?" said Noel to his image. Rising, he spoke again to Sandy and Phil but did not cut off dialogue with himself. "Looks like I've got a stiff neck. Inside it feels like it's tied in a knot—in the *back* of my neck, that's where I really feel the tightness. Tension inside my shoulders too, and my upper arms. I'm holding my arms so close to me as I go to the board, clenching them against me, because I'm afraid if I open up, I might be blown apart. God, I can barely bring myself to lift the chalk."

Sandy and Phil were no longer looking at the monitor. They did not have to, for Noel was miming himself so adeptly that in effect, he had *become* his electronic likeness. At the same time, there was a marked difference. From behind the anxiety-stricken, brittle figure being captured so faithfully by the living Noel, a spontaneity was coming through, the fluid working of creative process. *This is how he heals himself*, Sandy thought.

"I must be able to accept myself," said Noel. "It cannot be just verbal. I've got to see into myself and *be* the self I see, consciously put on that body without passing judgment."

"Love. You mean you have to *love* yourself," Sandy said.

"Which could be narcissistic," remarked Phil.

"Could be," said Noel with a smile. "But Narcissus was passing judgment. His self-love depended on the perfection he thought he saw in the surface of the pool."

"And you want to get *beneath* the surface," said Phil.

"Yeah. It's necessary."

"You want to go down to a deeper self-perspective."

"Yes Phil, but more than that," Sandy earnestly injected, "it would be the deeper Self.—Wouldn't it be?" she asked, turning to Noel for confirmation.

Innerman agreed. "It's the Self that doesn't deal in fixed images and rigid expectations."

"You relax your self-concept and your weaknesses then can be accepted?" offered Phil.

"I can accept my*self*," Noel replied, "which could mean overcoming weakness, if I'm determined enough. In the last analysis, weakness comes from non-self-acceptance."

"From shutting out the Self," Sandy added.

Phil looked away, spending several moments in private reflection. "So the longer you're caught on the surface of the pool . . ." he began.

"The stiller and colder grows the water," said Noel, "until the pool freezes over into icy caricatures, stilted self-images. I'm in pain. Immobilized. I can't even lift the chalk.

"That's the way it happens," Noel continued, looking intently at Sandy and Phil. "Images harden, become so hard to break that you hear people say it's impossible. 'It's human nature,' they say, 'and human nature cannot be remade.' They're wrong, of course."

"Noel thinks we should do something to break the ice," said Phil. He extended his hand to Sandy and she took it.

"Well yes," laughed Noel, "but since you put it that way, I'd emphasize that it's just as much a matter of letting it happen *to* you."

"Because we're not strictly on our own with this," said Sandy to Phil, squeezing his hand.

"You're *conspiring*," Noel said. He went over to them and put his hand in theirs. "*We* are conspiring, working in creative collusion with something deeper."

 **15**

A Vision of Planetary Transformation

Noel peered from his window at the con-
struction workers on the street below and repeated to himself the
goal he had set five years before: *To write a novel that is more than
a novel, to find the literary space between fiction and fact,
between the present and the future.* Though he was close now to
the end of his book, it was clear to him that he had not yet
succeeded. The gap had not yet properly been bridged.

Closing his eyes, he opened himself, made himself receptive.
But on this occasion, the needed inspiration did not come. He
went back to his desk to continue his attempt at the keyboard.

. . .This morning the sightless theoretician
awakens with an image crystallizing in his mind's
eye. For the first time, he senses the true nature of
the paraphysical energy he has been studying.
Dimly, he can visualize its contours, glimpse its very
shape. He pictures the peculiar curvature of this
ultimate source of energy, and mentally tracing it,

finds it leading back to **himself**.

His absorption increases. Entering a state of deep contemplation, he can feel the energy flowing through him. In an exhilarating rush, it surges from the core of his being, streaming outward through his limbs and head to his environs. From his depths, the paraphysical energy pours forth to penetrate the depths of others, joining them to him in a most intimate way. He senses this living, core-to-core current as a flowing outward that is also a flowing within, a being-to-being circulation embracing **all** beings, enfolding them in but a single self.

And there is more to the theoretician's curious waking encounter with the energy of self. He is aware that the inside-out self, of which he is part, is itself opening outward, flowing toward a Self that is greater still. He and his soul-bonded sisters and brothers are approaching a Being of Light.

With this the vision ends. The theoretician sits up in bed, throws back the covers and swivels his legs to the floor. There he remains, reflecting on what he just has experienced.

He believes he has glimpsed a momentous event, a climax of epic proportions about to be reached. It is as if the innermost workings of Nature have been laid bare for him, as if he has been given an insight into the essence of organic process, a glimmer of a Cosmic Seed in the instant before its conception. Selves bonded at the core, consciously returning to their deeper Self for Self-impregnation. In this way the Seed will be formed. It is metamorphosis on the grandest scale imaginable, the theoretician intuits. It is a process that **strains** imagination, for space and time themselves are to be transfigured in Nature's evolutional leap. And he has witnessed a foreshadowing.

With crystal clarity, the sightless theoretician now sees that the government's military strategists will not be able to tap the paraphysical energy as they have planned. It will be impossible for them to mine and manipulate it to direct at America's enemies. Nor can the Eastern European opposition have succeeded from their end, as many have feared.

The theoretician recalls covert meetings with uniformed officials, heads of departments and agencies. He senses again the coldness of their manner, the stony insensitivity that disguises their paranoia, the desperation with which they struggle to protect the status quo. Behind all their machinations is elemental fear, the theoretician knows, terror at the prospect of their own transformation. At any cost, they strive to hold the center, maintain the rigid boundaries of their egos, the time-hardened, truncated sense of who they are, with all the trappings of habit-worn values and fossilized institutions that support it. It is to this end that they would harness the paraphysical energy, and the theoretician recognizes the irony of this, for unbeknownst to them, the paraphysical energy is the energy of the very transformation they wish most to forestall.

The blind theoretician sees this ultimate energy as the energy of Creative Process. It is the energy of Self welling spontaneously from the primal, collective subconscious with a purpose and direction of its own. Old structures of self and society disintegrate and cannot be redeemed. In every sphere of life—

economic, political, cultural—at every level of
being—individual, social, global—old images and
familiar patterns deform and collapse. The theoretician sees the energy of Self rising to wash away
the debris and offer a wellspring for creative rebirth.
It invites and challenges the whole of humanity to
participate in its own metamorphosis.

But what open souls we must become, the
theoretician thinks. Can we end our stubborn resistance, loosen our desperate hold on what we have
outgrown, accept our own transformation? Is it possible to be as open as that, surrendering our old
selves so fully, giving them over so freely in a spirit
of intimate collaboration with each other and co-
creation with our deeper Self?

The would-be engineers of paraphysical energy
cannot have succeeded. The theoretician feels certain of that, for the engineering approach is
designed to preserve the very self that must be surrendered, if the energy of Self is truly to be tapped.
His mind now turns to accounts of paranormal hap-
penings, reports of bizarre episodes in which physical structures were impossibly twisted, turned inside
out. Was this the result of psychotronic sabotage
deliberately perpetrated by an insidious foe? The
theoretician thinks not. And what of the widespread
accounts of **minds** turning inside out, of private
thoughts being shared directly by others, of telepathic bonds being formed? To the theoretician, links
such as these are clearly not contrived by engineers.
They are spontaneous indications of the working of
Self. He sees the inside-out linking of selves as part of
a creative coming together, a rush to organic unity
in that moment preceding Self-impregnation.

Is it authentic, this heady vision of his? For a moment, he doubts it himself. Surely it must be invisible to most who hold power, the scientists and technicians, the policy makers and high government officials. In the East and in the West, a blindness seems to prevail. With the rising of Self not perceived, the paranoia escalates. On both sides, the pressure builds for decisive military action to preempt the fantasized control of bodies and minds by mechanical means. The species moves toward the precipice.

Is it truly a blindness? the theoretician wonders. Perhaps we are only asleep. Perhaps we can awaken, open our eyes before reaching and crossing the brink.

We need to awaken, he thinks and fervently feels. We must wake up to Self, act to recreate ourselves, or be undone.

A smile is on his lips. Though telling what he has seen may be close to impossible, the sightless theoretician intends to tell the world.

. . .Others awaken this morning. They too realize the struggle they will face in finding the words to express the insight into Self they have gotten and the impulse to evolve that goes with it. But from this vision of their own future embryo, there is no turning back.

The awakened begin to conspire. Even as sleepers continue to drift, somnambulate toward the brink of destruction, dreaming paranoid dreams of eyes watching eyes—the awakened start breathing as one.

They are becoming aware of each other. A

network of conspirators is forming, every participant uniquely contributing to the critical mass that
is beginning to build. The threshold of metamorphosis is being approached . . .

Gazing at the rows of small green letters he had typed onto
the screen, Innerman shook his head. He was having misgivings.
*Have I gone too far, come too far away from the central characters
developed in the first part of my book? Have I changed my form
of expression too drastically, departed too radically from the more
conventional narrative style I used earlier? Or perhaps I have not
gone far enough.*

I want *to come out of the fiction,* thought Noel. *That is my
intention—to leave the narrative flow, leave the politely indirect
symbolism of literary convention behind and make immediate
contact with my reader. But it has to be done in the proper way.*

The gamble is that the reader at some level knows already
*what I am getting at, that he has had his own awakening. Then
—just by understanding the perspective I offer—she will be conspiring with me to bring our shared vision into sharper focus. But
the responsibility for that understanding largely is mine.*

*Yes, I must break with literary tradition, step entirely outside.
But at the same time, I somehow must remain* within. *If the break
is too abrupt, the wrong message will be sent, and the reader will
only be startled and confused.*

Innerman looked beyond the computer monitor to the piece
of graphic art that hung on the wall. Yet another time, he followed
the expansion of the boy in Escher's "Print Gallery," marveling
once more at the smooth transition, at how the character *in* the
picture fluidly transcends it, comes to view it from outside, from
the artist's own perspective.

A literary "Print Gallery," Noel thinks. *That is what I must
create.*

Phil sat alone in his office, grading papers at his desk.

As he was drafting a remark near the bottom of an exam page, he became conscious of the movement of his hand. In mid-sentence he stopped writing, put down his pencil, held his palm open for scrutiny. This was his hand, of course, but he could feel, almost see, the presence of *another* sharing its space. A smaller, narrower, more delicately ligated hand was kinesthetically sensed.

Sandy, at home doing yoga, could also sense another in and as herself. She was perched on her heels, leaning all the way back, slowly stretching her torso. As back, chest and abdomen expanded, an *alter torso* was experienced, inwardly, tangibly felt. *How strange is this squareness, this muscular fullness,* Sandy thought. *The angles and alignments of bones are all wrong.* Yet in the odd new sensation, she also could discern something old. And the maleness within her made her feel not less than a woman, but *more.* She could palpably feel the promise of completion.

How will it happen? thought Noel. He was attempting to sharpen his vision of the near future, bring into focus the scenario that could make planetary transformation a reality. *How will the conspirators awaken to each other, by what specific means will they be joined, their minds become linked, their selves bonded at the core?*

Will there simply be a flash of lightning, a clap of thunder, then instant metamorphosis? That is not very likely, Noel said to himself. *Some kind of framework or scaffold should be needed, a* platform from which global awareness can be launched. In the early stages before fertilization, the Planetary Organism should require support.

It occurred to Noel that a global nervous system of sorts was already in the making, and at that very moment, he was sitting before one of its germinal "neurons": his computer. He had just had a modem installed, and it was now possible for him to communicate with colleagues who were similarly equipped. Noel knew of many such kindred spirits scattered far and wide. Insights now could be exchanged at a moment's notice, images transmitted almost instantly over thousands of miles. Of course, this was not linkage at the core, not telepathic bonding. But could it be part of the *framework*, Noel pondered, the initial support system that itself would be transcended when preparations were complete for the more intimate contact? Could the information-processing, image-generating units now turning up around the globe in fast-growing numbers be the "future neurons" of the *truly* organic nervous system yet to be incubated? Might the worldwide network of computers form a kind of chrysalis from which the Planetary Organism would emerge?

Perhaps, thought Noel, *perhaps it could happen that way*. In his mind's eye, he fancied Khomo Bandrinko and Marissa Vlatkin poised before their own computer terminals, and the cinema director was stationed in front of his. Even the blind theoretician was included in Noel's mental picture. He sat at a terminal of special design fashioned with a monitor that was meaningfully alive to his touch. There were many other conspirators in Noel's vision who were making first contact by computer, electronically "crawling" before they could fly.

It was a scenario worth considering, in Noel's estimation, and he began to set it forth.

```
ANDERSON A, BANDRINKO K, BEIJING MED COLL ENVIR CNTR, BOHM D,
BRAINMIND NET, BRUNER J, CAMBR U COMM LAB, COEVOLNET, COOPLINK
STUDYNET, COSMON PEACE BRIG, CYBERNCO INC, DELTA FORCE...
```

It is the near future and a conference by computer is in progress. Independent researchers and consultants, self-organized networks participate. Interested parties from businesses and governments are included, academic study teams and private think tanks take part. For several months, the conference has been developing. Dozens of sites around the globe are going on line.

```
...WORLDHEAL CLUSTER...
     COMPATIBILITY PROFILE:  NATIVE AND WESTERN MEDICINE
     COMPUTE INTEGRATION POTENTIALS...
...ECONBUS CLUSTER...
     DISPLAY NONLINEAR TRENDS SIMULATIONS:
     "CATASTROPHES," NONEQUILIBRIUM SHIFTS, QUANTUM JUMPS...
...HOLOSCI CLUSTER...
     SCAN ARTLIT, THEOPHIL STORES FOR SOFT CORRELATES OF
                                         FOURTH DIMENSION...
...SPACEPAX CLUSTER...
     TRANSMIT REFS 16, 137, 883-916 TO ECOLNET, COSMON PEACE
                                                        BRIG...

...MEDIACOM CLUSTER...

     ...SOCIOPOL CLUSTER...


          ...CONSTUD CLUSTER...



               ...PSIPROBE...



                    ...EVOLQUEST....
```

The Creative Visions Conference is many confer-
ences in one. Each cluster of groups and individuals
operates from its unique perspective on the totality.
Working from computer terminals geographically
remote, cluster participants share common memory
and knowledge-processing capacity. Information
and ideas are input, questions raised, comments
exchanged; explorations are pursued and themes
integrated. Multilateral transactions unfold fresh
insights, novel realizations.

Time is no more a limitation than space. Input
may be given at any time. No participant is tied to
his or her terminal at a particular moment and
expected to contribute or react. All cluster proceedings are recorded, stored and are accessible when-
ever convenient and desired; a response may then
be evolved, may be allowed to ripen until ready for
inclusion in the collective cognizance that organi-
cally grows.

As within clusters, so in the Conference as a
whole. The operating system helps orchestrate.

```
POSITIVE SUM GAME ⟨--⟩ POLY-OCULAR VISION ⟨--⟩ EMPATHIC KNOWING...
  AUTOPOIESIS ⟨--⟩ SELF-REFERENCE ⟨--⟩ HYPERNUMBER...
    ARCHETYPE ⟨--⟩ MORPHOGENETIC FIELD ⟨--⟩ "HUNDRETH MONKEY"...
```

New integrations occur across fluid cluster
boundaries.

```
            EARTHSPAN NET
            ENG F
            ESSER A ...
```

A roster of prospective participants continuously develops.

```
REFER CULTURESCAPES QUERY TO WORLDHEAL, TECHSYS...
COORDINATE EDSPECT, MEDIACOM...
INTERLINK SPACEPAX, ARTLIT, HOLOSCI...
```

Cluster interactions are harmonized.

And through the general operating system participants are reminding themselves and each other to

```
STAY OPEN TO SELF AND TO OTHER
BE MUTUALLY SELF-ATTUNED
CONSPIRE
```

Though perspectives are many and varied, those who take part are coming to consciously know, to **feel** and to **see** the Conference's single purpose and challenge. The shift in perception is occurring. It is an awakening, a momentous transition from the fragmented view of myriad fragments of problems to a grasping of the one and only authentic problem presently faced, the problem of healing by self-transformation, of transformation by Self.

```
THE PROBLEM:  TO SEE THE WHOLE IN EVERY PART
              TO WORK THROUGH THE WHOLE

THE PROBLEM:  TO ACT NOT JUST BY DOING
              BUT DIRECTLY BY SEEING
              TO ACT BY CREATIVE VISION

THE PROBLEM:  TO GO BEYOND THE SELF BOUND BY HABIT
              COLLABORATE WITH THE SELF THAT IS DEEPER
```

```
THE PROBLEM:  TO BRING TO LIFE AND KEEP ALIVE THESE VERY WORDS
              THESE WORDS PRINTED BEFORE YOU
              SO THE PRINTOUT IS PRINTED WITHIN

THE PROBLEM:  TO WORK THROUGH THIS VERY MEDIUM
              THIS COMPUTER CONFERENCE
              TO GET BEYOND IT.
```

The participants know that the operating system is only their tool, that **it** cannot accomplish the
transformation they seek. But the system does a
great deal, especially by way of the generated
image. . .

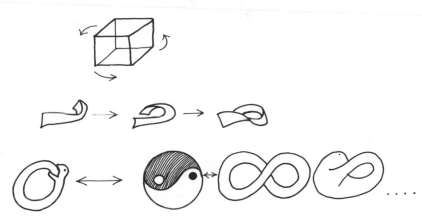

The abstract is made concrete, graphically
rendered for instant comprehension. Complex pro-
cesses are simplified, dynamic relations
simulated—computer animation deftly capturing
details of movement, overall patterns of flow.

Modes of artistic expression are extended,
audial as well as visual. Applying the system's syn-
thesizers, new colors are blended, new notes struck;
the unpaintable picture is painted, the unperform-

able score is performed. What once could be but vaguely imagined becomes tangibly imaged, the mind's inner eye and ear reaping their outer harvest as never before. And what of the harvest of mind's Mind? Shadows of Infinity, echoes of Eternity, symbols reaching so far within themselves they go beyond themselves, beyond symbolizing to touch the heart of Self?

In an African hut, a Bavenda shaman sits in trance at an electronic drafting board drawing a simple curve with his light pen. Through him speaks the tribal spirit, coiled serpent, closing upon itself, returning to itself. Now the circle opens. Spiraling outward, it expands.

Two thousand miles away, a William Blake poem is input.

AWAKE!
AWAKE, O SLEEPER IN THE LAND OF SHADOWS,
WAKE! EXPAND!

A third voice joins in from far to the north. From the Soundart Laboratory of Amsterdam comes J. S. Bach's "Canon per Tonos," a harmony advancing by keys, moving further and further from its key of departure. After six outbound turns on the musical spiral, a surprise for the ear is discovered. The original key has been restored! Was there ever a departure? a worldwide audience wonders. But the voices of Bach are now all one octave higher and can begin afresh their expansion/contraction.

A planetary artwork is in the making.

Interrupting his train of thought, Innerman looked away from his computer to question himself again.

The vision seems right, it appears to be taking the shape I

*intended. But what of my form of expression? Have I not come
still further away from my fictional format, gone from a novel to a
poetic meditation?*

Noel decided that his problem of literary form could wait a
while longer. He would press his vision of the near future to its
conclusion. As he began another session alone at his keyboard,
Sandy and Phil were completing a session of their own.

They sat face to face on their living room couch, gazing
intently at each other in a special way. "The Moebius Gaze," they
had named the exercise, in honor of Noel. Pupil to pupil they
stared, corresponding pupils separately locked in continuous contact, like the separate sides of Noel's twisted surface which nonetheless were one. By following this procedure, Sandy and Phil
overrode the natural tendency for their eyes to come into focus on
but a single eye of the other at a time. They seemed to experience
more of one another in this way and to experience each other more
deeply, for the gaze resulted in a powerful sense of
interpenetration.

When Phil went out for a paper, he felt like he was wearing
Sandy's body in addition to his own. It was a peculiar sensation, yet
somehow also quite natural. He felt very much himself and at the
same time, sensed he was not. He sensed that he somehow was
more than himself.

A flower cart had been set up beside the newsstand. Following an impulse, Phil stopped to buy carnations, and back in their
apartment, Sandy smelled a definite sweetness.

At the outset, the scale of the Creative Visions
Conference is small, a handful of participants
operating personal computers linked by telephone
lines and limited to the east coast of North America.
Seemingly overnight, with no central organization,

no formal campaign to marshal support, involvement spreads to every corner of the Earth. The Conference is truly a phenomenon, an **événement
sociologique** without precedence or peer.

"It is **insanity**," say skeptical observers. "The
world must be going insane," they declare. They
look but can find little rhyme or reason to the Conference, little that is clearcut or coherent. Is there
any specification of realistic goals? Are any practical problem areas identified and sensibly
addressed, any measures, feasible methods, definitive programs of action described? How then could
the Conference be attracting such wide attention,
ask the skeptics, winning such strong endorsement,
hard backing from sources that in the past were
always so reliable? It **must** be a form of global
dementia, in the skeptical view.

The "insanity" continues its advance, gaining
new advocates in circles of influence, administra-
tors of United Nations agencies, senior officials of
governments, associates of powerful transnational
commissions. The Conference goes on satellite, and
televideo facilities are incorporated to enhance
communications. Commercial and public television
stations, sensing ripe world markets, **help** to ripen
them by broadcasting Conference proceedings on
a continuous basis.

The "Global Psychosis" intensifies. Earth blinks
half-comprehending as She glimpses her own transformation. And comprehending, He is transformed.
The planetary Artwork progresses. . .

A picture of Earth is transmitted live from the
first Earth-orbiting Conference participants. The

response initiated below at the Mathflex Imager of Stanford University is a curious topographic progression:

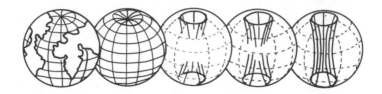

indentations appearing at opposite poles, deepening, a channel opening through the core of the planet, a tunnel from pole to pole. . .

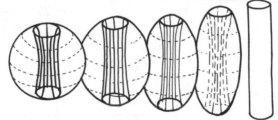

hollowed sphere elongating, stretching lengthwise to form a narrow tube. . .

north polar orifice drooping downward, approaching its antipode.

The poles seem about to be joined, Earth's openness resealed. But union is achieved in a peculiar manner. In ghost-like self-penetration, the north polar mouth of the terran tube passes

through the tube's lower wall, fuses with the south pole from inside the crust:

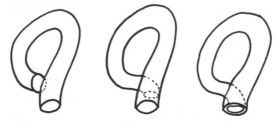

A "Klein bottle Earth," the model is called, an inside-out Earth that is closed and yet open.

The imaging process is carried still further. Now taken up in the Prajna Cooperative of New Delhi, a further transmutation is enacted.

It is this image of Earth as Embryo that is chosen for the pilot trial. The state of the art shifts upward a gear, a dimension is added to the unfolding poem. At three separate test sites, the Earth Child is projected holographically.

Presently more "madness," **true** hysteria now. For how can the Embryo be seen in full relief, seen protruding beyond the flat screens of computers not technically equipped? With transmissions of new holographic forms, the "madness" redoubles, multiplies out of control, thousands succumbing before ordinary television receivers all around the world. Reports come in that the Conference's images are viewed even where no receiving equipment of any kind is present, on walls and ceilings of homes, in theatres and churches, department stores and open markets—any place and every place the sightings are occurring, the depth of their effect evidenced in the powerful outpouring of emotion, a sense of awe and elation verging on ecstasy.

Among three selected outposts, Conference participants themselves are holographically projected, appearing to each other in full body, as if in the flesh. These are nothing but transmitted pictures, of course, phantoms woven from laser light. Then what new madness accounts for allegations of tangible impact? Can a projected likeness stir a current of air, audibly thump the side of a cabinet, visibly ruffle papers on top of a desk? It must be the power of suggestion, the skeptics proclaim. But the "abberation" is worse than that. Beyond detecting the palpable presence of the others in their midst, each member claims to sense his **own** presence amidst his counterparts, sense herself abroad in their environs, viewing details that have not been projected. And what is this talk of **rapport** that begins to be heard from the centers involved, of unspoken thoughts being shared, of core-to-core contact being made, what besides the advanced symptoms of a grand dementia?

Contageously, it spreads. In an instant, the "madness" of intimate knowing infects the Conference as a whole. A moment later, it flares up beyond, great numbers enveloped. The madness that heals is taking hold of the planet, the global dementia working its metamorphosis. Spontaneously, the Earth is enfolding, turning inside out, forming Itself into the Seed from which the Earth Child may germinate. . .

A Literary Surface of Moebius

A SEED, REFLECTED NOEL, CONTEMPLATING the closing passage of his chapter. He climbed out of his chair and went back to the window. The construction workers were gone and the sun was setting.

And the turning inside out, Noel thought, as he stared into the deserted street. *My fundamental image, the signature for my entire book. When intimate linkages are forming, when consciousness is creatively evolving, there is the turning inside out —circumversion à la the Klein bottle, which is just a Moebius strip in an added dimension!*

Noel, you win a gold star for content, he commended himself.

I've said what I wanted to say. What is left is the question I've avoided, the question of form. I have written about the inside-out Moebius process, but have I done it in the Moebius way? I've written about wholeness, but have I achieved a wholeness of expression?

Abandoning the characters and plot established earlier is not the way, thought Noel. *Breaking with fiction and waxing poetic, as I have, does not give me a literary Moebius strip. I have been aiming for a novel that is more than a novel, yet it seems I no longer have a novel at all. The ideas are coming directly from me, which is what I intended. But then how can I claim to still have a work of fiction? Must not the author of fiction express his ideas through his characters and plot?*

Can a middle ground be found between fiction and fact? Does one exist? Baffled by his literary conundrum, Noel left the window and walked out of his office. In the adjacent room, he pulled off his socks and fell onto the bed, not bothering to undress. Lying on his back, his hands folded behind his head, he continued to ruminate.

I suppose I'll have to rewrite at least the last portion of the chapter, do it so I am not directly involved. Perhaps I could use the same device as in the opening sequence. The Creative Visions Conference could be described from the perspective of my sightless theoretician. No, that won't do, either. The theoretician is not one of my established characters. He is a latecomer, and a mythological figure at that, one whose introduction is itself a departure from the standard narrative laid down in the beginning.

Then why not have an established *character serve as my stand-in?* Of course, thought Noel, immediately reminded of his central figure, the college professor whom he had used as his surrogate in the first part of his novel. *I could say that the material is coming from his pen, that it is he who is writing about the blind theoretician, that he is the author of my vision of the future. The content of the chapter would stand as it is, and by attributing it to a character who is integrally grounded in the plot, the unity of the book would be maintained.*

It is still not enough, Noel thought, shaking his head in dissatisfaction. *The technique would only bring me back to a straight fictional format. There would be non-fictional material embedded in the novel, but structurally, it would be* only *a novel, not any more. To create a literary Moebius strip, I* literally *would have to come out of the fiction — but not the way I have done it so far. It would have to be smoother, more fluid. To bridge the gap between fiction and fact, the book would have to remain a novel, yet at the same time be something more.*

Is that even possible? Noel asked himself. Confounded by the paradox of writing technique he had posed, he turned on his side and went to sleep.

Without waking up, Noel was aware that he was dreaming. *Is it just a dream,* Noel wondered, as the characters in his book came before him. He saw Khomo Bandrinko emerging from her cave, Marissa Vlatkin orbiting the Earth in a satellite of the Creative Visions Conference, and the near-sighted theoretician was mopping his thick-lensed goggles as he spoke of H. G. Wells. Sandy and Phil also appeared in this dream about Noel's book, for theirs was a pivotal role. And there were others. A group of men were playing a high-spirited game in the courtyard of a building, a freckle-faced youth was jogging through the snow with a radiant glow on his face and in a laboratory, a white-coated scientist conducted a demonstration for a man he called Supervisor.

The "Print Gallery" entered Noel's vision, and as he watched it, it grew to enormous proportions, filling his entire field of sight. His eyes were drawn to the figure pictured in the lower left-hand corner of the artwork, the boy whose head had been enlarged by the clockwise expansion around the empty center. Following that expansion, Noel witnessed the boy's metamorphosis. Curving upward from left to right, he changed into Merlin the Magician with high-pointed, silver-starred cap and long flowing robes. Moving further toward the apogee, the image of Merlin was transmuted into that of Noel's awakened cinema director. It was his holographic magic, Noel knew, that was making the print three-dimensional.

When the top of the arc was reached, the picture itself disappeared, leaving only the transformed personage. He was now a living, breathing, full-bodied individual, but Noel could not make out the details of his face. Presently the man approached him, and as he drew close, his features came into focus. Noel recognized himself.

. . . This morning Noel Innerman awakens with the solution to his literary problem. He will use his central character, after all. At the beginning of his novel, he will hint that this *college professor* is writing a novel. The specific contents and title of the work will not be revealed until the climax. Noel then will disclose to the readers that the professor's novel is the very one they have been reading —that it is *Noel Innerman's* novel the professor has been writing. So the character written about in the book will become one with the writer. Like the boy in Escher's expansion, he will begin as but a detail in the literary tableau, take the Moebius twist and wind up outside, with the author's perspective — the author's very identity — now his own.

This is how Noel will speak to his readers directly, come out from behind his third person cover and make firsthand contact with them. Yes, a fictitious figure will describe the transformation of Earth, but in the end, the figure will turn out to be Noel Innerman himself. By bridging the gap between author and character, author and readers, Noel intends to overcome literary fragmentation, achieve literary wholeness. He is not content merely to write *about* wholeness. He feels it must be built into the very medium in which he writes, if the idea of wholeness is wholly to be conveyed. Noel views his novel as an act of conspiracy that may contribute to the widespread awakening he believes is in progress. Noel calls his novel *The Moebius Seed.*

∞ 17

The Moebius Seed:
A Visionary Novel of
Planetary Transformation

R EADER, I CAN SEE THEM ALL NOW, ALL THE CHAR-
acters in my novel. And I can see myself.

It is the near future. The world-wide computer network
already has formed and is transcending itself. The intimate madness sparked by the Creative Visions Conference is turning Earth
inside out.

But I also am witnessing the resistance. It continues even now.
The Committee for Sense and Sanity still perceives only mass
hysteria in the linkages that form. Forrest Reynolds and his skeptical colleagues stage a forceful appeal for reason and calm, a return
to sound thinking. They call for sober minds to regain control.

A more dangerous form of resistance can be sensed. Even as
the awakened stand at the threshold of self-transformation, the
threat of self-extinction is palpably real. General Hagger and
Supervisor Malek are unyielding. They refuse to comprehend the
passage of matter through matter, the loving embrace of minds.
Blind to the signature of Self, the imprint of creative advance, they

tell themselves they see the footprints of their enemies. It is the enemy's decisive assault, they are convinced. In Washington, Hagger presses the White House for immediate action. In Moscow, Malek warns Premier Provokin against further delay. Both are urging the ultimate, that a first strike be launched.

I am in New York City. At a terminal of the Creative Visions Conference, I stand beside Sandy and Phil. We watch as Escher's "Print Gallery" is rendered holographic. As the full-bodied image jumps forth, my fellow conspirators go out of their bodies.

Brush strokes are still individual brush strokes, but the artwork as a whole is all and is none. It is more. Notes are still single notes, but the symphony is all and none, qualitatively more. Sandy is Sandy, Phil is Phil, but the Sandy/Phil self is joyously neither, more than both . . . yet somehow *still* incomplete.

The colors do not run. The focus stays sharp, the tune distinct. The dream is *not* a dream, the magic not magic. Can it be magic when nothing goes up in a puff of smoke, no one floats through thin air unsupported or dissolves in it? Space seems yet a space, time a time. The chairs are still the vinyl chairs they were, the tables still piled high with trays of diskettes and sundry manuals, the keyboarded, video-equipped terminals remain terminals, the hologram projector remains that. Yet Sandy/Phil's angle of viewing all this is odd in the extreme, the field of vision distended in undreamed-of directions.

The perspective is panoramic, a wrap-around view that comes close to revealing all sides of objects at once. The angle of sight is so greatly stretched that the *insides* of objects are being exposed; it is twisted so radically upon itself that objects become subjects, are seen as if from within. But here the optical adventure just begins, for while an aspect of Sandy/Phil's visual sphere is contained in the firm-standing walls of the conference room, another opens outward.

Perspective quickly enlarges. It grows to encompass all six floors of the university science building, balloons up and out to embrace blocks of city streets. Much faster yet does the vista expand, all structures human being swiftly dwarfed, all features natural, drastically shrunken in scale. Now starkly encountered is the curve of the planet, and queerly, in the wrap-around, inside-out way.

Absurd, but this way of seeing is also a way of hearing and touching, this way of sensing a way of feeling and knowing. And in this moment out of time, Sandy/Phil knows too there are others, feels their intimate presence, senses them in his/her midst.

A new horizon falls away, a virgin direction is broached. As if being yanked around, twisted into an impossible stance, Phil/Sandy sees themself from the other selves' eyes—Khomo Bandrinko, Marissa Vlatkin, Merlin Mises, Constantin Nesor, many more "I"s, yet still not complete. . .

General Hagger sits in his CIA office before the modem of his own computer terminal. He is remembering the words of a poem. "If you can keep your head while those around you are losing theirs and blaming it on you, then my boy you will be a man."

He must be a man. . .

Not yet an embryo, not even a seed, the community of self-seeing, all-seeing selves does not yet see All, has not yet touched Self. A boundary still stands, a membrane unpassed by the Soul-mating "I"s. But they are approaching, coming close now to Self-impregnation. . .

So many boys, thinks the General. *So many lost their heads. Even the top, even the Head of State is lost, poor weak bastard.*

And I—God, I must keep my head. It is happening to me. *The bastards are reaching me, worming their way inside my skull. Stay out, mother fuckers!* shouts Hagger, *I know who you are!*

Oh God, he blinks, suddenly ablaze with a vision past enduring, *I really know . . .*

They move through a tunnel. Darkness gives way to light as the selves near a Light that is neither, and more than both. They move toward the open, to an Outside beyond inside and out. But the Planetary Egg is not yet fertile, the Moebius Seed not yet conceived. . .

The General really knows. Part of him truly is undeadened. Will it stop him?

He has gotten the strike code from a White House in shambles. *It has to be used,* Hagger thinks, *an order must be given, a program carried out.*

He stares at the keyboard, gripped by a sense of stretching and inflating, his visual angle oddly distended. "Pay no attention!" the General cries out to himself. "It is extraneous. Disregard it. INITIATE THE SEQUENCE."

The hand moves upward, starts toward the first command key, closing toward activation. Yet now the finger falters, the mechanized digit delays. Will the sequence be completed, will inertia run its course, if not here, then at some other robotized, lunatic command post? It has not happened yet. . .

It has not happened yet ... The Seed of transformation has not yet been formed. And it will *not* happen with mere words and lines of print or even with pictures, and not with pages enclosed in a book.

But it is a Moebius book I have written, and an inside-out book such as this does not simply close. The circle is closing, the Moebius work nearing an end. And yet it opens *outward.* It points beyond my private vision, inviting *yours.*

With these closing words I reach out to you in the Moebius way, hoping that we may conspire...